THOSE WHO BURN
THE BRIGHTEST

KAYLA MORTON

First published in the United States of America May 2025 by Lake Country Press & Reviews.

Cataloging-in-Publication Data is on file with the Library of Congress.

ISBN 979-8-9922275-2-9 (Paperback edition)

ISBN 979-8-9922275-3-6 (Ebook edition)

Author website: www.kaylawriteswords.com

Editor: Tara Sexton

Cover Design: Angelica Gregori https://linktr.ee/Ormolu

Formatting: Juliet Bridges

Lake Country Press
Publishing & Reviews

To those who fight darkness that feels insatiable:
you have the power to set the world alight.

"As the saying goes, 'The best blaze the brightest in adversity.'"

ハウルの動く城
    HOWL'S MOVING CASTLE

AUTHOR'S NOTE

THOSE WHO BURN THE BRIGHTEST features content that may be distressing to some readers. Though a few of the things listed below are sparsely featured, they are there nonetheless; and whilst I hope to have addressed these topics with care in mind, I would implore you to please read ahead with caution. Always put your mental well-being first.

Content warnings include:

- Absent parental figures and familial loss
- Allusions to sexual content
- Cursing
- Death (on and off page mentions)
- Discussions of mental health and substance (alcohol) abuse
- Emotional abuse
- Grief
- Hallucinations
- Homophobia (challenged)
- Kidnapping and confinement

- Mentions of needles and medical equipment (with allusions to being tested on)
- Misogyny (challenged)
- Public humiliation
- Suicidal ideation (briefly mentioned in end Acknowledgements)
- Unstable sense of reality
- Violence and gore (on and off page): body horror, bruising, burns, depictions of weapon-induced injuries, scarring from confinement, suffocation
- Vomit

I have done my absolute best to ensure this list is as comprehensive as possible; but in any case, if there are things that have been missed, you will be able to find the updated list on my website.

PRONUNCIATION GUIDE

This list includes the most prominent names of characters and places in THOSE WHO BURN THE BRIGHTEST, as well as their phonetic pronunciation, formatted alphabetically. Please note that the purpose of this guide is to assist readers and reviewers who seek direction for the pronunciation. It's not to say that you won't have your own way of pronouncing things—my Australian accent plays into how I perceive these intonations, as well—but I do hope this helps people who find this sort of thing useful!

Akela Kalama
uh-ke-luh ka-lah-ma

Celimene
ce-limene

Eira Isolde
aye-rah i-sold-uh

Enyo Telema
ihn-yoh te-le-ma

Erebus
air-eh-bus

Etsumi Eimi
eh-tsu-me eh-me

Exilis
ex-ilis

Haneul Eodum
ha-neul eo-duum

Meilin Azelie
may-lin ah-zeh-lee

Sila Atuat
sihl-aa ah-too-at

Silvia Herminia
sihl-vee-uh her-mi-ni-ya

Tufani Faven
too-fah-nee fah-ven

GLOSSARY

Celimene
The capital city of Erebus. This is where King Durante, and The New Reign, reside in.

Erebus
An island that exists between the fabric of mortal and fae realms, which is ruled by the Durante bloodline, and was said to be established after the Treaty was created.

Exilis
The mortal world. Only accessible through one pathway from Erebus which no one but the Durante bloodline know of.

The Demir Trials
A series of trials designed by King Durante, created as a way for him to judge The New Reign.

The Higher Courts:
An unseen plane that is ruled by The Fates (also commonly

referred to as Deities), non-binary figureheads whom The Seelie Court worship as divinity. More commonly known as Light, Moon and Time. All three Fates make up The Higher Courts.

The New Reign
Nine fae heiresses—one from each of the nine Seelie courts—who were born in the same year. Their birth was the first of its kind in the history of Seelie and marked the beginning of a strange turbulence between the courts.

The Rite
A coming-of-age ceremony for every fae, occurring during their eighteenth birth year. Considered to be sacred tradition, participating in the Rite is what immortalizes the fae, and brings them to the full extent of their power. It falls on the same day yearly, so all fae who turn eighteen that year participate in it, even if their birthday is passed/yet to come. The ceremony happens on the first of the eleventh month in the year. It is a particularly coveted celebration for the heiresses, who were due to return to Seelie in time for the commencement of the Rite.

The Seelie Court (Seelie)
Nine courts make up The Seelie Court, the fae realms. All courts have their own power systems, and landscapes, based off of elemental magic, as well as ruling royal families, from which the courts take their names: Court of Atuat, Court of Azelie, Court of Eimi, Court of Eodum, Court of Faven, Court of Herminia, Court of Isolde, Court of Kalama and the Court of Telema.

The Treaty
A set of contracted rules, created by the earliest fae and mortals,

which outlines the duties both parties must abide by in order to keep the peace between the kinds.

The Unseelie Court (Unseelie)

It doesn't exist.

PROLOGUE

"He's an abomination," Light spat.

Before the babe could be reduced to ash, Moon snatched him from the reach of the other figures that loomed frighteningly close, their presence not one that evoked any feelings of kind intentions.

"This bloodline is ill-starred," Time huffed. "I foresaw this vision a great while ago, yet you refused to listen. How did we allow this to happen?"

The silence that lingered thereafter was ominous and it clung to all three Fates, only stirred by the sound of a harsh cry. It drew them from their solemn thoughts.

Clutched against Moon's chest, swaddled and suddenly silent despite the momentary outburst, the cursed child was unaware of the weight that its existence held. With pupils the size of rounded pebbles, Moon assessed the others with a newfound craze. "Don't you *see?*"

"What are you doing, you fool?" Light hissed, reeling back from Moon as if their words were acidic. "Do *you* not see that this child is condemned?"

Time's gaze was more forgiving, though there was a sternness in their face that wasn't melting away, even as Moon frantically looked to them for some reassurance.

There was a silent plea in Moon's eyes that Time had to turn away from, shaking their head.

"We can't let this child grow up to become something we have no control over. We don't know which nature within him is more dominant," Time explained. "The anarchy this boy could bring upon The Seelie Court is unlike anything perceivable."

Moon shook their head, unwilling to believe in the cruelty of their counterparts. "He's the new beginning. *This* is the new beginning! You'll see."

"You'll have no one else to blame when he turns the world to ash," muttered Light.

Moon's gaze was unmoving, locked on the child.

"Let it burn," they whispered.

PART I
THE MEETING

CHAPTER I
AN UNLIKELY SANCTUARY

The pressure of the stale air was like a knife against Eira Isolde's throat.

She felt its weight against her jugular as she finished her second glass of amber hued ale.

The entrance to Amzi opened.

As one of the Kingdom of Erebus's most notorious taverns, Amzi invited in a . . . *colorful* array of customers through its worn oak doors.

Mortals were too fun when inebriated.

Alcohol, combined with the shadowed curtain of nightfall, made spots like Amzi breeding grounds, catered to Celimene's grimiest. This is where they came to play. Eira was a regular herself, though she didn't consider herself of the same caliber.

This just so happened to be her favorite spot to people-watch.

Another round of dismal patrons entered.

Eira wondered if tonight was the night she finally snapped. If one wrong look from a too-far-gone mortal would spoil her amusement; if she would let loose the long-simmering contempt that kept her belly aching for something more than Amzi's signature ale.

The new patrons dragged their feet as they clambered inside. The lag in their step made it appear as though they were being unwillingly lured into the tavern's viscous grasp. Some part of their long-buried sensibility had already given up on its effort to urge them to retreat out the door.

Eira knew that wasn't the case.

Even with her dulled senses, she smelled their intoxication from where she sat. As if it were a tangible thing, the alcohol-ridden stench writhed around the patrons as they bumbled through the crowd. The smell worked promptly to contaminate the small pockets of untouched air that meandered in the still-filling spot. Eira wasn't opposed to the smell of alcohol—quite clearly—but something about the haze that followed them was so severely off-putting that she nearly second-guessed the very reason she was there to begin with.

And yet, Eira didn't move from her spot.

It was like this every time.

Her companion was due to arrive soon enough.

Eira's attention stayed on the group, who successfully made their way to the bartender, who crinkled his nose at the patrons' combined stupor but would not refuse them service nonetheless. Men and women alike enjoyed their obscenities when the moon was high and only the stars bore witness to them—and who was the bartender to deny profiting from this?

Business was business.

Something bitter snagged in Eira's throat as she continued to watch the group talk amongst themselves. They communicated in broken syllables and gargled barks of laughter so loud that even the other, equally as drunken patrons, began to throw annoyed glances their way.

How many other taverns had they frequented that night?

Were their pockets still heavy with coin, even after what could've been hours of drinking?

Did they leer at mortals who passed them by with downturned heads and hurried steps?

Were there women, or men, who waited in dark, quiet bedrooms for them to return home?

Were there ones who wished, instead, that they never would?

What a great privilege it must be to look upon the silhouettes of the city and not fear its vastness; to live a life so small, so monotonous; to not fear the anguish that pulsed through the veins of its seeping heart, to not mull over how much resentment its people held within its towering walls before it all caved in on itself.

What a great privilege it must be to be anywhere but here, Eira thought.

Of course, when she wasn't moping, Eira acknowledged that being a fae heiress trapped in the skin of an unassuming mortal had its benefits. One being that she could sit in the most decrepit joints in Celimene, the Kingdom of Erebus' capital city, without anyone batting an eye. She could even work in them, too. Meet people. Exchange secrets.

Deities forbid, if anybody knew who—or what—Eira truly was, she wouldn't be doing any of that. She would be strung with bound wrists and ankles, showered with silver bullets, or burnt alive, perhaps. Whatever the mortals of Erebus believed would be the most effective method to banish scheming fae from their midst. They lived in a world threaded with magic, moulded thanks to the combined efforts, and fragile allyship, of fae and mortal alike—but that didn't rid them of their fears.

Or their preconceptions.

Eira supposed she should also be grateful she wasn't in

Exilis. A mortal world, through and through, where people either didn't know of the existence of the fae at all, or on the opposite side of the spectrum, chose to live with the dream of dismantling The Seelie Court in its entirety.

Eira's tongue brushed the bottom of her lip, catching on the skin that had been drying up in unfortunate little patches. She wanted to make a mental reminder to better moisturize them.

Instead, all Eira could think of was the bitter notes of ale that lingered there. A phantom kiss. It would be rude to order herself another round whilst she waited. The thought lingered nonetheless, and she did her best to distract herself.

Eira wondered how the mortals around her passed the time in Celimene, in Erebus, when the sun came up. She pondered if the alcohol and tavern hopping made their *little lives* bearable.

When the nights blur together so seamlessly, does it really matter where you are in the morning?

It had been enough for Eira, too, in the beginning.

But in her third year of living in Erebus, Eira long tired of the routine.

Yet, with so little time left, she made the choice to see her articulately crafted regime through. Thus, Amzi became a part of her every-other-day nightly schedule, meaning Eira ended up in her trusty spot—indulging in the same two to three glasses of ale—about three to four times in a week.

The only issue this left Eira with (besides a steady, ever-growing sense of shame) was a monetary one.

Another group of mortals made their way through Amzi's entrance, bringing with them a gust of crisp evening air. With the swiftness of a sharpened blade, the cool wind sliced through the muggy mess that had been made of Eira's mind. She rubbed her eyes.

What time is it now? A tsk fell from her lips as she spotted a clock, mounted on a far wall.

He's late.

Who was she to ever trust a man, let alone a man to be *on time.*

Goosebumps rose and littered the bare skin across Eira's arms as she remained unmoving, eyes now locked on the display of liquor decanters. They glittered and danced in the dim light of the tavern, things of strange beauty in such an unsightly place that had become far too familiar over the past few years.

Eira knew every crack and crevice in the rickety framework that held Amzi on its last standing legs.

She knew the rotation of customers, both old and new—though the painfully obnoxious group of mortal men that still meandered around the bar boasted faces Eira hadn't the plea-sure of committing to memory—and she'd heard all the secrets the tired walls offered to anyone willing to listen. On slower nights, Eira resorted to counting the spots of ever-growing mold on the ceiling.

She'd frequented Amzi since her first year in Erebus, at the ripe age of fifteen. For the first few months, Eira only ever wanted to sit in the tavern and observe. Observe and listen, *of course*; to the mortals who poured their hearts out after a slow but steady coaxing from a liquid that looked innocent but burned on the way down; to the guards who spoke in hushed whispers, that weren't hushed enough, about their days on duty to the king of all kings; to the way they spoke and sobbed and serenaded one another. Eira listened so intently so that she could, eventually, mimic them.

It was Eira's way of survival. What better way to live amongst mortals than to take on the worst parts of them.

The barkeep allowed her visitation to begin with because she didn't cause a fuss—and because Eira offered to work behind the bar to make her time there worth his while, as a patron who sat, and observed, but never drank herself. She once cared little for the colorful liquid, as she didn't yearn for it the way mortals did; Eira just enjoyed being in a place where she could drown the incessant ring of her own heady thoughts.

Eira had no formal training, no previous experience nor a soul to vouch for her credibility as a person, let alone a worker.

He took her on nonetheless.

Eira turned sixteen halfway through her first year living in Celimene. She and the barkeep, the owner of Amzi, barely talked outside of what was necessary in the workplace. Over time, the unlikely pair cultivated a companionship of sorts.

It was around the same time, after six months of washing dishes and scrubbing away mortal waste and greeting the morning light bleary eyed and bone-tired, Eira decided she deserved a taste of what brought so many bodies through Amzi's doors to begin with. That was the beginning of the end for her—and not once had her employer, or anyone else for that matter, bothered to ask Eira her age—so Eira reaped the benefits of that blessing, and curse, for the rest of her meagre existence in Erebus.

Now, eighteen, the effects of the accumulated years of drinking long caught up to her weakened mortal body.

And mind.

Eira felt her eye twitch.

"Do you plan on getting another round, or will you just sit around and mope all night?" a once familiar voice asked, snatching the fae from her stupor. "You're puttin' off the other customers."

As if any mortal here cared for someone other than themself.

Unlikely.

Eira smiled up at the barkeep, Alfie, standing at the corner of her booth. "You know I like to savor my drinks," she replied, sweetly, despite the effort it took to draw the words from her mouth.

Alfie never seemed to truly forgive her for the random day, late in the year prior, that she stopped showing up to work, despite letting her linger in his establishment, night after night thereafter, until the sun poked its head through the mottled windows.

Eira assumed he still had a soft spot for her.

She couldn't understand why.

Alfie's flushed brown skin gleamed under the dim light, similarly to the decanters, slick with sweat. Stray, grey-streaked bits of hair came loose from the spot where he attempted to keep the rest of his tight honey curls at bay with a small, leather band. Even in the shadows, Eira knew that the pressed purple under his eyes deepened exponentially over the past few months, indicative of the fact that being a body down in help hadn't done Alfie any favors in aiding his state of perpetual exhaustion.

Eira couldn't remember the last time she'd seen him up close like that.

A pang of guilt stabbed her in the gut, sobering her up, just slightly.

Alfie's nose crinkled. "You're lucky that I don't charge you the cost of the tab as soon as your gloomy ass darkens my front door. It's never just one glass with you, is it?"

Eira hoped her expression didn't falter. His words were not untrue, but they were cruel, in some ways. Perhaps she would never be used to Alfie looking at her like she was a burden. "Do I look like someone who would leave before paying my due?"

"I can't say that you've proven yourself to be entirely reliable in the past," he shot back, voice sharpened with hurt.

"She's with me."

The voice that joined their conversation, if you could call the terse exchange that, made Eira's heartbeat stutter in the worst way possible. She recognized the baritone of his words but familiarity, and inebriation, couldn't numb the constant wariness that settled itself into the foundation of her bones, fashioned from her time amongst mortals—who she had come to learn enjoyed stabbing one another in the back just for amusement, just to watch the other bleed.

Eira's eyes moved to the figure behind Alfie, the visual affirmation in the lines of his face allowing her to settle. "Finally," she mumbled.

The man pushed past Alfie with no amount of subtlety, situating himself in the empty seat across from Eira. Once sat, he placed four copper coins with crescent moons pressed into either side on top of the table in front of them.

"Two of her regular," he said to Alfie, who had not yet moved his crumpled expression away from Eira, seemingly angered at the fact that her mortal companion didn't bat an eye at the two already empty glasses in front of her, not needing to question whether he really could cover the full tab for them both.

Eira knew her companion to be more than capable of doing so. Alfie knew this, too. This was a part of her routine, so of course he did.

That didn't mean he liked it, though.

Alfie mumbled something under his breath before picking up the glasses and the coins in one well-practiced scoop. He nodded in the direction of the bar. This was the way he told patrons that his services didn't extend to table delivery unless there was something they had that *he* wanted.

Alfie had nothing left to say to them. To Eira.

That much was clear.

Two rings of condensation marked the wood of the table. Eira's gaze lingered on them before they were obstructed by the outstretched arms of the mortal across from her.

Eira swallowed the regret of being unable to throw a response back at Alfie before he slipped away. She despised him for getting the last word. For making her feel bad.

Instead, her eyes moved to the face of her companion, pushing down any guilt that festered from her interaction with Alfie.

He broke the silence first. "It's been a while since you've called me out this way," he said, something accusatory in his tone. Eira wouldn't be surprised if she simply imagined the intonation. She struggled at reading other people's emotions when they weren't made crystal clear. Subtleties were often lost on her.

"My apologies, dear friend," Eira spoke with a tongue heavier than what lingered in her mouth, "but I have had as little need for your services as you have for mine."

"But that has changed now, has it?"

She nodded.

The man seated across from her was cloaked in a coat of material so fine that its craftsmanship was notable even in the lackluster light. Eira and the well-dressed, but always unshaven man, never exchanged names—not on the night they met nor any after that.

He was a sneaky bastard.

One of the self-proclaimed advisors to the king himself—a fact that Eira was initially skeptical to believe based on his word alone—she didn't know how her little rat hadn't found his head missing from his neck yet.

He was ruthless in his whispering, and she sensed it would be the end of him. If he cared, Eira didn't know—and she didn't dare to ask either.

They weren't that close.

Before their conversation progressed any further, a sharp whistle from the direction of the bar told the pair that their beverages were ready for collection. Eira's companion excused himself, much to her surprise (maybe chivalry wasn't dead after all, though she'd be the last person to know), and it was only moments later that he was back at their booth, drinks in hand.

How he managed to weave through the churning tavern crowd with such ease was beyond her; an acknowledgement that served as a reminder that she was not his only client. He had spent many nights seducing secrets out of mortals and fae alike, unbeknownst to him.

In a flurry of movements familiar to them both, Eira and the man clanked the crystalline rims of their glasses against one another with no amount of grace before taking large swigs.

"So," her companion choked the word out, "what is it that you wanted to tell me?"

They met every other week. Eira's companion knew when she had something valuable to offer him. It was an exchange that became habit seemingly out of nowhere. He saw an opportunity in her.

Some weeks were quiet. Some weren't.

A louder week brought them to the spot they were at.

If Eira had no secrets to spare, she would be short in coin. If she were short in coin, she didn't have an excuse to sit and eavesdrop in Amzi. It was a cycle of destruction, but it managed to sustain her.

Eira felt the broken skin that stretched to make room for her grin burn with the movement. "Now, now. I can't go spoiling all the fun before payment, can I?" She placed the glass down.

Her lack of subtlety made the man sigh, and yet, he didn't reject her request, moving to fish deep within the inner lining of his superbly crafted coat. Suddenly more awake than she felt in hours, Eira was acutely aware of the desire that gnawed at her insides, almost in expectation of what this payment would give her in the weeks to come.

The information she was going to offer was well worth it. All information was, whether it was secrets or not.

What Eira would *not* divulge in was secrets of her own— that this money was to keep her afloat for her last stretch of time in Erebus; that she had long spent all the allowance King Durante intended to last for the three years of accommodation; that she didn't believe she had it in her to last even three more months without this stupidly sacred part of her routine.

A velvet bag, bulging crudely at the sides, passed between them.

Eira pocketed the payment in a swift exchange that could be mistaken for an over-the-table handshake, as one should do in a joint like Amzi.

Her companion replaced his now empty hands with his drink. "All fifty is in there, just as you requested."

Eira would have to trust him. Despite the irrational part of herself that wished to do so, she couldn't be seen pouring out the bag's contents and doing a headcount for the coins given right then and there. If tonight was the night he finally chose to betray her, Eira deduced that maybe she deserved it.

It would serve me right.

It was what her parents might say if they saw her.

Eira leant in over her half-full glass, lowering her voice to speak to him. "I've received word that the ninth heiress will arrive tonight."

His eyes widened. "The fae heiress?" There was a subtle urgency to his words despite the quiet volume with which he spoke. Uncharacteristic of his usual calm, cool demeanor.

"Are there any *other* heiresses due to arrive in the kingdom?" she chided. The ridicule earned her a sharp tsk in response, paired with a look that told Eira her companion would reach over and snatch the velvet pouch back right then and there if he was so inclined to do so.

If only he knew.

Eira allowed herself to chuckle inwardly at the thought.

And perhaps he would've known who she was had King Durante not accounted for that possibility, too; that the sudden appearance of new citizens in a city such as Celimene wouldn't draw the attention of its people. The king assured the fae that their time in his kingdom would see them protected—hidden with mortal skins, preconceived histories and forged identities to match—and that meant any and all mortals to come in contact with the cloaked fae would be none the wiser.

But it remained that Durante's methods were as curious as his connection to the fae themselves.

Eira continued. "I can't tell you which of the courts is left, though. Don't know which one she belongs to."

"How can you know for sure that this is true?" Yes, he was listening, but whether he believed Eira or not was another matter entirely. "I struggle to grasp the concept of *you* having found out this knowledge before myself."

Eira shrugged. "Look, old friend, you come to me in search of words whispered in the corners of this tavern. This is the stuff you won't hear in gilded hallways and grand rooms. Why you didn't hear it first is cause for my payment alone—because it means someone may be stepping into your territory, stealing business from under your nose—and I was first to find out."

Her *informant* was a royal guard who frequented Amzi with wide pockets and an even wider mouth. Eira heard a slew of off-handed confessions and (not so quietly) muttered commentary from him regarding his thoughts on the court proceedings of Erebus for many months.

Now *he* was someone whose survival she truly didn't

understand—how word of him blabbing hadn't gotten back to Durante was beyond her.

But some fear mongering for her companion wouldn't do her any harm, surely.

It would give him something to do. A reason to stay on his toes.

After all, guards with loose tongues put *everyone* in danger.

Eira's companion considered her, and her words, in silence. A few moments passed between them before he finished off the rest of his ale in a swift and singular gulp.

"Go on," he said.

"I know she's due to arrive tonight. Assumedly around midnight." Eira's eyes fell to her own glass. "I heard she's been making Durante wait, purposely delaying her arrival."

He tightened his empty fists atop the table. "To be there for something like this . . . it would be immeasurably valuable. If I had known earlier . . ."

Eira wondered, morbidly, if he watched her own arrival. She supposed he wouldn't be here, sat with her, if he had. After all, it was only the king's closest associates (business advisors didn't make the cut, Eira assumed), his tightest inner-circle and his wait staff that got to make a spectacle out of the event. They were the only mortals saved from Durante's mental manipulation.

They knew exactly who the heiresses were, even in their mortal skins. They were sworn to secrecy—and it's not like Eira was privy to what the crowd looked like. Donned in masks made of intricate lace, covering any discernible facial features, the peanut gallery was protected.

The night of Eira's arrival in Erebus had become something of a gruesome blur that she didn't linger on. It was probably better that way, too. It wasn't healthy to simmer in her anger, so she opted to drown it instead.

That's what the ale was for.

"The arrival of the last heiress is a big deal, but so late? Why did he allow such a delay?" He spoke at her, not to her. "Is he trying to incite more fear of them?"

This piqued her curiosity. She bit down on the lead he offered. "Why *shouldn't* we fear the fae?"

Eira's companion thought on this for a few moments. He seemed to disappear into his own mind. "Those that are different *can* exist at one time without one fearing the other," he said, simply, "because it has been done before."

She scoffed. "Or maybe Durante thinks it's easier to neutralize a threat when it's forced to move in next door and you're not told until a few years later—then, the fear and the mystery—everything that makes *them* different from *you* doesn't seem so distant."

"Hm," was all he said in response.

Then, "In any case, there have been whispers around Celimene . . . there's change in the air. I don't know what Durante is planning with all of this, but it's not good."

Eira spread her palms out on the table in front of them, an ease to her movement that seemed to agitate him further. "When is it ever good?" she asked half-heartedly. But she was grateful the mortal man couldn't peel back the layers of her falsified demeanor to see what squirmed underneath—Eira herself was unable to deny the significance surrounding the arrival of the last heiress. An event that a version of her three years prior would've wanted to witness.

Something that would've fueled the fire in her veins; the need for answers, or evidence, to bring back to her parents to prove that a partnership with Durante, in any form, wasn't worth the trouble.

Her companion narrowed his eyes. Another pause.

"I need you to be there when she arrives."

18

It was a simple statement—not a question. An instruction. A very clear one, at that.

Eira had never been more confused.

"Do I look like an inside man to you?"

He smiled. "You'll do."

CHAPTER 2
LAST TO THE PARTY, FIRST TO THE FUNERAL

Her companion could be convincing when he wanted to be.

Or maybe Eira was *just* sober enough to see, now, how the situation she'd agreed to put herself in was an incredibly foolish one—even for her standards.

It hadn't helped that the ale gave her an unfair confidence boost. It thrummed under her skin like a living thing, matching time with her thundering heart as she listened to her companion rattle off his plan.

Eira hadn't felt so awake in weeks.

Months, maybe.

And that, alone, was bad grounds for decision making. Horrible grounds—to chase a high that would be gone in a matter of hours.

So Eira decided that she would make the most out of the situation. If she made it out in one piece, it would be means to celebrate.

That is what she told herself as she unceremoniously stripped out of her clothes. Eira's companion was convinced that if she got ready quickly, she would arrive in time to watch the event unfold.

"*What would happen if I were to arrive too late?*"

"*People will think you're a drunkard playing dress up—that you've escaped the confines of the palace to gallivant in the streets.*" He shrugged. "*Play the part and you'll be able to slip away just fine.*"

Eira's face warmed.

"*Why can't you escort me, then, you old bat? Get me through the gates without any additional humiliation.*"

"*Too risky.*"

Whatever that meant.

She donned the gown given to her in a cluster of trees close-by Amzi. Their limb-like branches brushed along her exposed skin as she dressed, occasionally snagging on the flimsy fabric. Sure, her companion didn't make her entrance into the palace all that easy, but he sure seemed to have a knack for pulling the right props out of thin air.

Eira had raised an eyebrow when he told her to wait outside Amzi after their debrief—telling her, simply, that the cool night air would "sober her up". She was even more confused when he slipped into the shadows, returning no more than ten minutes later to shove the evergreen, silken dress and mask into her hands.

"Hurry along," he said, ever impatient, "we don't have all night."

Eira caught a glimpse of his back, facing away from the spot where she got changed. The fae offered him a crude gesture as she finished fighting with the material. It was a size too small, and she was painfully aware of how the fabric shifted with every movement she made. The mask, discarded in her efforts to get the dress on, was covered in a light layer of dirt.

She brushed it away to reveal the craftsmanship beneath. Lace and jewels were woven with care, made to cover all the discernible features of her face. Goosebumps littered her skin at the sight and feel of it—an awfully mortal sensation.

The audience at her arrival had worn the same. Slightly varied iterations of the same haunting vision.

Hers was white, the color of eggshells, with an obnoxious stretch of fabric sewn into the spot where it would sit at her hairline. A veil. It made Eira want to gag.

At least it would cover her hair.

The copper layers, falling just above her shoulders, had a spattering of silver streaks right down from her widow's peak. Too obvious not to hide from anyone paying attention.

Eira emerged from the trees like the ghost of someone's wronged wife, the mask clutched between her fingers, her other clothes forgotten in a sad pile behind the shrubbery.

"No shoes?" she asked as her companion turned around to face her.

He shrugged, the impatience in his expression starker from the front. "The less noise you make, the better."

Eira's stomach tightened. "Have you been to one of these before?"

A smug smile painted his face as he said, "What do you think?"

Maybe he seemed so unwilling to escort her in because, once she did arrive (left to walk alone almost immediately after they moved away from Amzi), mask donned and feet out in the finest part of Celimene's city center, the fae slipped into the mingling pool of finely dressed, masked mortals with ease. It was simple to slip into a crowd that assumed you already belonged.

She arrived just on time.

"You took your time, Meilin Azelie."

Eira's breath caught in her throat.

She *should* despise the fae heiress who stood there with burnished umber eyes and a grimace painted across her face. Eira grew up being told tales of the other courts, of the heiresses that shared her birth year—and none of what she heard was positive. They were all enemies to the Court of Isolde, threats to her home and her throne.

Despite focusing on that very threat and the leaps of space between them, Eira could summon none of the expected emotions in the presence of Meilin Azelie.

Instead, the heiresses' name made something ancient, and unfamiliar, awaken inside of her—as if the monstrous thing craved the sound of its syllables for centuries. Eira had to steady herself from its impact, only able to focus on fighting the sickness that rose to meet it at the sight of King Durante.

The mortal King of Erebus peered down his nose at Meilin as he spoke, all but spitting her title like it was a profanity and not something to be proud of.

Meilin cast her eyes downwards, but Eira read no shame in her posture.

Eira hadn't been able to snatch a spot amongst the rows of courtiers closest to the fae heiress. Nonetheless, even from the few rows of distance, she wouldn't be spared the details of everything unfolding before her. She could see the lines of Meilin's tall, willowy build, the curtain of ink-black hair tied back in a haphazard updo, the billowing dress that was simple in both fabric and color but made her look as if she was better suited to sitting as the subject of a painting, rather than being placed on display in the chamber they were all in.

Before the attending crowd, and Eira, found themselves in the room—which was draped in a haze of smoke and smelt of bitter liquor before they stepped in—the guests were ushered into the palace's great ballroom to linger before the real show was due to begin.

A string quartet, perched atop an elevated stage, played melodies all too jovial for what they were about to witness.

Eira supposed this was the regular practice for the arrival of a fae heiress, as none of the courtiers around her questioned the sequence of events. They moved with purpose and familiarity, so Eira did the same.

This was despite the fact that she had no clue how the mortals mingled and talked amongst themselves, hands full with flutes of sparkling wine and lips curled into expectant, knowing smiles, with the lingering thought of what lay a few rooms over. Eira hovered around, so as to not arouse suspicion, accepting an offered glass of her own from one of the king's servers. The staff working for the night, those that weren't guards, wore crimson masks and plain clothes of the same shade; and despite being less ornate than the ones the guests had been given, the masks did a perfect job of obscuring the facial details of the wearer, as if Durante cared to protect their identity.

As if a fae heiress would ever dare target the mortal staff of the king.

Those same servers and guards stood waiting in the room they led everyone to only moments prior. Lining the walls like an arsenal, with their darting eyes behind their strange masks, they were more fearsome than any armed guard.

Eira swore she could see Meilin doing calculations in her mind—after all, her magic hadn't been stolen away just yet— not before the berating to come. Was there anything she could manipulate to her advantage? Would she dare to do so?

Which of the forces was hers to wield?

What would the power of the Azelie's manifest as?

Eira made a mental note of everything she'd known about

the other kingdoms of The Seelie Court—granted, it wasn't a whole lot—but she knew that each was tied to their own powers. She had never seen their faces, only reassured she would know such a thing when the time was right and she was ready.

Eira also knew names.

The Court of Atuat—*as swift as a slicing breeze.*

The Court of Azelie—*as beautiful as an unwavering flower.*

The Court of Eimi—*as free as the ever-flowing current.*

The Court of Telema—*as forceful as the strike of a steady sword.*

The Court of Eodum—*as unknown as a shadowed night.*

The Court of Faven—*as unforgiving as the strongest storm.*

The Court of Herminia—*as giving as the earth beneath us.*

The Court of Isolde—*as unrelenting as the winter slate.*

The Court of Kalama—*as brutal as an irrepressible flame.*

They were lines from the younger years of her childhood. Whispered in the shadow of night, her father spoke the stanzas in his sweet, soft voice when she'd been unable to sleep.

Her mother would've had his neck had she known.

What did a flower mean for Meilin Azelie? What was the extent of her magic?

A grating voice chimed in, filling the heady silence. "I'd like to let you in on a little secret, if you're inclined to lend your ear to it."

Durante's paper white skin was so thin that it was almost translucent. The color of it reminded Eira of fishbones. She fantasized for a moment about the experience of opening the king up, if only to see how he functioned on the inside. To make sense of someone she couldn't bring herself to understand. To rip white flesh from chalky bone.

Her stomach continued to curdle.

The king's head of close-cropped hair was mousy at best,

balding at worst. Even the striking blue grey of his eyes couldn't convince Eira that he had once been anything resembling handsome. Durante was hunched forward in his throne, his thin frame draped in a matching set of cream colored linen attire. If he didn't sit atop his dais, Eira could've been easily convinced that the king was a citizen playing dress-up.

He looked like he'd just been woken up from a deep slumber.

But Eira also couldn't ignore how the decadent jewelry that adorned his leathery hands twinkled like stars trapped in blanketed darkness. She hated that the pieces were so elegant, so beautiful, and wasted by being worn atop the fingers of such a loathsome man.

Perhaps his cruelty aged his soul quicker.

Living on Durante's land was one thing. Being in such proximity to the king, in a scenario like this, was another thing entirely. Eira had to steady herself—and her emotions—but sense felt too far and few in-between for her to grasp.

"It would be my pleasure, Your Highness," Meilin responded, tone flat despite the heat that dyed her cheeks in a violent splash of crimson. The color started at her collarbones and spread upwards, making her neck a similarly flushed shade of red.

Eira's own skin took on the same hue when she was either one of two things: enraged or on the verge of tears.

She could take a guess what emotion the other heiress was feeling at that moment.

The sound of Meilin's voice only made the beast that made a home of Eira's insides thrash and rattle, screaming to be acknowledged. The words, though sharp, bore curved edges that were sanded down by the honey-like way in which she enunciated them.

Each court of Seelie had their own dialect but most spoke the common iteration of the mortal language.

It was a practice that came about after the signing of the Treaty.

Durante's grin cracked wider, the broken skin of his lips splitting more severely. "You're the last heiress to grace my kingdom with your arrival, and with the end of the third year nearing, no less!"

He threw his head back, an obnoxious bellow of laughter coming from deep inside his chest. A spattering of chuckles in support of the humorless remark filled the room.

Meilin took the very brief distraction as a moment to really examine her surroundings. Eira watched her gaze trace the room. There didn't seem to be anything of value—anything that she'd be able to pull her power from—but Eira couldn't be sure.

It was only when she saw her settle on a selection of potted plants, dotted alongside the wall, that Eira finally understood. They appeared exotic, though poorly maintained. Sporting wilted leaves and what she assumed was near toxic soil, Eira wondered if Meilin ached to call out to their roots, to urge their bodies to come and shield her with their limb-like foliage.

Durante sucked in a short breath of air before pushing on, Meilin still so solemnly silent all the while. Her focus was razor-sharp, though—back on the king without anyone having noticed. Eira was glad she could pay attention, the thick of the liquor clearing.

"Who would've known the Court of Azelie was unable to pass the importance of manners onto their treasured heiress?" King Durante's sneer was incredibly, delectably punchable. "It seems you, like the others that share your birth year, are not accustomed to the expectations of behavior outside your court,

Heiress Meilin. Have you already forgotten the role you're due to play here?"

Meilin hadn't a chance to respond, to even open her mouth in defense, before her body was slammed into the ground.

Eira caught her lip in her teeth and bit down hard, tasting copper. It was the same unseen impact that swept her feet from underneath her, the same weight of *wrongness* that she hadn't noticed until it already descended upon her.

Meilin's lungs emptied themselves on impact, the crude sound of skin being slammed against marble now echoing in the chamber, amplified by the crowd's silence.

Durante barely lifted a finger.

A fat pendant, resting at the base of his throat, thrummed with energy. Eira could feel it from where she stood. The foulness that bled off it and into the air seized her heart, taking her back to the night she'd been subject to the same act of humiliation, and abuse, from the unmoving hand of the king.

The piece of gaudy jewelry was weighted with the stolen magic Durante stripped from The New Reign. Eira didn't understand how—a mortal accessory should *not* have the capabilities to hold captive the combined power of all the courts—and she couldn't fathom who adorned the king with the ability to wield it . . . but just as he had done to Eira three years prior, King Durante used the pendant to suck the magic straight from Meilin's veins.

Invisible fingers peeled back layers of the fae's skin, making her endure a pain so terrible that it brought her hands to her head, muffled screams erupting from her still floor-bound body. Eira remembered the feeling. The searing of her internal organs, the tightening of her mind, the wrongness of something foreign rummaging through your soul to slip away with the most integral part of your identity, leaving you hollow, unfamiliar with what once was entirely your own.

28

Whatever force he used to control her with was unfamiliar —unnatural.

Whilst the mortals could only see, could only fathom, the outward reaction, Meilin's blood was boiling her body from the inside out. As Eira's did, the heiresses' body would try to reject the pull of the pendant. It would fight.

Inevitably, it would lose.

Durante spoke over the sound of Meilin's quieting screams, his voice resounding. "Here, in this world, I am your King! You are a welcomed resident of this city, in *my* world. Shouldn't you apologize to your king for being so late?" Durante tsked. "Now, now, Meilin. That's no way to introduce yourself to the fellow subjects of my kingdom—your new neighbors."

The increasing feverish tone of his words made Eira recoil. He had been no different with her, if not angered by some other unknown reasoning. He was always angry about something.

But even for Durante, this seemed . . . extreme.

There were supportive jeers that came from the crowd she nestled herself in to, and when they came from mortals that were all too close, their disgust brushing over her own skin, Eira made herself smaller.

When Meilin's screams morphed into stifled whimpers, Eira knew it was done. The pendant took on a jade glow, blinking in and out of color momentarily, as if to acknowledge the success of the extraction.

A few beats of terrible, terse silence passed before Durante sighed. He exchanged his grin for pursed lips. Disappointment lined his expression, like Meilin was a child to be scolded.

"The powers of your court are surely something to behold," Durante said, tone flatter than before. Eira saw, as Meilin lifted her body to rest on her knees, that blood—red as wine— trickled down from her nose. "Your blood *sings*, Meilin. What a gift."

The pain that pulled at her features made Eira's head pound. Meilin seemed to muster enough spirit to spit at the ground, at his feet. "A shame that it will never *truly* be yours."

Small gasps came from the crowd.

Onlookers became unsettled.

Meilin was no danger to them. Not anymore.

But they had the audacity to act as if she could cause them harm. Eira felt their mortal anxiety cloud the room. It wept from their pores. She wore it like a second skin. Warm and oppressive.

Let them be scared.

It was the least they deserved for playing a part in the madness.

"No need for concern, my comrades," Durante re-assured them in a sing-song tone, "we show our hospitality to even the most *uncooperative* of heiresses. There is nothing to fear. The eight before her have, and will continue to, live amongst us—as one of us. They will be the pedestal of peace. Even stragglers, like our dear Meilin.

She may just need a little more...*encouragement.*"

The room held its breath as Meilin's body lifted up from the ground, pulled taut by the invisible tethers that heeded Durante's call. Eira knew, expected, that her fellow heiresses had their own tragic renditions of arriving in Erebus. Durante was consistent, of course. But it wasn't lost on her—the horror of a mortal king wielding magic from fae blood to inflict hurt on the owners of said power. This wasn't *peace*. It was a mockery of the Treaty.

And he was getting away with it.

Making a show out of it.

Eira didn't understand *how*.

Surely this wasn't what her parents imagined for her,

allowed her, to suffer through when they signed that letter of agreement.

Eira had to believe they were none the wiser.

The alternative was too much to bear.

Meilin's body rose, higher and higher, and Eira felt the world around them bleed from meek color to complete monochrome. Blood continued to trickle from her nose as the heiress hung in mid-air, arms and legs spread outwards like the points of a tortured star, suspended in space. Eira's gaze moved between Durante and Meilin. The king's fingers flexed and unflexed, just slightly. The mortals around them were not as fazed by the brazen show of otherworldly power—in witnessing this multiple times before, it wasn't the dizzying display of magic that had them enthralled.

It was how Durante wielded it to bring the fae to their knees.

The room burst into color again when Meilin's mortal flesh collided with the cold floor once more. Snickers and sneers grew in volume, the crowd emboldened. They didn't fear Meilin. They didn't fear the mortal girl that was crumpled in front of them. They had no reason to.

Durante thrashed Meilin's body around a little more. Too caught up in the display of it all, the mortals didn't seem to care to notice how—since having her power stolen—the fae changed. On the outside, she was still *her* (as much as Eira knew of what she looked like before Durante's hands made her bruise, bleed and shift into something entirely different).

There were markings, though not easily discernible from where Eira stood, that connected Meilin to her court. Eira had them too, as did every other heiress of Seelie.

They were gone now.

The pointed tips of her ears, noticeable before the room fell to chaos, were rounded to that of the mortals. They were the two changes most prominent to her.

But Eira was the only one who knew, *truly knew*, the changes she had undergone.

Meilin may notice that, with her powers gone, she wasn't feeling the emotions of the mortals around her as viscerally. But she would hear their jeers. She would be able to feel the pain coursing through her newly fitted body. It would be dull for the time being, a minor comparison to what she withstood during the extraction of her magic, but the transition would continue to be an uncomfortable one.

Eira was taken back to her first night, the memory an added element of distress in an already confronting situation; she knew what was coming for Meilin in the coming weeks, what the other heiress had not yet experienced. But Meilin's healing would prove to be even harder, considering the additional pain that Durante subjected her to.

Bruises sprawled on Eira's own skin for weeks after her arrival.

They were a sickening reminder of Durante's power over her, and whilst she recognized this wasn't the place or time to compare their pain, Eira was sure her treatment was nowhere near as bad as Meilin's. She was bed-ridden for her first week in Erebus, having shattered at least a few of her bones.

Concern for her fellow fae should be the last thing for Eira to feel—but it surfaced nonetheless, and she couldn't get it to quiet.

In reality, Eira didn't know what she was supposed to be looking out for, what her shadowed companion expected to see in Meilin. If something special would show itself in the wake of the heiresses' arrival, Eira assumed it would've done so by now.

Was it worse, or better, to learn that the heiress before her was not the horrible fae she had been told she was? That she didn't bear fangs and have skin that seeped poison; that, if anything, she was just like Eira, stripped of her powers; that she was a fae, like Eira, victim to circumstances they never truly had a hand in controlling any part of?

Had her family been lying to her?

Had her companion expected this?

And why couldn't Eira deny the feelings that burned her throat like acid when she looked at Meilin? In a time where they may have once been stars that circled one another, they were born enemies. Their magic made them different. Whatever pulsated in the pendant at Durante's throat sung to her and recoiled from her—a mixture of stolen powers that didn't belong together—awakened in the presence of the heiresses. She wondered if Meilin felt it, too.

The ale and adrenaline fought for control of Eira's nervous system. Her skin had taken on a sickly pallor—she knew it without being privy to her reflection.

Durante continued his ramblings, Meilin still splayed against the crimson-splattered floor.

White noise filled Eira's ears.

The queens and kings of Seelie protected their daughters fiercely whilst also having absolutely no idea what to do with them. It would seem that the two were mutually exclusive.

Maybe the families thought that the distance would give them the answers they needed to figure out exactly what to do once they were due to relinquish their thrones to their cursed daughters. A matriarchal society that cared little for its woman wasn't an irony lost on Eira.

I need to get out, her mind screamed.

She wondered what Meilin's family would think of their choice had they been privy to viewing the arrival ceremony; if they would feel so certain in their decision when they saw their daughter's limbs splayed against the unforgiving marble of the palace floor.

Eira felt her body teeter on the brink of shut down. She clenched the fabric of her dress in one hand whilst the thoughts in her head fought for her utmost attention. *I need air.*

For someone who claimed to truly care about the wellbeing of the fae, and the strong retention of a healthy relationship between them and the mortals, King Durante seemed to truly revel in causing them pain.

Did Eira's family understand something of Durante's game plan that she couldn't see for herself?

Her fists clenched and unclenched around the fabric—she couldn't, and shouldn't want to, help her fellow heiress, especially not without further endangering them both. Eira possessed all the power and none at all whilst she stood there, morphed into a crowd where she didn't belong.

The heiress was a fool to think anything other than pain would come of this experience.

What was she supposed to tell her shadowed companion?

"Well, she didn't get a pass for arriving late. She got the beating that the rest of us did. He definitely didn't spare her any humiliation."

But through the pain and rage that seared like hot-white flashes behind her eyes, Eira could see that something *was* different about Meilin. Maybe she was forcing it to compensate, and thought it was impossible to perfectly pin down in, the ninth heiress was special—but to what extent, Eira doubted she would find out.

Not now, at least.

The last of Meilin that Eira saw before her and the ogling crowd were escorted out was the heiress slowly pushing up to a sitting position. She didn't speak, didn't open her mouth to give

Durante the pleasure of spitting vitriol, even as he continued to berate her, words spoken softer and more directly this time.

When all was said and done, Eira struggled to settle her racing mind on one thing.

Eira felt like she was leaving with more questions than answers. More concerns that she was not prepared to shoulder.

Time felt altered inside the palace walls.

It all happened so quickly, and yet, once Eira found herself outside again—shocked by the sudden cool shift in the night air—she couldn't be so sure of how many years her experience in that room had stripped from her life.

Thinking of the satisfied sneer in Durante's voice made Eira grind her teeth.

He spoke in the same way he wrote. Cocky. Durante wore an air of arrogance more prominent than the crown atop his head.

To the esteemed Family of Isolde,

I have been waiting for some time to share this correspondence, and my dream, with you.

It is nearing sixteen years since the birth of your daughter, who is only one of the nine that make up The New Reign. This is not knowledge lost on me, despite my ruling priority being that of mostly mortal folly.

As the bearer of Durante blood, continuing the lineage of those before me who ruled the lands born out of our beloved Treaty, you would know it is my duty to ensure that the allegiance between mortal and fae kind is honored.

You must also be aware of the unrest in Erebus and Exilis alike. I have also been told of the tensions that trouble the courts in Seelie. The birth of your dear heiress, whilst a great blessing, has caused uproar that refuses to cease. The mortals of Exilis, those unlike myself, do not know of your temperament, let alone that of your daughter. They are not quick to trust what they do not understand.

They are becoming restless. I'm hearing word of mortals preparing weapons of iron with the intent to present themselves to my kingdom, requesting permission to pass through our world to yours, to strike the courts. Whilst I write to you, they ready to march. Whether to eradicate the looming threat they see in the unexplained nature of the birth of The New Reign, or in an attempt to harvest your power, I'm unsure.

It is a reaction that stems from fear, but it is not something to be so easily dismissed. If word makes it past my ears, to the people of Erebus, there may be a disturbance at your door that is much closer to home.

Alas, it is not all bad news. I come to you as

an ally, with the best intentions for both fae and mortal kind at the forefront of my mind.

My proposal is a compromise.

The rest of the letter, the details of said compromise, was read through blurred vision. Eira hadn't assumed him to be serious.

Despite unbid tears welling in her eyes at scanning the words, Eira *scoffed* after reading it for herself.

"Is he serious?" Eira asked, her tone indignant. The words came out choked.

She remembered the way her parents looked at one another. The way her stomach sank.

A near-sixteen-year-old Eira had thrown the parchment paper to the ground, fists clenched as she stormed out of her mother's office. She remembered the way her skin burned hot, like she'd dripped the fresh molten wax of a flickering candle directly atop it. She remembered the tears that stung her eyes, that fell freely in the isolation of her room. Eira didn't sleep that night.

How am I to blame for a birth that I had no say in?

Queen Isolde sent off her own correspondence, with an additional sign-off from Eira's father, not even a week thereafter. Her daughter was a living, breathing sign of the unyielding loyalty and strength of their court—Queen Isolde honed the perfect weapon from a revered daughter. She saw Eira living in Erebus, presenting herself in front of Durante, as an additional star on her belt.

Eira was said to be blessed by The Deities—despite being treated as nothing but one of a nine-fold curse—so surely living in mortal lands for a few years would do her no harm.

Besides, Durante's knowledge of the fae courts, and of the strange circumstances surrounding the year when The New Reign was born, was both unsettling and impossible to deny. It made Eira uneasy to think of the way the mortal king offered a way to safely have the nine fae heiresses reside in his kingdom without any of them being able to identify one another; it made her uncomfortable to know that Durante understood the heiresses' bodies and magic were more malleable to manipulation prior to the Rite; it made her question the will of the Higher Courts, to give a mortal lineage so much say in the business of fae.

Nonetheless, he had given them no other real alternative than to heed his call.

If court relations were tense before The New Reign was born, they grew deadly that year—and he knew this. No court seemed to have insight to offer on the unsettling circumstances of the nine heiresses' birth. The Higher Courts wouldn't heed their calls for help, their questions and prayers and concern shouted at starless skies. Deities gave them the cold shoulder, their message clear.

Figure it out for yourselves.

Eira didn't know for sure what sort of answers the fae expected from them. Signs could only come in such subtle ways, and the superstition around it all was what made it so revered, made it a tradition. But maybe that was also why the birth of The New Reign was the final straw to break the back of a hierarchy with a millennium of unsolved problems. All it took was a bad omen.

Because things tended to get bloody between fae when they misunderstood each other. Unwilling to test the vitriol of mortals who existed in masses larger than the fae could ever imagine—who were ready to die in the thousands to see their odd sense of justice through to the end—were just as danger-ous, in their own way.

The Treaty, brought about to keep the peace, was guidance.

If avoiding war of any proportion meant sending the heiress to live amongst mortals for a few years as a show of goodwill, then so be it.

But was this truly in Durante's cards?

Was the cruelty so necessary?

Eira ambled along the path to home, mind swimming. She emptied her stomach multiple times along the way.

The night sky above her was altogether beautiful and terrible.

Once in her cottage, Eira flung the mask from her hands so violently that you could be fooled into believing the fabric seared her skin. She would sweep it into a corner later, when she was ready, and move on from the night with the composure of someone who wasn't suffocating under the weight of their mismatched emotions.

But for the time being, Eira succumbed to the heaviness of it all, and her body crumpled at the foot of the door. Once on the floor, she drew her knees to her chest, suddenly fifteen again.

She cried, and cried, and cried.

CHAPTER 3
CHORDS OF DESTINY

Eira might as well have signed her death certificate from the moment she agreed to her companion's palace escapade.

What more could a little curiosity cost her, in the grand scheme of it all?

The thought was comforting in the beginning, at least. She had woken up that morning with spirits higher than usual—and with the garments from the night prior shoveled away, out of sight for the time being—Eira felt refreshed. Born anew, with a purpose.

Gone was the usual pounding in her head after a night at Amzi. Her bones didn't ache and protest as she moved out of bed, and the smell of the early forest air wove its way through her window, coaxing her up. It was only the redness that rimmed her eyes that gave her away.

A small glimpse beneath the newly crafted façade she donned for the day.

Eira was going to learn more about Meilin Azelie—and what better way to do that than to find her herself?

Was it in her best interest to seek out Meilin, if only to satiate her morbid sense of curiosity?

Probably not.

But if she could learn something of value, her companion would be sure to compensate her. Eira would be free of the fae thereafter, using her coin to waste away the remaining few weeks in Celimene in comfort.

She wouldn't acknowledge the small voice that nagged at her, that wanted to see how Meilin had fared from the events of last night. Would she be able to answer the door? Would she be willing to linger in the presence of another mortal so soon after?

As she readied herself to take on the city outside the weathered but familiar walls of her little home, Eira filled her argumentative stomach with slices of fruit and bread. It grumbled and murmured as she did, as if begrudgingly accepting the sustenance. With the bread loaf near done, and her unknowing of when the next delivery would arrive, the heiress made a mental note to visit the city's best bakery. In the heart of Celimene, its interior aways smelt of warmed butter and honey, and whilst Eira rarely ever spent her earnings outside of Amzi, she indulged herself in their signature tarts or seasonal cakes when she bothered to take the trip out to grab a fresh loaf.

Fed, and promptly dressed soon after, Eira paused at the washroom mirror to observe her reflection.

Three years had made its mark on her.

Her face, though not as harshly angled as it once was, suited her more. There was a roundness to her cheeks that, back home, wouldn't withstand the strenuous training regime that was an integral part of her life. Eira liked the way she grew into her skin, even if, technically, it wasn't hers at all.

What she didn't fancy was that the purple hue under her green eyes had darkened exponentially. She sighed, wondering if grey strands would come next.

Eira pictured them cutting through the copper layers and together, with the singular silver strand already closest to her brow, the monochrome hued hair would swallow any pre-existing color.

She and Alfie would match, then.

It wasn't that she minded the thought of aging. Eira just didn't think that the face of an eighteen-year-old, fae or mortal, had any business looking so *drained*.

How foolish she felt, suddenly, to be scrutinizing her reflection in the face of everything she experienced. *Of course* she had changed.

Perhaps Meilin looked in her own mirror that same morning, wondering of all the ways that the mortal king could change her in just the few weeks that she would darken his doorstep.

The questions that danced in Eira's mind from the time she woke up to the moment she turned away from her reflection became more persistent, and their drive pushed her further, and faster, out the door.

Yet, once outside, it hadn't taken long for hesitation to make Eira falter.

The same way she had done the night before.

This wasn't the same as donning a costume to crash a party. Eira was already in the skin of someone else. If she were to slip up—to somehow give Meilin any inclination that she was anything other than mortal—it would mean that the three years she'd stuck out in Erebus would be for nothing. She shivered at the thought of what a true disruption to Durante's *project* would mean for The New Reign, especially whilst they were just within his reach.

Everything seemed to progress as he planned, and it would be just like Eira to step in and screw it up, all at an unfathomable cost.

Eira bit her tongue and drew blood. The tang of copper

brought her back to her feet, planted firmly on the floor of her cottage.

She wouldn't spiral. It wasn't the time.

Nothing had gone wrong yet. She would give herself this— this well-deserved rush, the luxury of true misconduct—for just a short while. Amzi had been her reprieve. Would it hurt her to find that elsewhere?

Still sweet morning air wrapped itself around her in an embrace so familiar, so intimate, that gooseflesh danced along the bits of Eira's exposed skin when she stepped outside.

The Seelie Courts didn't have seasons, as such. Just a perpetual state of whatever climate best suited their respective powers. That was one of the very few facts about the other courts she could be certain was true.

The reasoning *why* was less widely understood.

Deity knows, was what her father responded with when Eira was younger and more curious, asking any and all questions that came to her mind.

But Eira had come to enjoy the mortal's rotation of seasons. Autumn, as it was known in Erebus and Exilis alike, brought crisp air and the changing of leaves. The heiress remembered watching, fascinated, as shades of varied greens gave way to yellows; enamored as they were then swallowed up by oranges and reds. In her first year, Eira had taken daily walks for weeks, excited to watch as the trees performed for her in their own special way.

It was that very time now and although Eira was not as dazzled by the ways of the weather, she never stopped loving the way her forest home transformed under Autumn's touch. She had to remind herself that she was in Erebus; a mortal world, with mortal seasons, ruled by a mortal king, whose cruelty outweighed the beauty that his land bore beneath him.

She felt as if she were constantly fighting a battle within

herself. The mortal rendition of her that enjoyed watching leaves change color and counting stars in the sky with drunk, bleary eyes. The other, true version of herself—fae heiress with the future weight of the crown looming over her, who trained in combat her whole life and knew nothing of the joy a regular citizen of the Court of Isolde may experience.

The bitter thoughts made it hard for her to enjoy a lot of things.

Leaves crunched under the weight of Eira's less-than-graceful steps as she maneuvered through the shivering forest, the leather of her shoes cracked and worn from constant wear but somehow still intact. Eira was grateful they'd lasted her so long, her trusty boots.

She wasn't one to know what did and didn't look good when it came to clothing combinations, but the light brown shoes seemed to work perfectly with all of the items she'd brought along with her, which happened to consist mostly of sparring and comfort wear. Loose-waisted pants and shirts that billowed around her figure were worn more than anything—the form-fitting sparring clothes had only seen the light of day in her first few restless months.

Luckily for her closet, and to compensate for her wish to avoid any of the city's seamstresses, Eira barely left her cottage during the warmer seasons (unless migrating to Amzi under the cool kiss of night-time).

That much made sense for a fae born of the ice court.

Not so much for the same fae cursed with an unnatural fire running through her veins.

Easily distracted by her own never ending thoughts, Eira willed herself to focus on the path ahead, despite being some-what unsure of what exactly she was meant to be looking out for.

One of the many reasons she had become akin to the forest was that it was consistent.

The heiress familiarized herself with its winding pathways and overgrown branches; and despite it growing and changing as she did, Eira never struggled to pick up on what shifted. She was able to accommodate it, as it seemed to do for her.

So, when something was different—out of place—Eira suspected that it would call out to her.

What she hadn't prepared for was that it would occur in such a literal sense.

Following a path that wound deep into the center of the woods, Eira's progression was paused when a new sound joined the melody making up the forest's morning song. The usual titter of birds and breeze whispering through trees was silenced by the sudden, unfamiliar sound of music that came from a place just out of reach. It felt as if the forest had paused with her, ears perked and back stiffened at the intruding sound.

Unsure of a source that could be anything other than who she was seeking out, Eira picked up her pace.

The notes, rising in volume as she moved, only drew her deeper into the mouth of the great woods. To be guided through the trees by a sweet and sorrowful melody was probably not the smartest move, but again, it blanched in comparison to others Eira made in the last twenty-four hours.

The further she went, the more the forest lamented under the rhythmic steps of her feet. As if deciding to trust Eira, and whatever intention it felt from her, the trees parted to reveal the truth she sought.

A small mansion, nestled in the deep stomach of the woods. The melody wept from open windows on the lower level of the two that made up the manor. A wilted willow tree curved over the top of the structure, the crescent-like twist of its trunk making it appear as though it were embracing the side of the building it grew over.

Eira's appreciation for the flora and fauna of Erebus came from biology books and thick slabs of text, mostly kept hidden in the library of her home. To learn about mortals—their homes, their landscapes, the trees they sheltered under and picked fruit from—was something her mother had been particularly against.

After all, if a war were to come about between the mortals and fae, how could Eira be expected to stomach slicing the throat of someone who was born of a land where she could name the native trees and fruit and insects?

Her mother believed that with knowledge came connection.

Her father's opinion was not considered.

Maybe that was why she was never taught anything about the other heiresses of The New Reign.

Eira rejected the notion as much as she could allow herself to without getting caught. Her training had done her well and would continue to do her well as she grew. She knew her responsibility.

Eira Isolde would not—*could* not—falter.

But even as a young heiress, she craved knowledge. She craved connection. Why should she be starved of either?

Stubborn, and set in her way from the beginnings, Eira would hide away in the library and, in the rare moments of seclusion she had, the fae would thumb through books on mortals. Their bodies, their ecosystems, their seasons.

If Eira listened to the will of her mother wholeheartedly, she would've had a conniption upon arrival to the mortal lands. Instead, a younger version of Eira was as ready as she could've been to uproot her life to move to Celimene.

Erebus was as close to Exilis as Eira would ever get. Yet, it only made sense that the lands gifted out of fae and mortal alliance would retain magic. It manifested itself in unexpected, unpredictable, and often unnoticed ways. A deer with eyes like silver or an enchanted flower that bloomed deep in the untouched groves of the forest, and only during a full moon. The latter was one that Eira hypothesized, whereas she'd seen the silver-eyed doe during her first few months in Erebus, believing it some sort of good luck omen.

The manor in front of Eira was another thing with magic wound through its foundations. It was a feeling she got, deep in her bones, that told her as much—and, more strikingly, the fact that she had never come across the mansion in years prior, despite its sizeable presence.

The curtains that hid one of the forest's best kept secrets parted, and Eira was granted a view of its insides.

An odd sense of accomplishment rippled through her.

She continued to examine the front of the home, the melancholy sound of the piano pulling her closer and closer to its front door. She didn't dare brace the thicket of overgrown rose bushes, their warped bodies swallowing what may once have been a beautiful, wrought-iron fence. The skeleton of the fence spanned the distance of the property, from the front to the back, and it gave Eira the illusion of something that was once grand.

With a tentativeness that her sense of curiosity cursed at, Eira followed the withered path and walked up the crumbling steps, hoping that her footfall was lighter than what she felt.

She tried to look for signs of a long-term resident, but all she saw was a front porch covered in a thick layer of forest sediment that bore the signs of multiple seasons passing atop it. There was the disturbed pathway she'd made on her way in, and accompanying footsteps were marked in the dirt and dust, showing Eira that the arrival of whoever was inside the manor now was only a recent one.

They hadn't the time to trim back the overgrown bushes or

patch the gaping holes in the floorboards, let alone brush away the mess from the entryway. Alternatively, maybe they just didn't care to do so.

Especially if they weren't planning on sticking around for long.

Eira, despite her best efforts, was not as quiet as she'd hoped to be.

The floor creaked beneath her every few movements and the noise rung out in the woods like an accusation. The pianist didn't stop playing, so she would let out a terse breath of air and try to angle herself closer to the window for a better auditory experience. If she got closer, maybe the heiress would hear a voice, too. Maybe the pianist would curse at themselves for missing a beat only they could pick up on.

If Eira heard their voice, she could know for certain whether or not it was Meilin inside. Once that was sorted, she would sit with the next steps. She only hoped the knowledge would make her feel like less of a creep.

This is so wrong, the rational part of her brain muttered indignantly.

Her body was already in the act of doing the very thing her mind resented her for, so it was all too late for that sort of thinking.

Eira, lost in her own mind, decided to assume her original position in front of the door. So preoccupied with what to do next, she hadn't paid heed to the abrupt pause of the piano, the notes no longer tumbling towards her from out of the nearest window.

The next thing she registered was the sound of the door crashing open and being knocked off her feet.

Eira tumbled ungracefully, curses falling from her tongue as the weight of another body bore down on her, the force of it taking the pair of them off the front porch, down the withered stairs and onto the forest floor. Pain flashed behind her eyes, white-hot and needle-sharp, throughout the base of her neck and all the way up to the top of her head.

In too much agony to open her eyes and feeling the effects of her recent lack of training, Eira very quickly found herself pinned with little effort from the opposing party. The earth was surprisingly cold through the fabric of her shirt.

"What do you think you're doing?"

Meilin.

She had been right, but it cost her. Of course it did.

Meilin's voice was commanding, her tone rigid. When Eira finally focused her gaze, she found that Meilin's own narrowed eyes and accusatory expression were just as powerful as they'd been from a distance. Instead, now, she wasn't directing her hatred towards the king—it was being directed at Eira.

And that wasn't the only thing Meilin wielded.

Eira acknowledged the cool lick of silver pushed against her throat and swallowed, her mouth painfully dry.

Meilin was faring better than Eira had done the day after her arrival. Being up on her feet, and reactive enough to end up on top of her fellow heiress, was testimony to that.

Neither of them spoke, communicating through short, ragged breaths as Eira used the cursory silence to scan Meilin's face. She needed to think of a good enough answer to begin with.

Despite Meilin being strong enough to get them into their current predicament, signs of Durante's abuse were not so subtle at close range. Already, darkening splotches of indigo littered her skin. There were swollen spots on her jaw and fore-head and the shadow of dried blood lingered around her nose, as if she hadn't been able to scrub it away the night prior. Eira saw the way Meilin's eyes twitched when she wielded the blade with headier force, applying a more urgent sense of pressure to Eira's neck.

A hiss of air escaped through Meilin's clenched teeth, which her lips curled back to reveal, daring the other to move.

"I don't mean any harm," Eira murmured, her voice low. She feared that if she spoke in anything above a whisper, the dagger would shift and slice through her exposed jugular.

But she didn't flinch. She didn't shudder away from Meilin's grip.

Eira didn't plan to play the part of the squirming mortal. She was already approaching the heiress with a pocketful of secrets. To yield beneath her, to cower and beg, would only be another falsified part of her personality to maintain. Eira was too stubborn to relent in playing into that role.

She also didn't fancy losing her head.

Meilin barked out a laugh. "You were lingering by my window to do what, exactly?"

That insatiable monster in Eira's gut perked up at the sound of her voice. She smelt of jasmine and had a spattering of freckles across her nose, just a shade lighter than the mahogany of her eyes.

Eira felt her face go warm.

Meilin shifted the position of her legs. Her knee, poised to dive into the other's stomach should the blade not be an effective enough warning, moved lower on Eira's abdomen as she re-adjusted to get a better view of their surroundings.

With her non-dagger-wielding arm holding the heiresses' arms together at the wrists, Eira didn't have any room to wiggle away. She watched, with interest, when Meilin's eyes scanned the vast forest around them.

"No regular citizen of Celimene is going to come stumbling into this part of the forest," Eira chided, "so I can assure you that we aren't going to be caught in this . . . *compromising* position."

Meilin narrowed her eyes, focus directed back on Eira. "That is not at all comforting."

Eira felt the beginnings of a sheepish smile break out on her face. "I have a knack for bad first impressions."

"At least we can agree on one thing," the other hissed. Meilin's grip on the hilt of her dagger was unrelenting. A sharp sting of pain promptly humbled the heiress. The faint smell of copper tainted the air between them. "As much as I *relish* in learning of your downfalls, I don't have the time to continue entertaining this conversation. Tell me why you're here—and who sent you to spy on me—before my hand slips."

"You're misunderstanding my intention," Eira hurriedly assured her, which was apparently anything but the right answer, as the blade continued to hover dangerously close to her trachea. "And I came here of my own volition. It was the sound of your piano playing that intrigued me."

Meilin, still unconvinced, didn't retract her weapon. Eira pushed on, the lie leaving metallic residue on her tongue.

"Unlike the other regular citizens of the city, I happen to have a great appreciation for this forest—so much so that I actually live quite close by in a cottage much quainter than this. You'll have to come by some time to see that my word is true, but I hadn't realized I had a new neighbor until that sweet, sweet melody drew me out of—"

A harsh tsk cut Eira's monologue short.

Meilin, having decided that the heiress was a nuisance rather than a danger to her immediate safety, pushed off Eira with no amount of gentleness. Air rushed out of her stomach as Meilin made a point to shove her knee directly into it upon rising, using the softest parts of Eira's body for some sort of leverage (as if she really needed the help to balance to begin with).

Stood above Eira, who still lay flush against the forest floor, Meilin brushed her hands clean of the other. She just as swiftly concealed her blade, moving aside the decadent fabric—which was the color of a clear, blue sky—to slip the weapon into a thin holster, which almost looked handmade.

When had she found the time to do that?

More importantly, Eira still couldn't understand how the other fae had managed to get a weapon in with her. She was told before her own arrival that their bags, and belongings, would be searched at some checkpoint prior to standing in front of the king. Eira assumed they did it when she had been out cold during the guard-assisted journey to the city. Anything considered to be contraband would be taken away from them.

Eira hadn't thought to bring her own daggers. She figured she would be forbidden from using them nonetheless.

The heiress that stood there, observing Eira with a cautious gaze and a deepened scowl, was as confusing as the king himself. She was secrets wrapped in secrets—which Eira couldn't fault, if only to avoid being a hypocrite—but she was strong-willed, that much was already clear, and as bright as the silver of her blade.

She was a mystery that Eira, in that moment, chose to cling to.

Eira wanted to unravel her. Selfishly, foolishly so.

"It seems your life lacks excitement, but I will not be the trinket you poke at for amusement," Meilin finally said. "Get out of my sight, and off of my land, before I retract the pity I've chosen to take on you."

Well then.

As eager as Eira may've been to learn more about Meilin, she was not a man—she knew what no meant—and was unwilling to test the boundaries of the fae who was as much a stranger to her as any other mortal in the city. Trust was not so easily earned.

And rightfully so.

By the time Eira had gotten herself off the ground, Meilin moved to stand on the porch of her crumbling home, her jaw set. She hadn't turned to go inside, to close the front door that seemed to swing, ever so slightly, in the morning breeze. Meilin just observed Eira at a distance.

Their scuffle left unusual markings in the dirt that kissed the bottom steps Eira tumbled off moments prior.

It all happened so *quickly*.

Eira had enough left in her, not yet spent on the emotional whiplash of the brief—yet achingly long—encounter to bend her body at the knees. A sloppily formed curtsy that earned her a slight twitch of Meilin's right eye.

Eira could've sworn that the house shuddered in laughter at her retreat as she turned and walked away.

CHAPTER 4
FRIENDSHIP

"You're not going to believe the morning I've had."

Alfie's expression was that of someone mildly perturbed, rather than excited. Eira couldn't blame him—she'd burst in the moment that Amzi opened, the need to talk about what happened to her so strong that it flowed out of the heiress and manifested in her uncharacteristically early arrival.

"Try me," he scoffed, half-heartedly. Their voices were loud in the empty space. Eira couldn't remember the last time she was able to make a beeline directly from the entrance to Alfie, behind the bar, without having to shove and stumble her way through the cramped crowds made of drunken mortals.

As she approached him, Eira saw that Alfie's focus was not on her but, instead, on the rag in his hand, which he dragged unceremoniously back and forth across the seemingly spotless bar top.

Eira didn't particularly fault him for this, either.

On most nights, he avoided speaking to her altogether. The unhealed, still festering wounds of the abrupt end to their companionship was never properly addressed, and they moved around one another in a strange dance; interactions jaded and cruel at worst, disinterested and indifferent at best.

Eira was grateful that he was entertaining her presence enough to respond. It would be unbearable if she was made to speak to the empty air. Alfie couldn't pretend she wasn't there if she was the only customer to grace Amzi's doorstep.

A smile tugged at her cheeks as she tried to sum up the happenings of the morning with enough ambiguity to not give away anything she wasn't equipped to share.

Alfie was . . . *Alfie*—there were no secrets shared in Celimene, and in Amzi especially, that made it past him. As the owner and barkeep of the renowned joint, he had no need to monetize his knowledge.

Eira, on the either hand, wasn't so coy.

Still, with the detailing of fae heiresses, she chose to tread with caution.

"I followed the sound of piano music," she started, hands placed flat on the bar top as Alfie wiped around her. The feeling of the damp wood under her fingertips sent a shiver down her spine. "Then, somehow, the next thing I know, I'm underneath a woman!"

He barked out a humorless laugh, still not looking her way. "Oh, so your dreams were extra vivid this morning, then?"

Eira's splayed fingers curled into loose fists, which she brought down with a half-hearted thump. "This wasn't the work of dreams, dear friend!"

She noticed him recoil, just a little, at the word—*friend*.

Something in her chest ached at the sight of it, but she moved on quickly.

"This was flesh and skin and the feeling of the forest floor—entirely, utterly real!"

Alfie raised an eyebrow, gaze finally settled on the over-dramatic heiress. "The forest floor is definitely a choice. Not one that I would make but, then again, who am I to judge?" He smiled to himself. "I was young once, too."

Eira found herself sputtering around an explanation in the next breath, the barstool shifting beneath her weight. "*Okay*, I was not taking that in the direction you seem to be heading in."

He shrugged, eyes back on the work he made of wiping down an already spotless surface.

"She's more striking than anyone I've ever met," Eira pushed on, "and I don't know nearly enough about her to make sense of this nagging feeling I have to want to learn more—to learn *everything*—about her. Alfie, I've barely known her for the sum of a singular day!"

"This is the most you've spoken to me in weeks," he mumbled. "I can't say I'm surprised that it's because of a woman and not anything else."

If he was waiting for an apology, Eira thought, *he would be sorely disappointed*.

She was too prideful for that. Besides, in order to apologize, she would need to possess the ability to reason with Alfie.

As is the nature of an apology, Eira would have to explain to him why she'd stopped working, why she'd changed so much, and why her will to do anything but the bare minimum to survive had become so small she felt as if it were her only path to walk for the rest of her time in Erebus.

Alfie's face bore the beginning of a smile when he spoke next. "But, from the sounds of it, this mystery newcomer is quite the charmer."

Eira didn't think she could claim the nature of their meeting to be charming.

Nonetheless, she smiled back at him. When she did so, that small but familiar ache unfurled inside of Eira's chest, warming the hollow spot that ached just moments prior.

But Alfie's face was quick to slacken. The smile gone just as quickly as it appeared, his eyes narrowed on a spot behind Eira's head. Windows on either side of Amzi's front door gave him the perfect view of the sky just outside the tavern's walls, the intensity of the oncoming evening shadow a clue as to when the busiest periods of the night were due.

He looked back to Eira, seemingly having found the answer to whatever he was looking for in the swollen sunset skies. "Don't bother sticking around tonight," he said, matter of fact.

Eira cocked her head. "You want me out that badly?"

"I just know that whatever you're not telling me the full details of is being reserved for that rag you meet here every other week. But I can tell you that I know he's not showing up. Not tonight."

"What, he let you know that himself?"

"You know as well as I do that no secrets go unheard here."

Eira, still confused, leaned back in her seat, which whined in contention at the movement.

Alfie pushed on. "Last night, when you went out to seek whatever he led you to, your friend stuck around after sending you off. Drank some more. Talked some more."

"And you listened?" The accusatory tone in Eira's voice was not lost on him.

"Was that not already established?" He scoffed. "When do I *not* listen?"

The irony was that she couldn't fault him for that—not when she did the exact same thing. He knew this just as well as she did.

Alfie's lips pursed. "Bumbling on about how things had changed and talking of his impending escape to Exilis."

He shrugged, the movement so casual despite the way his words made Eira's ears ring.

"I presume that it all just became too much for the fool. But whatever the reason, he is gone. That much I can promise you."

Eira couldn't remember the last time anyone made a promise to her.

She couldn't think of anything she wanted less in that moment.

Eira was meant to come to Amzi the night after her palace escapade to meet her companion, to tell him what she'd come across. She was due to meet him in the later hours of the evening—but her whole body buzzed after her encounter with Meilin, and she'd itched to be out of her cottage and in the tavern, if only to tell Alfie small licks of her experiences in the last day.

Eira was dumbfounded.

She sat there for a few moments, quiet and unmoving. Alfie's head tilted to the side, and he watched the heiress, his movements paused. He just as quickly shrugged off her emotions—nonchalant again—and grunted, arms folded over his chest.

"If you're not going to stick around to get your exuberant tab covered," he said, "then I'm going to need you to leave."

The doubt that roared inside of Eira was only worsened by the flood of information, and Alfie's change in demeanor didn't help.

What was she supposed to do next?

The disappearance of her shadowed companion—and for Alfie to know this before her—was not a situation she could've predicted for herself. Between the added confusion of Meilin's arrival, and the feverish search for knowledge her companion had wanted so badly to secure, Eira was lost.

She swallowed a surge of bitterness and clambered down from the barstool, turning away from Alfie.

The quiet that followed her out the door let Eira know that he had stopped whatever he was moving to do to watch her retreat.

The semblance from her earlier experience with Meilin made Eira grit her teeth.

So, for the first time in a long time, Eira left Amzi whilst the sun still dawdled in the sky, making way for night with lazy intention. Another first was that the heiress was sober—not only in body, but in mind.

Not even the familiarity of Amzi's ale would be able wash away the apprehension that nuzzled between an open slat in her rib cage, weighing heavy on her lungs and making it hard for her to breathe.

What do I do?

It only occurred to Eira then—the extent of her self-made solitude—and how alone she truly was.

CHAPTER 5
A MORTAL DILEMMA

As a part of the ceremonial path to adulthood for the fae, the Rite was a time that Eira eagerly awaited.

She'd be granted access to the full breadth of knowledge required to sit atop her throne and rule her court—finally, Eira would come to know, and understand, the inner workings of her world.

The secrets that Eira's parents whispered when she left the room would be secrets no more. Information in books, with pages rotted by age; intricate, leather-bound covers, locked in places she could only dream of knowing the location of; texts that detailed the reasoning behind the tense relationships within the courts of Seelie—the real explanation as to why the trade lines between the kingdoms had closed when The New Reign were born.

Maybe, even, the next steps to take to strengthen the bonds between the fae and mortals, as she took responsibility for the royal duties required by the Treaty.

Eira pondered on all of this, as she often did.

At the end of her third year, moving into the start of the fourth, Eira was due to return to her court. Then, and only then, would she be able to participate in the Rite.

Occurring on the first day of every fae's eighteenth birth year, it was a court-wide celebration for all.

Many other fae her age would be sharing the day with Eira.

It was not only the heiresses who underwent the Rite—it was just made out to be a much bigger deal amongst the ruling families of Seelie.

She was so close.

So close.

She would be made to drink the ichor of The Fates, to bathe in a moonlit pool and everything in her life would fall into its neat, pre-destined place.

Everything would be fine, then.

But things in Erebus were not tied up, not clean cut. Eira's companion was gone, she was inexplicably drawn to a fellow fae heiress—*enough of a problem in its own right*—and her hatred for the king burned as bright as ever.

She wouldn't be able to suffer through the pleasantries required.

She wouldn't be able to forget the image seared into her mind, one of brown eyes and a silver dagger.

Eira didn't trust that she possessed the strength to swallow down a bitter acceptance, to work in favor of a relationship with the mortals that she—as the queen—would be entrusted with maintaining.

Even in the safety of her own court, with her crown and her throne secured, the thought of having to come face to face with Durante once more made her skin crawl.

She wanted to make his blood run cold. To make him suffer.

Doubting any benefit of stewing in her emotions for a moment longer, Eira decided to embrace the prospect of the new day ahead of her. Her sleep was fitful the night beforehand, due to either the evening she'd wasted away sulking, or because she'd gone to bed sober.

But the morning air was kind, at least.

It tended to be amid Autumn.

Remembering her need for a fresh loaf of bread, and to get out of the house, Eira set her sights on Celimene.

It took less than five minutes for her to get ready.

Her trusty boots found their way onto her feet, and she filled her belly with the same serving of fruit. Eira's stomach grumbled in disagreement. Maybe it knew there was an element to her already dissatisfactory meal that was missing.

She could almost convince herself that all was well and normal, as it should be, besides that.

But the knowledge that the coins she carried like a secret in her pocket came from her missing companion made that task difficult.

Like a forlorn lover, so many things reminded her of him—of the situation that tied him and Eira to Durante and Meilin, and the complicated web that seemed to ensnare them all.

The walk to the bakery was treacherous.

Warm, clay-colored tops of cottage homes not unlike hers, soon gave way to taller and more banal looking structures once Eira crossed over the threshold, abandoning the security of the high-reaching forest.

Eira passed Amzi—unfamiliar, as always, in the daylight—with a pit in her stomach. The shadow of Durante's palace looming on the otherwise clear horizon made Eira's fists clench.

Bile rose in her throat when she spotted a flash of a guard in embellished red or a courtier in a pale blue gown.

"This isn't helping as much as I thought it would," she mumbled to herself.

The heiress only felt a semblance of relief flood through her when she caught sight of her destination in the near distance.

Plentiful Pastries was nestled between two buildings that towered over it, the blush lined roof and matching door a sight for sore eyes. Its front-facing window allowed her to peer inside its cozy interior, boasting a similar inner belly of softly hued furniture.

Greedily, Eira devoured the vision of the small row of sitting chairs and a front counter, which shadowed a buzzing kitchen over its shoulder, occupied by fast-moving bodies. Even the seated patrons, talking over flaky pastries and around mouths full of crumbs, seemed like they had somewhere to be once they were done.

Behind a bay shielded with frosted glass was a vibrant array of pre-made treats, both sweet and savory.

When Eira would step inside, she knew to expect the fragrance of freshly cooked bread and sweet undercurrents of rich vanilla.

Everything would mingle in a cohesive, consuming concoction that she itched to swallow a bit of with every breath.

There wasn't any real rush in Plentiful Pastries; just something electric and pacey in the air that Eira got an immediate sense of, even from outside.

The same as always.

The only thing out of place was a fae heiress, stuck in a skin that wasn't her own, with a wave of onyx hair and a violet dress, stepping up to the counter.

Eira's breath hitched.

All reason seemed to float away.

How could The Deities expect Eira to stay away from Meilin when they kept throwing them together?

Selfish as it was—*foolish* as it was—Eira stepped towards the front door to Plentiful Pastries.

She could've turned away.

She should've turned away.

Yet, there was something about the way that Meilin flinched away from the worker behind the counter.

Silvia.

Her warm brown skin was snaked with vines that travelled up from her right wrist. The black ink went up and around her elbow, disappearing under the pale cream color of her bakery uniform. Amber curls fell over her shoulders and into her eyes, which Eira saw flash at Meilin with not-so-reserved apprehension.

Meilin was overdressed, perhaps, but not enough to warrant the knitted eyebrows and bitterness on Silvia's face. The hard working and slightly terrifying till-keep was magnificent in a way that made Eira remember her name.

There weren't many instances where Eira interacted with the same mortals multiple times over.

Alfie and her shadowed companion were the extent of the faces and names she remembered and one of the two she didn't even actually *know* the name of.

But as much as she could chalk up remembering Silvia due to her beauty, it was more due to the fact that, despite having the demeanor of someone on the receiving end of a constant threat, she offered Eira small smiles and discounts on her bi-weekly loaf of bread once she'd warmed up to the heiress.

That warmth wasn't present in the expression she was offering Meilin.

The sound of a bright bell announced Eira's arrival into Plentiful Pastries. "Your payment comes to five copper coins," Silvia said, voice just as stoney. Her palm was upturned.

From the back of the line, Eira watched the heiress fumble

for a few moments, trying to navigate the non-existent pockets of her gown.

Durante, wicked as he was, hadn't given her any money.

Of course he hadn't.

Meilin's fists balled at her side. Eira wasn't in earshot to hear her response, spoken in a whisper compared to Silvia's previous sentence.

Before she could second-guess herself, Eira maneuvered her way around the line, ignoring the disgruntled murmurs of upset mortals.

"Sorry for being late," she said breathlessly at the counter. Eira placed a handful of coins into Silvia's open palm, enough for her to add her own loaf to Meilin's order. "Add my usual to this one, please, Silvia." She smiled down at the heiress, whose reciprocating gaze told her that she was the last person Meilin wanted to see. "She's with me."

Meilin's harsh intake of breath beside her was drowned out by Silvia's scoff. Surprised by the new arrival, she looked between the pair, a question in her eyes.

"You can't come in here and hold up the line"—a pointed look at Meilin—"and cut in"—a pointed look at Eira—"because, *in case you failed to notice*, I have other customers to serve!"

Eira donned a smile. "I don't cause trouble for you all that often, do I?" Silvia's fingers curled in on the coins as Eira pushed her luck, watching the other's reserve crumble. "Just this once? We'll be out of your way right after."

Silvia, already resigned, dropped the payment in the open mouth of the till with a non-committal sigh. She moved back towards the wide bay beside her, where strawberries with hardened sugar coatings winked back at Eira under the gleam of the morning sun. They stood out amongst the rows of delicacies, their half-split bodies sat atop the golden brown crust of small, rotund pies.

Silvia picked one up to package for Meilin, grabbing a savory cheese bun along the way. She did so with nimble fingers and a mild expression, rolling her eyes when Eira's smile widened in her direction.

The loaf of bread was the last thing to go on top.

"Go on, then," Silvia said, pushing the food towards the pair.

Eira scooped up her bread and Meilin grabbed her crinkled brown paper bag of treats. The heiress was just as quick to turn on her heel and leave, and Eira scurried to catch up to her.

"Thank you," she mouthed over her shoulder to Silvia, who just rolled her eyes again before beckoning forward the next customer.

There was no change given, even though Eira definitely paid extra. She didn't complain, too busy focusing on making it out of Plentiful Pastries in one piece—without losing Meilin on the way.

Once outside, and a few steps in front of her, Meilin whirled around to face Eira. "Are you following me?" she asked, her voice shrill. Her cheeks were a deep shade of red.

"This *is* the second time in two days." The beginnings of Eira's grin only seemed to grow. "Maybe the world is trying to tell us something?"

A tsk fell from Meilin's lips. She held the brown bag of food close, as if expecting Eira to snatch it away. "I know what it's telling me and it's nothing good."

Eira raised her hands, bread still held tight in one. "The circumstances of our meetings have been *unfortunate*, sure, but I truly mean no harm."

She rearranged her expression into something more sincere in an effort to relay her intentions. The line between teasing and honesty was not one so easily established in her interactions with Meilin. In all fairness, the heiress seemed to struggle locating that line in any interaction at all—that wasn't a new development that came about during her time living in Erebus.

It was a vice that Eira held close to her heart all her life.

She told herself that it made her unlovable. That her presence in the company of others was always uncomfortable if she didn't fill silence, no matter what words she used to do so.

Social interactions never seemed to come easy to her.

They were as unnatural as the fire that flowed through her veins in place of ice.

So, Eira boasted bravado as protection. Cockiness in place of sincerity. It served her well enough in Seelie, and the same could be said for Erebus. But the strategies she'd long implemented in her life, with strangers and family alike, seemed to falter around Meilin.

Eira didn't know what face to show her.

As soon as she decided on one, Meilin would talk, and Eira's mind became a slippery landscape, impossible to navigate, even harder to control than it always was.

She wondered, with a dull ache, whether the Rite would be able to teach her the best way to talk to people. How to form words that didn't feel wrong once they translated from her mind to her mouth, strategies to shed the pride she donned like a coat to keep herself from being hurt.

A cocked eyebrow told Eira that Meilin wasn't so sure of her, even with the genuine infliction she tried to line her words with.

"Try something like that again," Meilin seethed, arms still tight around her chest and over the brown bag, which made it crinkle even more, "and I'll cause a scene."

Eira didn't know why the idea of them running into one

another again, in any other scenario, made her skin surge with an unfamiliar electricity.

Mortals passing by considered them with raised eyebrows. They exchanged whispered words and quickened their steps.

They were still close to Plentiful Pastries, lingering near the bakery's storefront, and Eira could *feel* Silvia's questioning glance from behind the till.

Customers that Eira cut in front of came out soon after in swift waves—a testament to Silvia's quick service—and regarded the pair with distaste as they did so. Eira shifted her body out of the direct entryway. Upon noticing, Meilin did the same, a cringe making her face fold in on itself the way the bag did in her unrelenting grasp.

"I would venture to say that a scene has already been caused," Eira tittered.

The other heiress narrowed her eyes.

"Whilst I'm absolutely delighted to see the humor you're dragging out of this interaction," Meilin's spoke with renewed venom, the humiliation angering her even further, "I don't think someone who makes use of their time peering into the windows of other's homes is fit to comment on whether or not *I'm causing a scene!*"

"Can you truly blame me for being drawn in by the sound of such a provoking melody?" Eira shrugged lamely, unable to keep the words from continuing to tumble out. "I didn't plan to do anything with the knowledge of its location—but learning that it was coming from an abandoned property, I mean, of course I was curious. As anyone would be!"

Meilin's lip curled but Eira rushed to finish her spiel. "Curious is the word I want to emphasize here. Curious. Not dangerous. I'm nothing of the sort."

The other heiresses scoffed before she spoke again. "You mean to tell me that if you'd become so curious that you wanted to see if the door was unlocked—if you couldn't find a way to scramble through the windows first, *of course*—that you wouldn't have come in? If that door handle turned, and I hadn't been on the other side of it, you wouldn't have stepped over the threshold of curiosity and edged into intrusion? The house was abandoned, wasn't it? So, you—drawn by the melody and that which you don't see nor understand—would excuse the act of barging into someone's home due to the conviction of your own curiosity?"

Meilin waited for Eira to answer.

When Eira didn't, her fellow fae set her mouth into a stern line, lips pursed. "*That* is dangerous. Your curiosity and lack of means to control it means danger for others around you." Her eyes flicked to Eira's throat. "Or yourself."

Eira remembered the press of Meilin's blade there.

The smell of copper. The disturbed earth beneath their bodies.

She saw then that Meilin's hurt—her rage—came from her in different ways. It seeped from her pores and fashioned itself into sharp words and high walls. Whilst it was just as much the bruises on her skin and the darkness under her eyes, it was also present in ways Eira would never be privy to knowing.

Just the same as it had been for herself.

And though she felt a terrible sort of empathy for Meilin's situation, Eira didn't stay silent.

Her next words came with an ease that was uncharacteristic of the moments of terse quiet shared between them. Just as quickly as she deployed her sincerity, in hopes that it would bridge the endless gap between them, Eira retracted it.

"Unlocked doors do no good for anyone but thieves and criminals, of which I'm neither, for the record. Although I *am* known to steal hearts, but that's beside the point."

A rigid noise of exasperation tangled with frustration tore

from Meilin's throat as she stormed past Eira, cutting short their conversation, having deemed that she wasn't going to get anywhere worthwhile with the fiery-haired mortal who didn't know when to keep her mouth shut.

Eira held her loaf of bread to her sternum, letting the dwindling warmth from its sealed mass radiate through her. Drawn towards Meilin again by means of her own curiosity, she'd managed to leave the situation worse off for it.

She really had wanted to help Meilin.

Now, Eira not only most likely left a bad taste in the other's mouth, but also left her with the feeling that she was somehow indebted for the purchase made on her behalf.

That's definitely *not* what Eira wanted.

But what *did* Eira want?

Feeling more like a fool than on any of the nights she'd drunk herself blind at Amzi, Eira turned away from Plentiful Pastries.

Away from the oblivious mortals lingering inside the bakery and from the watchful eyes of Silvia.

She walked back to her cottage alone, doing so at a pace slow enough that ensured that even if Meilin happened to be on the same path back home, they wouldn't run into one another at the crossroads where the city and the forest met.

CHAPTER 6

HER LIPS, MY NAME

Eira's situation made her restless.

A tether to her fellow heiress had been drawn by a shadowed companion who was now nowhere to be seen.

He moved in the darkness, and then, he didn't move at all.

Eira didn't know why she and Meilin were linked to begin with and now their connection was taut with the stress of the unknown, at least on Eira's end.

Thoughts of all consuming night and fraying rope cycled in her head on a sickening loop which seemed to have no end. Surely there were answers to her questions somewhere, waiting to be found—but Eira couldn't pin them down.

She didn't even know where to start looking in order to do so.

She spent her time worrying she'd make herself ill with the mixture of unfamiliar concern and all that came about as a result of it it.

Everything before this—before Meilin—came in waves, according to a schedule. The unpredictability was what made it all worse.

As dull as life in Erebus became, it was monotonous. It was

routine. Begrudgingly, Eira saw it as familiar. Because of that familiarity, in turn, it became wanted.

But just because Eira wanted for Amzi did not, in turn, mean it wanted for her.

"Eira, I don't know if my dismissal wasn't clear enough last time, but you're no longer welcome here." Alfie's tone was steel, his eyes just as cold. He was resolute in his decision and was set on making the heiress know she was no longer welcome in the place she once called home. "Without a friend to pay your dues, I dare to presume you won't be affording my services, so—"

"*Eira!*"

The heiress only *just* walked into Amzi, drawn by the morbid comfort offered by its dank interior, and was already being berated by Alfie when the sound of her name falling from the lips of someone behind her struck a chord inside her chest.

Alfie's eyes, which were locked onto Eira's only the moment prior, mirrored her own shock.

Meilin.

The melody of her name falling from Meilin's lips for the first time made that aching chord pull even tighter.

The creature from a few nights prior stirred, stretching, its claws now unsheathed and lodged into her soft insides.

Eira turned to face Meilin, standing in the doorway of the still quite-empty Amzi. She was windswept, her cheeks a tinted rose instead of darkly strawberry stained, her hair unkempt.

Evening had barely broken behind her.

The smile Meilin wore was one of someone not wronged by Eira the day prior. They saw each other yesterday morning, and after a day wasted away in her own worry, Eira found herself on the receiving end of a smile that could've washed away all her problems.

It was as if hundreds of years lay between them.

Eira struggled to breathe, as she always seemed to do around her.

"You would not *believe* how long it took me to find this place!" Her tone was exasperated but not unhappy, as if Eira should've been expecting her arrival. Meilin tilted her head when the heiress didn't respond, still standing in the doorway. "Are you going to get a table for us, or do you expect me to do that, too?"

Eira looked back to Alfie, almost expecting him to shoo them both out, but the barkeep just raised an eyebrow before nodding, once, back in her direction. She took that as a sign to pull out one of the few seats positioned at the bar—the same ones she sat in when Alfie essentially barred her from coming back to the tavern.

Meilin seemed satisfied with that.

She closed the space between them with a few strides, the shimmery fabric of her chosen dress of day making waves around her.

It was the color of a tangerine, bright and rich.

Eira was still yet to recover from the way her name sounded falling from the other's heart-shaped lips.

When Meilin took her seat beside her, the heiress was silent. Words struggled to form, to fall from her mouth. It was only when Alfie took that as his cue to wander to the other side of the bar, most likely preoccupied with some imaginary task, that Eira finally spoke.

"Did you hear Alfie berating me?" she asked.

For the first moment since she arrived, Meilin appeared confused. "What do you mean?"

"Isn't that how you know my name?"

A pause.

Then, laughter.

Meilin sucked in a short breath before responding, her tone

airy. "I was surprised you were able to keep it from me this long, to be completely honest. In the very brief time I've known you, I've come to learn of the joy you get from the sound of your own voice."

"Talking fills the silence," Eira murmured, cheeks impossibly hotter than they were only a few moments prior, "and it's the silence I don't like."

She expected Meilin to say that she knew as much. She prepared for the back-handed jab. Instead, Meilin met Eira's gaze and simply said, "Maybe I would like to see you squirm."

Was she flirting with Eira, or threatening her?

Either way, the heiress was intrigued.

Meilin's eyes fell to a spot behind the bar. "He doesn't want you here?" She nodded her head in Alfie's direction. "Your friend?"

She'd *most definitely* heard Alfie berating Eira.

"It's complicated."

"Are things always complicated with you?" The question was a lighthearted one, and even so, Eira felt a weight beneath the words.

Her body was strung tight with nerves but she willed herself to smile, calling her courage forward once more, bit by bit. "You would have to stick around long enough to find that out for yourself," Eira responded, tone teasing.

Meilin scoffed. "And if I did so, would I find myself indebted to you again?"

"I'm not going to hold you to the cost of a few sweet treats," she said in earnest, "and I didn't do that to gain some sort of advantage over you. You don't owe me absolutely anything."

And she was telling the truth. If anything, the decision she made at Plentiful Pastries was for *herself*. Eira could've turned away from the shop window and ignored the sight of Meilin. It would've been the smarter choice.

Yet here they were.

"Hmm," was all Meilin replied with, the unconvinced answer sent through pressed lips. Her eyebrows knitted together, as if deep in thought, and just as she was about to say something, Alfie sidled back over to their side of the bar.

Eira didn't know whether to hug or to hate him for it.

"Can I get you something to drink?" he pointedly asked Meilin, like the heiress sitting beside her simply didn't exist in his realm of consciousness.

A smile tugged at the corners of Meilin's mouth. Eira felt the familiar sting of red hot embarrassment in her cheeks as the heiress eyed the options available to her, displayed just beyond Alfie's shoulders.

Meilin pronounced, with ease, the name of some fancy liquor that tumbled out of Eira's mouth like rocks whenever she'd been made to repeat it back in an order during her serving days. Alfie nodded approvingly and turned to prepare her drink, grabbing a beautifully crafted glass on his way to the shelf. Eira knew he kept the finer serving glasses for special occasions, but she couldn't quite understand what about this scenario in particular was bringing him so much joy.

Maybe he had glanced over at the right time, immediately understanding the awkward and out-of-character air that settled around Eira. Despite her best efforts, she was *shy* in the presence of Meilin. Meager attempts to raise her own confidence levels didn't seem to aid in that.

Eira didn't usually care to bear the weight of rejection—but her interaction with Meilin the morning prior left her defeated. Everything made her feel defeated as of late, and it all added together to only deepen her humiliation.

"Two, please," Meilin said suddenly. Alfie, bottle at the ready in one hand and glass poised in the other, raised his eyebrows in question once more.

Meilin just smiled.

Like the businessman he was, Alfie didn't deny her. He silently passed the tall, jade colored bottle of liquor to free his hand and grabbed another glass. The second was not as beautiful, but still lovely all the while, and he filled them both with equal amounts of ice.

The rich liquid came next, poured with a careful, yet generous, hand.

When Alfie took the full glasses and slid them over to the seated pair, Eira moved to offer her own coin.

She had enough left.

This was worth it.

After all, when would Eira ever have the chance to come back to Amzi? She doubted Alfie's generosity would be extended again after the night ended.

But Meilin drew her own hand forth first, her fingers curled around a handful of copper. Eira bit her tongue against the questions that arose. Where this money came from was not her business, not now—but whatever the cause, she had enough of an inkling of Meilin's personality to know that if she had the same amount yesterday, Eira wouldn't have needed to buy her that food.

"This one is on me," Meilin declared after having paid, fingers now wrapped around the glass.

The gesture was a kind one but Eira grimaced. She had been nothing but a nuisance to Meilin thus far—and it didn't really feel right that she was being bought a drink she didn't deserve.

As if reading her mind, Meilin clicked her tongue against her teeth. "Stop overthinking this," she said, voice softer than before, "because it's just one drink. Consider it as me repaying you for yesterday."

Knowing better than to start an argument she presumed

she was bound to lose, Eira lifted the glass up to cheers with Meilin.

After the rims clinked together, the noise resounding, Eira brought the drink to her lips. The liquor went down with a burn. Notes of citrus and something sweeter, like vanilla, were unfamiliar to her but not undesirable.

"Good choice," Eira said after her first sip.

Meilin's widened smile was enough of a response. The tells of her pain were clearer to Eira in that moment, as if the expensive drink had somehow sharpened her senses. Meilin winced even after her initial sip, which told the heiress that it wasn't just because of the heat of the liquor rushing down her throat. Her smile was wide, yes, but her cheeks twitched before her eyes focused back in on the bar top. Her wrist bent awkwardly with the weight of the glass, and though she was good at hiding it, Eira saw the way Durante's marks settled into her skin.

Eira's heart squeezed with empathy.

None of what Meilin made her feel was truly familiar; and she struggled to separate her anguish over what the king stripped from them both and the odd sense of gratitude she had for The Fates that intertwined their paths.

But fate didn't excuse the bruises that darkened her complexion.

After a few moments of quiet passed between them, Meilin cleared her throat and turned her focus to Eira. "Don't make this weird," she mumbled, "I'm trying my best to be . . . kind."

The word—*kind*—tumbled out with a cringe, as if it were painful for her to acknowledge aloud. She ground her teeth, sullen again, chewing on the sentence—tasting the words in her mouth.

Maybe Meilin, too, detested the silence and wished to fill it at any cost.

It was Eira's turn to raise her eyebrows in question. "You going out of your way to seek me out was a *definite* surprise—"

"Is that so bad?" Meilin interjected with a huff.

"Not at all. I apologize if I made you think so." Eira leaned forward, a little closer to Meilin. "If this really is the last of any interactions you wish to share with me, I will happily oblige to your wishes."

"Why is it so hard to believe I just want to be kind for the sake of it?"

"Because *I* don't believe that you owe *me* any kindness."

Meilin grimaced.

Maybe that was the wrong thing to say, Eira thought.

But the other heiress was quick to respond. "Look, I won't stick around here for long—and if you can't beat them, I guess you can stalk them back, at the very least."

Eira choked on a laugh. "I've never heard of such a saying! But I have *not* been stalking you."

"Maybe not intentionally," the other muttered. Her eyes twinkled with humor, though, and this told Eira that whatever compromise they'd made in understanding their strange encounters was enough for Meilin. She didn't trust Eira entirely, and rightly so, but she wasn't set on being turned in the other direction.

It was an impressive change from the day prior.

And because she didn't have the courage to ask what had prompted this change of heart, Eira made the most of it.

"I can't say your gawking upon my entry was making this decision much easier for me," Meilin added.

"Can you really blame me?" Eira swallowed back the regret that coated her lips once the words left her mouth. Being brave proved so impossibly difficult in her presence.

A softer smile. "Not particularly," she said. Meilin's eyes fell to her glass. "Kindness—it's something I'm not entirely familiar with giving or receiving. I decided that I want to open myself up to strangers, even if it terrifies me. Even if it is something I take on one very small step at a time."

Eira couldn't fathom the right words to show just how incredibly impressive she thought Meilin was.

She chose kindness, reserved it for Eira, despite having no real reason to do so. She made that choice because she *wanted* to.

When Durante left Eira beaten and bruised, rightfully filled with doubt in the goodness of fae and mortal kind alike, she resorted to numbing her pain.

Meilin confronted it head on, in her own way.

This humbled Eira more than she could articulate. So, they continued to talk, Eira nodding in understanding and Meilin taking a sip of her drink in a silent, solemn cheers to her decision.

They breezed through topics of conversation and Amzi continued to fill with people as the hours ticked by.

As the volume of the tavern rose, their talking quieted, heads leaning closer to one another to avoid the need to yell or speak over the mingling mortals. They discussed everything and nothing.

Eira shared her own truths—the foods she despised, her favorite season, suggestions for the best time to walk around the forest if Meilin wanted to clear her mind—but danced around anything too close to home.

Her childhood, her family, her court. She talked of them like they were distant things that caused her pain to discuss, which wasn't *entirely* false.

Meilin didn't mind. It was much the same for her.

Unsurprisingly so.

Soon, their interests fanned to the others in the tavern. Eira whispered of what she heard in weeks prior, of petty secrets and things that she knew would make Meilin laugh.

No one paid them any mind.

Alfie would occasionally peer over at the pair, eyebrows still raised in question. But he didn't move them on. He would periodically hover close to refill their glasses, to ask if Meilin was enjoying herself, to give Eira a once-over.

Then, the point in the night came where the fire-haired fae was comfortable enough to ask the things she always wished to discuss with the friends she didn't have.

"What do you dream of doing one day?"

This was the first question that made Meilin stutter in her answer. She paused for a few moments, contemplating, before responding to Eira's prompt. The future was a safer topic to discuss.

Bearing the skin of mortals meant that their future was unspoken for.

It held endless possibilities.

"I haven't been dreaming about much of anything as of late, let alone what I'll be able to achieve in the years to come," Meilin replied breezily, despite the somber implication. "That *dwelling* is far too haunted for me to sleep soundly. It sounds foolish, but I haven't yet shaken the fear that I'll wake up one morning to find that my body has become a host to all the spiders that took up residency there long before me." A visible shiver ran through her body. "Webs and all."

Eira thought about that for a moment, slightly taken aback by the candid nature of Meilin's answer. The heiress existed in a world of fae courts and costly power—yet she, too, had never gotten over her aversion to spiders.

At least Eira wasn't alone in that fact.

"If I hadn't seen the place for myself, I would think you were exaggerating," Eira acknowledged.

Meilin sighed. "Speaking of those dusty corridors," she started, eyes turning to look out the window over their shoulders, "I'd best get going back to them. I worry that another wandering intruder will get bold if I'm away for too long."

If she suspected that there was something special about the home, and the forest they both resided in, she didn't show it.

Eira sputtered out a laugh, taking a generous final swig of her drink. She didn't know how late it was, especially considering that Amzi continued to teem with life so far into the night, but the ache in her lower back was indicator enough.

They'd sat at the bar for hours.

She swallowed down the surge of doubt that threatened to purge itself from her throat.

"Should we make a deal?" Eira asked as Meilin turned back to face her.

"That depends. Does this deal involve purchases from a bakery?"

"*This* is a deal in an effort for me to make it up to you. It won't remedy everything but . . . if I were to bring the supplies to assist you in cleaning your mansion . . ." Eira started the proposition tentatively, watching for any change in Meilin's expression. "Would you consider keeping me in your company a little longer?"

I'm not sure I'm ready for us to part ways indefinitely.

Those were the words that she couldn't bring herself to admit aloud, though they may have helped spare Meilin some of the confusion that momentarily crossed her face. Sure, the heiress was practicing kindness. But that didn't mean they would cross paths again outside of Amzi.

It didn't secure Eira a chance to see Meilin again.

"I don't know if a promise from me will be worth much to you at this point, but I won't require anything in return," Eira rushed to add. *Just your company.* She splayed her hands openly in front of her, on either side of the glass between them. "But I'd be lying if I said I didn't want to see what that place looks like without all the grime, especially on the inside."

Meilin let out a laugh of her own. "And you have all this free time to scout out maidens in peril and offer up your services *because?*"

Eira winced at the implication, having realized how the situation looked from afar.

After years of luck that could be considered as rotten at best, it was an odd play of fate that Eira ran into Meilin as many times as she did.

She didn't initially wish for the company of another.

In reality, Eira yearned for the no-contact reprieve that made her time in Erebus as seamless as it was, despite how deep loneliness had nestled into her tired bones. People at Amzi were passing. Alfie was passing. Her shadowed companion, clearly, was just the same. It was safer that way.

But Eira wanted Meilin to be a constant.

If only for a few more weeks.

"I have wasted too much time alone," was the best response that Eira could come up with.

Meilin considered her. Then, with a resolute nod, she said, "If you're at my door tomorrow morning by eight sharp, I will take you up on your offer—but only if you knock. No walking in uninvited."

Something warm and unfamiliar exploded in Eira's chest. "I'll be there," she said confidently, extending her hand to the other.

Meilin's smile widened. She moved to take Eira's hand in her own, chin jutted out proudly, gaze locked as they shook on it, sealing a deal that felt all too weighted for what it was.

Meilin's skin was soft.

Eira felt her cheeks go red with heat.

The interaction was an entire one-eighty from the last time their hands touched, when there was a blade against Eira's throat because Meilin was sure she was an ill-intentioned intruder.

Now, Eira was being invited in.

She clung to that warmth, holding it close.

Selfishly—like it were fleeting and precious.

Because no matter how much she wished to convince herself otherwise, Eira *knew* it was.

CHAPTER 7
THE SECRETS THESE WALLS HOLD

"You didn't think I was lying, did you?"

Eira would've made the walk to Meilin's residence, hauling buckets filled with various cleaning supplies, a hundred times over if it meant she got to replay the expression on her face just once more.

The early morning sun lit up Meilin's face, which was scrunched in an amusing mixture of surprise and confusion. There was a glimpse of something else underneath all of that, but Eira wasn't yet armed with the knowledge she needed to dissect Meilin's emotions to catch the meaning of it.

Meilin bore the appearance of someone who just woke up, disturbed from sleep by the sound of knocking at the front door.

Just as Eira promised she would.

"I didn't think you would really turn up so early," she murmured, rubbing the back of her hand across eyes that cringed against the full strength of the sunrays. The nape of Eira's neck was being kissed by the light, too. Her own head pounded upon waking up—thanks to last night—but she hadn't wanted to be late.

"Ah," Eira remarked, "I can leave and come back later, if you'd prefer that—"

Meilin grumbled something incohesive before reaching out to snatch one of the full buckets from Eira's hands. "Hush and get inside."

The other heiress obliged.

Luckily enough for her, Durante wouldn't have given her such a well-kept cottage without the expectation that Eira maintained its condition. She found out quite early on that the cleaning supplies were in a nondescript cupboard closest to the bathroom.

The space boasted wide shelves, four of them, with the highest going just above her head and the lowest at her ankles. Most of the bottles stacked inside them held liquid contained in cloudy-colored glass, and whilst Eira couldn't discern the contents, she spent some time opening and briefly passing the tops under her nose. The scents were clue enough to figure out what was for what. She found some shame in the fact that so much was done for her back at court. It was as if Eira relearnt all it took to live on her own, to take care of herself and her own space.

If anything, Erebus forced a sort of independence onto her that she would've never been able to embrace in Seelie.

When stocking up supplies to bring to Meilin, Eira settled on an assortment of bottles with liquid that varied in hues and consistency. She placed them in deep silver buckets that had handles strong enough to ensure the bottom wouldn't break under the weight.

She filled a separate bucket with rags and cloths, adding in smaller sticks of shaped wood with heads of feathers and cotton on the end. Atop everything was the long wooden stick she owned, fashioned at the end with a coarse head of weeds wound tightly with twine.

Once inside, Meilin inspected the contents of Eira's bounty, her face breaking into a smile.

Suddenly, she was awake. Eira's own skin danced with energy in response.

"Do you know what half of that is for?" Meilin asked, not unkindly, whilst bending at the knees to sift through it all.

Eira did an awkward shuffle around her, stepping a little further past the entryway to give the other some more space. She bit her tongue to avoid questioning why Meilin thought an azure slip gown was the best choice of clothing for a day of cleaning, worried it might be taken more seriously than intended.

She looked resplendent, nonetheless. That didn't surprise Eira.

The deep-set darkness under her eyes told Eira that Meilin may wear extravagant dresses as an escape from the fatigue that rippled through her daily existence.

Eira chuckled. "You caught me. I was actually bringing these to you to ask if you could identify their purpose for me. I'm not yet sure how to use any of them."

Meilin rose from the ground to scrunch her nose in her direction, taking one of the buckets in her hands as she did so. "I have no doubt about your cleaning capabilities," Meilin cooed, her expression saying the opposite, "though I will not deny, however, that I *did* have my doubts about you showing up."

Eira shrugged, feigning nonchalance. "I keep my promises."

"We'll see about that," Meilin shot back, already moving down the hallway. Eira picked up what was left of her cleaning haul by the front door and hurried to keep pace.

The contents inside the buckets clanked together loudly as the pair shuffled along.

The daybreak glow painted the hallways in a golden glow

that erased years off the wear and tear that was painfully present in every aspect of its build. Their combined movement stirred up dust and Eira saw clouds of it fill the pockets of sunshine reflected through the ancient windowpanes.

It didn't appear entirely unlivable just yet, but it also certainly didn't have the makings of a *home*.

"Where do you want to start, boss?" Eira asked. At that, Meilin stopped in her path, and the heiress had to steady her weight to avoid falling over the other.

"We can start off with you never calling me that again," Meilin retorted. Her exaggerated disgust made Eira grin. "Surely we're the same age."

She didn't linger on the topic. "That's beside the point. Just direct me where to go and that is where I'll be."

Meilin tsked. "If only you'd gone away when I asked the first time, maybe I'd be more inclined to believe that were true."

"And then you'd have no one to help you clean," the heiress sung in response.

Meilin just knitted her eyebrows together and gave Eira her signature once over, as if to check for a final time that she really *was* there to help and not to argue. Her hold on the bucket handle tightened before she gathered the longer front layers of her dress in her free hand and moved on. Meilin's restraint was much more refined than Eira's.

Despite her jabs, Eira really did want to help Meilin.

The home was beautiful once—she knew it even from her first look at its exterior.

The inside only reaffirmed her thoughts. Eira could swear that it whined underneath the weight of their combined steps, near begging to be loved—to be restored.

She wondered if its nature would reveal itself to her at any other points during the day.

Eira stopped following Meilin down the uncharacteristically long hallway when she came across the first closed door. Every other one they'd passed by that point was open, and she had indulged herself in sneaking in small glances at what they held inside.

"Should I start here, then?" Eira asked.

Meilin's expression creased with unbridled discomfort. "Go ahead," she said, turning to focus her gaze on the room across the hall. "I won't be venturing in there anytime soon. You handle that room and I'll be just over here. I think it would be most effective to focus mostly on dusting and taking off any old sheets or coverings. Make sure you open all the windows whenever you go into a room. I'll close them by nightfall, but the house needs the airflow for now. We'll start off with that and see how we go."

Eira nodded her approval before turning the handle to the door of the mystery room. It was unlocked, opening with no resistance. Despite the nondescript entryway and easy access, the room made quick work of Eira.

There was an energy stored in the air that she immediately detested.

Its velvet couches were anything but the material they may have once been. Their surfaces worn and tattered, the color fatigued. They may have been expensive once. Now, they sat uncleaned and unused in a room that had long aged passed its expiration date.

The decor wasn't the issue, though.

Not all of it.

The rest of the room was nothing like the grand illusion the aged furniture initially presented.

It was worse.

As Eira neared a cloth-covered set of shelves towards the far-back corner, she dropped everything in her hands. She doubted anything was alive under the muted fabric, but that knowledge didn't stop the erratic beat of her heart.

No smell emanated from the area—surely that was a promising sign.

Nothing moved or shuffled. Nothing shifted.

Somehow, that made it worse.

"I'm not going to be bested by a sheet," Eira grumbled to herself. She reached out in the next moment to pull the fabric back. In one jerky movement the malicious content underneath was unsheathed.

Two wooden shelves, as tall as her waist, dutifully lined with mason jars. The glass of the jars had long become opaque because the contents inside them were left pickling for however many centuries; and what she *could* identify out of the mismatched shapes didn't make her feel any better.

Eira would've had room to be surprised that they were left so out in the open if she hadn't been entirely too preoccupied with how mortified she felt.

It was a collector's shrine.

Each row of shelving looked to be categorized. The jars were placed purposefully—almost painstakingly perfectly—next to one another, sorted and separated by both the color of contents and the liquid within them, which varied in an uncomfortably wide array.

The fluids were anything from sage green to flaxen yellow, and the closer Eira got to the shelves, the more she could see.

The more she wished she hadn't.

Jaggedly lopped-off shapes, stacked so high that they rotated towards the top of the lid, swam around like grotesque fish.

Closer examination only confirmed that the strangely outlined bits were that of body parts.

Pointed ears. Fingers with the nails still on—some with the

nails off. Curved teeth. Squares of preserved skin. Pieces with less flesh. Chunks of indiscernible bone in their own dedicated jars, too.

It was kill memorabilia, so well packaged that even the stench of rot couldn't permeate through the jars.

And though some things were identifiably human, most were not.

There were fae in those jars.

Sickness burned Eira's throat with an acidity so strong that the heiress had to step back from the shelves. Rage bubbled up alongside it, making for an overwhelming wave of emotions that very quickly became all too much to stomach.

She remembered, vividly, being told that it was pointless to try and give reason to mortal cruelty—especially when, more often than not, there was no real reason.

It was what made their choices all the more terrifying.

Eira was grateful, then, for Meilin not being in the room. She didn't think she could handle the act of passing off a neutral reaction to a sight so deeply disturbing.

No wonder she avoided it.

It was clear that the sheets were untouched for years prior to either of their arrivals. Maybe it was a gut feeling, or knowledge of something darker—but for whatever reason, Meilin made the right choice in keeping the door closed.

She hadn't needed to see what horrors it held.

The Seelie Court *should* be made aware of the treachery—Erebus was bound to the fae by contract—and they were under obligation to not bring harm to Eira's kind.

Regardless of who these items belonged to, or where they came from, their existence alone was a clear violation of the agreed upon terms.

Her breath came out in short, reedy whispers of empty air.

In actuality, there was no way for Eira to reach out and

report such a thing; not this close to her leaving, and not without proof—and she didn't plan to steal a jar from Meilin's home to show off later.

Besides, if she questioned Meilin about it, for any reason, Eira would be running the risk of exposing her own identity.

She couldn't do it.

Not now.

Not when she'd only just been welcomed past the high walls of someone who she thought may become very important to her.

With a queasy stomach, and the image of pickled body parts burned behind her eyelids, Eira threw the sizeable sheet back over the scene, promising to herself to address it with her family as soon as she had the chance to do so.

If that made her a coward, it wouldn't be the first time.

And for now, it would have to do.

Eira would continue to clean, if only to discover the other secrets that the residence had to offer her. This room could wait.

It would have to wait.

But the heiress wished she could understand the house—wished she could know of its secrets, of the pain it held within its walls. Was there a reason she was drawn into the room?

Was there meaning to this cruelty?

To avoid giving any more power to the concoction of sickness and anger brewing dangerously inside of her, Eira made quick work of the rest of the space, which was fairly sparse in furniture if she didn't think about either the couch or the shelves. She opened the windows, just a little, pushing down the irrational fear that someone—somehow—may make their way in to take a peek like she had done.

It felt like both an hour and ten minutes passed before Meilin appeared in the doorway. Her hair was swept off her neck, held up in a makeshift knot of sorts. Her bare arms were streaked with misplaced lines of grey.

"Is everything alright?" she asked, suddenly. Meilin didn't dare to step over the threshold, but she watched Eira from the other side of it, eyes holding the type of concern that was unfamiliar to the heiress. There was no scrutiny under the weight of her gaze.

Eira just smiled. "Sure is. I'm just about finished up in here so give me a moment to pack up, and then we can move to the next spot!"

Meilin, despite appearing utterly unconvinced, nodded her agreement. She gave the room another once over. A barely noticeable shiver seemed to run over her before she turned away, the sound of her clinking bucket in tow.

Eira steadied herself with a few deep breaths.

It felt wrong, abandoning what sat on those shelves—leaving it there to rot even more. But she was resolute in her decision. Whilst it may not have been the right thing to do, it was the only choice she had. She didn't chase after her missing companion.

This may just have to be another mystery to go, temporarily, unsolved—for the sake of her own wellbeing.

Eira collected her cleaning supplies, putting them back in the bucket.

"We can get a start on the grand hall together," Meilin called out from the other side of the door. "Keep up or stay in there—your choice." The playful taunt in her tone made Eira's stomach swoop. It was a welcome break from the ache that the room plagued her with.

Eira didn't straggle after that.

The hours passed in a steady, comfortable rhythm.

By the time Eira took a break from cleaning, her clothes were covered in stirred up remnants of dust and her eyes watered from bits of dirt lodged in her tear ducts. Only upon stopping did she also realize that the sun had dipped to a much lower point in the sky.

The horror of the first room hadn't inhibited her ability to assist Meilin. The task that the rest of the house offered was a welcome distraction.

They brushed, scraped, pulled, and wiped their way through almost every room of the two-story residence, talking and laughing all the while. They shared jokes intermittently, when their minds weren't as busy as their hands.

Opening every window proved more of a task than Eira thought possible—the ancient handles to some of the panes had gone too long without being twisted, and the pair dissolved into giggles at how much effort it took to get some of them open. Their hands had gone red with the effort.

Eira didn't mind.

Meilin made a habit out of humming when she got lost in her task. It seemed to assist in directing her focus. Eira found it endearing.

She was happy to see the way that the other heiress eased into having her around. Eira's guard had fallen, too. Despite this being a dangerous mix of things that she should have been a lot more concerned about, they didn't bother her in the moment.

Tomorrow's problem, Eira promised herself—as if she would actually address it then.

When they took their break, Meilin stood to stretch.

She wiped her forearm across her brow, eyes cast on the reflection of the dimming light that still blinked through the window. "My room can be the last one before we call it a day," she advised with a nod in the direction of the hallway.

Despite Eira's exhaustion, and growing hunger, the thought of her time with Meilin ending made a resounding sadness echo through her.

The pair moved in harmony to the aforementioned bedroom.

"There's not much to do in here," Meilin announced, somewhat tightly, "but it does need a thorough dusting."

Eira could see that she had already settled into the bed.

The sheets were haphazardly strewn about, and there was an impression in the thin blankets. The rest of the room was fairly untouched, with the exception of the closet and vanity, but it would definitely be less work than any of the other spaces they'd occupied.

It was clear Meilin only hung around in her bedroom on a need-to basis. To sleep, to change.

Eira couldn't count the number of times her own space offered a type of comfort that saved her from crumbling, especially under the weight of what Erebus had taught her. Knowledge was heavy. Tiring.

She wanted to help make this space safer for Meilin, even if only for a little while longer.

Setting her sights on the windows on the furthest side of the room, Eira placed the cleaning supplies on the ground and paced over. Bringing her hands to rest under the clasp closest to the windowsill, Eira flipped it to the right, which left it open and allowed her to push the frame up with ease. She guessed the give of the handle was thanks to Meilin doing so a few times beforehand.

There were three generously sized windows that found home against the aged coffee wall of Meilin's bedroom. The detailing on their frames sustained the touch of time to an impressive degree. Etched flowers and vines were prominent markings in the wood.

Meilin twisted the handles with more care than Eira, more understanding of how fragile they were. The wood had withheld, but the panes were surely close to breaking. It looked like they would blow out with a ferocious breeze, and yet, they had held strong like the rest of the house—an impressive feat, really.

The property was a paradox.

When Eira turned to look at the rest of the room, she found that there was a similar motif of childlike wonder that danced around the walls and the various pieces of furniture inside of it. The vines from the window frames also ran up the bedposts and even across the top of the door frame.

Once she knew where to look for it, it became easier to spot.

Despite being large, the bedroom was unremarkable in comparison to everything else that the house already offered Eira. She almost found it comical that the most spectacular person assigned herself to the most unassuming room.

Meilin clapped her hands together, ridding the dust that coated her fingertips. It seemed fruitless, considering they were yet to truly get their hands dirty. "Right! You can start with the wardrobe"—her instruction was followed with a short gesture to the corner of the room—"and I'll clean what's already accumulated around these windowsills, since the breeze is going to stir it up anyway."

Eira agreed and got to work.

The stand-alone wardrobe was as old as the rest of room, towering about a head or two over her. Its darkened oak doors were worn, with curved brass handles that looked as if they had been opened and closed many, many times.

Eira wanted to get an idea of the state of the interior before she started her work on the exterior.

Spindly cobwebs were splayed from the top of the wardrobe and trailed all the way down, nestled into the corners and atop the railing which hung a row of dresses. Out of the corner of her eye, she saw Meilin already working diligently on cleaning the windows.

Eira busied herself.

She grabbed one of the cloths that was rung out earlier. It was still damp to the touch, enough so that when she wiped it across the wardrobe doors, everything came off cleanly. She held her breath as she dropped the fabric into the bucket, worried that any extra movement would end in an embarrassingly violent attack of sneezing on her behalf. A loss of composure like that would earn Meilin endless ridicule rights, so she couldn't have that.

The webs were easy to get rid of.

It took no more than a few broad swipes from the top of the furniture downwards for everything to collect under the fibrous head of the short-handed brush Eira swapped to. The dust and dirt clung to the grey threads, their ghostly cream carcasses wrapped delicately around the mane as if embracing.

Eira was particular with her handling of the gowns themselves.

She wasn't sure how to really clean them in the condition they were in—for the most part, they were the newest and most cared-for part of the room. There wasn't much work to be done in that regard.

The scent of vanilla lingered on the fabric, which wafted around the heiress with the stirred movement.

"Done," Eira called out to Meilin. She turned away from the wardrobe, sweetness lingering in the air, and began to walk towards the other fae. "Hopefully your gowns won't be so prone to being dust-smattered—"

Her sentence was cut short.

One moment, Eira's eyes were on Meilin's face. The quickly dimming light of sunset crowned her, and she was as undeniably gorgeous as ever. In the next moment, her vision was swallowed by darkness.

For the time that followed, despite being unable to see, Eira was acutely aware of one thing in particular.

Her ankle *throbbed* with a righteous fury.

No longer did the fragrance of vanilla fill her head. Eira could only comprehend earthy soil, the sting of copper and the burn of humiliation.

She should *not* have been so easily bested by a stray floorboard—but a mouthful of small stones and clumps of dirt were enough to prove otherwise.

Something about being in Meilin's company made Eira susceptible to everything in harm's way; first, a dagger to the throat and now, even the sentient floor of Meilin's undoubtedly haunted bedroom planned on taking her down.

It may have been humbling if not for the prominent concern that it caused.

A sharp cry rang out overhead. Eira wasn't sure whether it came from her or her companion, who only fleetingly missed meeting the same fate as she did. Whether a result of the added strain on a particularly weakened floorboard, or just bad luck, she was at least glad that Meilin wasn't down there with her.

"Are you okay?" The fae's voice was crystalline clear in Eira's ears, despite the wreckage she found herself in.

She hoped her response of *"I'm fine"* around the dirt wasn't as unintelligible as it felt.

When she shifted her right ankle even just the slightest, a sharp pain shot down her leg. It was the reminder she needed to pull herself out of the ground, and that her falling behind in the conditioning of her weakened side had done her nothing but harm. Though a meek attempt, the heiress was able to maneuver the sprawl of her limbs to something that mimicked an uncomfortable sitting position.

Good enough.

"I'm not hearing a response so I can assume your answer is not a positive one," Meilin shouted hurriedly, an unfamiliar panic laced behind her words. A few frantic-sounding thumps followed. "I'm going to find something to come down, okay? Just stay there!"

"I'd wait for you even if I *could* move."

Eira wasn't upset that Meilin couldn't hear and then, in-turn, dismiss her humorous answer. She may have been if she had the energy in her to feel anything but the pain that thrummed through her body with every breath.

Shifting her focus from it, Eira allowed her eyes to adjust to her new surroundings.

Although it was dark, the warmth from the barely-there daylight above dipped downwards, which allowed her to make out the curved edges of chipped rock and a path made deep in the ground.

By the grace of the floorboard, Eira was dropped directly into the gut of Meilin's residence. She wondered if it was here that she would be exposed to the fragile flesh which housed all its secrets.

Why else would there be an underground tunnel?

The lax nature of her own thoughts almost caught Eira off guard. She expected more chagrin and bitterness. After all, she was in an excruciating amount of pain. But Eira wanted to see more.

So, she waited—and soon enough, the sound of footsteps overhead told her that Meilin came back.

"I'm coming down, Eira!" she called out.

"I really am fine, so please don't rush." Eira swallowed the dryness in her mouth. "It would be awfully humiliating for you to take a tumble, too."

Meilin's laugh was airy and insincere and Eira startled at

just how distraught she was about the fall. A sudden *thump* behind her head made Eira look over her shoulder.

The following sound of feet coming down the creaking steps of a wooden ladder made the fire-haired fae's stomach swoop.

"How has it taken this long for that thing to give out?" Meilin mumbled the words as she climbed, loud enough for Eira to hear. "I have walked over it so many times now!"

"It's really not your fault," Eira said suddenly. The response seemed to shock Meilin, as if she hadn't expected the heiress to be listening. She could see the surprise etched onto the other's face only because of the lamp Meilin held in the crook of her arm.

Eira smiled, despite herself. "I'm thoroughly impressed that you juggled holding that whilst getting down the ladder."

She wasn't too worried to spare a matching smile in response. "I'm more impressed by the fact that I even found one. Who would've thought that this useless place would have a ladder hidden away in the linen closet?"

Eira swore that the mansion moaned in disagreement.

"It *is* full of surprises," she agreed.

Meilin sighed, though her tone was unsteady when she spoke again, seemingly taken aback by the full sight of Eira on the ground. "I'm starting to believe that's not a good thing."

"I never said it was," the heiress mumbled, cringing as she tried to stand. Meilin was quick to move, free hand slotting into the curve just under Eira's shoulder. She didn't push the assistance away.

The silk of Meilin's gown brushed against her skin.

With the assistance of allowing her weight to fall onto Meilin, Eira managed to stand. She couldn't fully rely on her ankle to support her just yet, but it was a start.

Using the arm that wasn't holding Eira up, Meilin lifted the lamp to the vast darkness in front of them. A warm glow spilled across the floor and crawled up the cavernous walls like paint being splattered onto a blank canvas.

The scene before them didn't look any better when illuminated; nothing became clearer, or less terrifying, as a result of the pooling warmth.

If anything, it was worse once the full thing was in view.

Under this aged property was an even older crypt.

A small lot of abandoned circular steps made a groove in the ground under their feet. Like stepping-stones, they led directly to a raised podium. Crude chips were made in the structure, bits missing from the eggshell colored dais. Discarded nearby somewhere was the floorboard that had taken Eira's ankle as its sacrifice, laying pathetically in the dirt, small enough that it seemed impossible that it brought her down with such ease.

Circled around the podium in a crescent moon were eight pillars, as tall as the overarching ceiling of mismatched masonry and stone. A foreboding sight to behold even in their worn state. Some had jagged tops, as if a chunk was lopped off, whilst others stretched to their full height. Littered further into the darkness were obscure shapes that the strength of the lamp's light couldn't reach—and as the wick began to flicker, the fire throwing out jittery shadows before them, Eira swore she saw the flash of something off-white, small and jagged.

She swallowed down a rush of bile.

"What *is* this . . ." Meilin murmured, sounding both skeptical and intimidated all at once.

Eira scoffed humorlessly. "Trust me, I'm seeing exactly the same thing and I have absolutely no idea."

"Ah," was all Meilin said in return, unconvinced.

None of this was a mirage.

Eira struggled to conjure an image of how this must've once looked—created in worship of some secret, higher being.

Glorious and expansive. Magical, maybe. A haven for whoever molded it.

Now, it was haunted more than anything.

Overgrown roots wound up and over it all, looping through gaps in the structure where chunks of stone had long been missing. The heiress wondered how they grew so ferociously in a lightless, lifeless chamber. Vines of varied colors, forest green and more distilled, sickly-looking hues, were proven to be persistent, at least, in their infestation.

They grew, but they were unwell. This wasn't a natural sort of growth. Wrongness oozed from the walls—and surely, it sunk into the soil beneath their feet.

Beyond everything were tunnels that spiraled deep into the abyss before and behind them. Even a glance over her shoulder made Eira shudder, unease stirring relentlessly inside of her bones.

Nothing in front of or at the rear of them evoked feelings of anything other than a creeping sense of dread.

She was no stranger to darkness or its companions.

The underbelly of Seelie was something gruesome and ill-omened at best—the need for survival had a way of bringing out those qualities in a place and in its people.

Eira herself had been trained in a manner that sharpened the most dismal parts of herself into pointed blades. She understood the importance that twilight played in the coming of dawn. There was no light without sacrifice—without the act of sinister things done under nightfall.

But this was a place, a feeling, she was not at all familiar with.

And she wanted to leave.

Meilin's quickened breathing seemed to mirror her thoughts. They were still, and unspeaking, for a few moments too long.

Eira turned her gaze from the discarded, broken shards that belonged to the carcass of whatever—or whoever—had been worshipped once in front of them. She faced Meilin, their eyes meeting immediately.

"Can we leave the cleaning of this room until later?"

Meilin barked out a laugh. It ricocheted off the walls, just as quickly banishing some of the darkness. "Even a fall like that can't stir the inventory of one-liners stored in that wondrous head of yours," she choked out, her tone awe-filled despite the sarcasm that outlined the words themselves.

Eira inflated her cheeks with a giggle that didn't pass her lips. She spared a final cursory glance around them before asking Meilin if she was ready to leave—and if she would, so kindly, assist her up the ladder.

Eira started her climb first, and quickly found out just how helpful the extra arm of support was as soon as she was made to trust her own body. Her impeded movements were sloppy, and when propelled by fear, they became rushed.

But Meilin was brave. Patient.

She cooed and coaxed just below Eira. She didn't push her or poke fun. Even as Eira said, "If you keep being so chivalrous, I'm going to start blushing", all the while struggling to keep steady with the strength of her upper body alone.

Meilin's kindness only made it so that she was grateful to be in front, and that the other couldn't see the redness she knew flushed her cheeks.

"You're not going to be talking much of chivalry when you learn that I'm making you stay the night here."

Choking on a response, Eira spluttered as she came to the top of the ladder, crawling with no graciousness out of the hole she'd made in the floor. The implication behind Meilin's words made her speed up.

"You barely know me," Eira countered weakly. It felt like a

pathetic excuse, considering the circumstances, but she wasn't about to burden Meilin even more. She'd done her due part for the day.

Meilin just laughed, an airy thing, as she finished her own climb, discarding the now flameless lamp off to the side of the floor. Her laughter was much more comforting in the safety of the bedroom—and it was the type of response that told Eira that a decision was made, whether she liked it or not. "And yet, here we are. You could've broken your ankle because you offered to help clean the house of someone *you* barely know."

Eira didn't argue against Meilin's points. Once they were both out, the pair knelt against the floorboards of her bedroom, working together to lift the ladder up and out. It was discarded, too, near the lamp.

Eira pouted, falling back on her uninjured ankle with a huff. "I mean, I did just cost you a floorboard."

Meilin rolled her eyes. "I'll cover the hole with a sheet—the brightest one I can find, so no one else falls in—and we'll call it even." A shudder ran through her body. "I don't want to think about what was down there anytime soon."

Jars filled to the brim. Sloshing liquid. Imagery forever seared into her mind.

Eira understood.

"I'll help you patch it up when I can trust my ankle to not give out," she promised, "but I won't take up space in your bed. You deserve a restful night—and you won't get that with me."

Meilin's eyebrow shot up.

"I've been told I kick a lot in my sleep," she added sheepishly.

But the heiress wouldn't relent. "By whom?"

When Eira fumbled over the opportune time to shoot something witty back, Meilin took her chance to continue speaking.

She sat cross-legged on the floor across from her. "That ankle isn't kicking anytime soon. Just be quiet and accept the offer."

"And what of dinner?"

"I can cook, you know," Meilin hissed.

The fire-haired fae grinned. "You really can't get enough of me." The words were lighthearted and their interaction was playful, void of any of the heaviness their shared discovery had impeded upon their previous conversation.

But even as every nerve in her body surged at the thought of spending the night with Meilin, of sharing a meal and a bed in any capacity, Eira couldn't discourage the unease that made her skin clam up—the pain was a stark killjoy.

She nearly broke an ankle *(damn these brittle mortal bones)*, had admittedly begun to fall for another in a capacity she never thought possible *(damn the loneliness Celimene cultivated within her)* and happily traded in the coziness of her cottage to spend the day cleaning a mansion built atop a ritualistic underground cave.

What is going on in Erebus?

Eira's mind buzzed with restlessness. The unanswered questions were like the fluttering of a thousand wings slamming against her skull.

What is going on with me?

Though those answers weren't found over a perfectly hearty, homemade stew and dinner table banter, Eira *did* feel a little better after having shared a meal with Meilin. The house seemed to come alive with both of them in it, despite their arguably subpar cleaning job (there was a lot of room to cover, of course).

When they couldn't navigate the kitchen or hallways without both holding lamps, it was clear that the time of night Eira was most nervous about had come.

Even that was made seamless, thanks to Meilin, who always seemed to know what to do—what to say.

When Eira protested to stealing space in her bed, Meilin demanded that she be quiet— that she worked hard and deserved to have a restful night, especially considering the state of her now swollen ankle. She told her that they were both grown women and that she trusted her.

Meilin trusted Eira.

"As long as you don't steal more of my blanket than you require, we will be just fine."

It was unnecessary. Unnatural—the amount in which she believed in Eira's goodness. Nonetheless, she was undeniably grateful for it.

For the first time in three years, Eira slept through the night without stirring.

CHAPTER 8
KISS OF DEATH

Eira couldn't remember the last time Alfie smiled at her.

She knew it was because Meilin was by her side, but it was enough, nonetheless. Compared to how he was a few days prior, this version of Alfie was warm and welcome.

Expectant, even.

He didn't berate Eira for daring to step foot in Amzi without her shadowed companion in tow. He no longer questioned her, or Meilin, for being in one another's company. Through the buzzing atmosphere of Amzi, Eira saw him nod to her regular booth in the far corner. She smiled back at him and weaved her fingers through Meilin's before any sense of hesitation could convince her otherwise.

The heiress didn't reject the touch. She just let out a small squeak of surprise, allowing herself to be guided through the crowd.

"It feels like a crime to be spending time with you in here," Eira said as they sat, "for a second time, too."

Meilin just laughed. "I didn't really give you a choice the first time."

That was the second time of many to come.

They made Erebus their own in the following weeks.

It turns out that bonding over a broken floorboard would benefit them more than Eira ever imagined.

Amzi's dimly lit booth became a place of comfort, where they talked over drinks every other night. More often than not, the drinks weren't alcoholic. Alfie began offering sweet mixes of fruity syrup and water that bubbled on their tongues and filled their stomachs without the buzz and following headache Eira usually nursed after a night spent at the tavern.

Whilst their time spent together was usually peaceful, the one time they encountered trouble was seared into her mind.

They sat across from one another, empty glasses lining the middle of the table, and Meilin had just scoffed as a means to brush aside some of Eira's commentary.

"What do you *truly* think?" Eira asked suddenly, breaking the lull of quiet that settled between them.

Meilin's nose scrunched in confusion. "About?"

"The drinks, alcoholic and otherwise," she clarified, hands splayed at her sides, "the overall atmosphere of this *renowned* establishment?"

The heiress grinned in response. Tension melted from her expression, as if she'd expected the question to be of a more solemn nature. "I think you enjoy frequenting the place where the barkeep looks like he wishes to skin you alive a little more than you're willing to admit."

Eira waved her off halfheartedly. "Alfie's always been a grump, but I've never caused him any real trouble, despite the faces he pulls at me trying to convince you otherwise. I bring in consistent patronage and have yet to cause a scene." The rest of their history weighed heavy on her tongue. She bit down on it.

Laughter bubbled on Meilin's lips, and just as she was about to say something else, her gaze darkened at movement over Eira's shoulder. Her mouth became a thin line. "That might change tonight," she said, tone stiff.

Without speaking, Eira craned her neck over her shoulder to follow Meilin's line of sight. It was like they'd opened the gates to the Unseelie—mortals crawled forward from the darkened corners of Amzi, their faces pulled tight with looks that were even more disconcerting in her state of sobriety. She could make out every line and crease in their expressions and suddenly wished she was drunk enough to not be able to note such intricate details.

The ambling bodies took their sweet time to slink towards them. Eventually, there were five men that surrounded their table. They were not the sloppy sort of drunk that Eira often saw on mortals—their movements were slow, but purposeful, and an unidentifiable source of *wrongness* cloyed the air that swirled around them.

The heiress struggled to hide her irritation. She felt it painted all over her face, staining her cheeks a deep red. Their shadows made the dim lighting of Amzi even darker.

It wasn't often that Eira knew men to approach with care for a woman's comfort in the forefront of their mind.

Both of Meilin's hands were curled around the half-full glass in front of her. She nursed it with apprehension and an entirely unimpressed expression. Eira spoke first, unsure that ignoring their presence all together would serve any purpose. "Can I help you?" she asked plainly.

The group of men snickered.

She couldn't care less about what they wanted. In truth, their reaction to the question made Eira want to surge forward and see just how malleable the whites of their eyes would be with her fingers pierced into them.

Another part of her—a much smaller one—recoiled at the brutality of the intention.

Meilin's face remained stoic, but in her peripheral, Eira saw the way her fingers tightened around her glass.

"We know what you are," one of them hissed with a voice like that of sharpened blades. "Your *kind* isn't welcome here, so how many times will you come here and do *this*?"

He certainly didn't know of her, or Meilin's, fae nature. That much was clear.

Their jabs were directed towards the closeness at which Eira leaned in when Meilin spoke, at the glasses that littered the table between them, indicating that they enjoyed being in one another's company. The men had been watching them. They may have done so multiple times before that instance.

Their assumption was bold—Eira and Meilin could've been close friends, for all these men knew—but Eira also suspected she wasn't as subtle in her growing feelings as she believed herself to be.

The heiress never questioned her love for women.

In Seelie, love was never dictated in that way.

She didn't know what it was like, really, in Erebus.

Eira only ever met women in the night. Affection was given, and returned, behind the closed doors of her cottage walls. But that was just the nature of the few encounters she'd had in prior months. She never sat with those mortals in somewhere like Amzi—never truly talked with them or reveled in their company, most definitely by fault of her own. Her adoration hadn't ever been painted across her face like it must've been with Meilin.

It just never occurred to Eira that she would ever be faulted for that—that in a world that meshed magic and mortals that people would have something to say of her liking women.

Eira only leant back into the seat of the booth, tilting her chin down. "And what would that be?" She looked back to Meilin. "I'm sure my companion would also love to be enlightened, considering you've already managed to interrupt our night out."

The one who spoke first curled his lip. "Do you not feel shame?"

She shrugged. "I can only afford confusion at this point in time."

The group had simpered forward, leaving no room between themselves and the table's edge. This close, Eira could see the stains of dark ale on their linens and hardened bits of food in their spotty beards. Though they were all different men, the characteristics of their cruel eyes and sneers remained the same. The type torn from the same wretched cloth.

Another leant forward, his knuckled fists thumping atop their table. "The last thing we want is for our wives to be *lead astray* in the dead of the night."

Another nodded. "This is your first and only warning—we will protect our women, so you better watch where you hunt."

Air hissed between Meilin's teeth and giddiness flash across her features. Suddenly, laughter bubbled up from inside of her. It wasn't loud enough to draw the attention of any nearby patrons, but it *did* draw the gaze of the group of men away from Eira.

The first man who addressed them—perhaps the leader of the gaggle—was missing the lobe of his right ear. Eira's focus flip-flopped between the men and Meilin. She knew she could hold her own, but No Lobe was getting more aggressive by the second. "Is there something amusing about this situation?"

When Meilin didn't bother to answer him, still sputtering with smaller fits of giggles, No Lobe inched closer. The fae refused to make herself smaller. She didn't shrink back into her seat. Adoration and concern swelled inside of Eira at the sight of it, as ridiculous as it all was.

"Are you a part of this, then? You know what she *is*?" Again, the words were acidic as they fell from his chapped lips. "Should we warn you, too, of the consequences that come about when fools try to take what's not theirs?"

Eira was utterly dumbfounded. If they were simply angered by the act of them enjoying one another's company, then the mention of *theft* made no sense.

A beat of silence passed between the two groups—Eira and Meilin, and the cohort of idiots. The buzz of background noise continued as though their interaction was nothing but added music to the tune of Amzi's interior.

Finally, Meilin spoke, laughter still edging her words. "As if women were ever such things—*belongings to be taken*—or yours to take to begin with!"

It was almost ridiculous to hear aloud; to have to remind these grown men that their wives at home had every right and will to walk out the door should they one day decide to do so— and that neither Eira, nor Meilin, would be the cause of that.

"You are just as bad as each other," No Lobe spat, "and you should be *ashamed*, sitting here like this, taking up space where you don't belong."

One of his companions bared his teeth. Eira decided he was to be named Black Eye—courtesy of the dark flower that bloomed just below his left temple. Discoloration carved a crescent moon covering his entire brow, bleeding onto his eyelid.

It seemed a miracle that the blow didn't blind him.

Black Eye leered. "The way you sit in Amzi and watch them —we've *seen* you do it."

Them being any mortal women who took their chance in the tavern for a night out.

Another nodded, grunting in approval. He had a low sitting ponytail and rings that adorned his meaty fingers. Long, dark hair curled across his knuckles. Silver Rings.

So far, Eira humanized three of the five men, and she had

still yet to be proved that any of them deserved it. No Lobe, Black Eye and Silver Rings.

The other two she dubbed as Ale Breath and Split Knuckles.

"I wish you boys would step away from our table," Eira seethed, growing tired, "so that my companion and I can go back to plotting about how to steal your wives to treat them better than you could ever wish to."

Ale Breath knocked empty glasses over as his hand shot out, grabbing Eira by the collar of her textured blouse. Soon, they were nose to nose. Meilin's intake of breath was sharp and quick.

"Do you think this is a *damned joke*?!"

Up until then, their interaction—whilst hostile—was contained enough as to not draw attention. But Ale Breath's actions made heads turn and voices halt.

The change in their air was palpable.

It worsened with a twitch in Eira's jaw. Spittle had landed on her cheek. She flexed her hand atop the table, just missing the shards of glass that lay scattered around them. This close, the heiress could make out every detail on his face. Lines of puckered skin and broken wounds. Glazed eyes.

She could do nothing. In this reality, Eira wasn't permitted to defend herself.

Durante's smirking face appeared in her mind.

The sound of a bottle being broken atop the bar top was what shattered the tension.

All eyes turned to Alfie. He stood, cloth-wrapped hand holding tight onto the jagged bottom of a bottle that looked to be *very* expensive. Deep amber liquid spilled out, and across, the surface of the bar.

"You *will* get your hands off my patron," Alfie instructed, simultaneously calm and authoritative, "and you *will* depart from this establishment immediately once you've done so."

He set the broken half down. Amzi was still silent.

"Or what?" Ale Breath challenged, fists not unwinding from the material of Eira's clothes. The other men paused with a more noticeable amount of hesitation. Their focus shifted from Eira and Meilin to the other customers in Amzi, taking note of their confusion—and apparent dislike—of what was happening.

Alfie just smiled. "I need to get a start on making good of the mess you've created, and if you don't leave, you're more than welcome to assist in that cleanup."

He unwound the towel from his fist, wiping his hands with it before he set it aside. The only thing that cut through the otherwise quiet tension was the soft creak of stools shifting, people moving to stand.

Alfie paused their movement with an outward jut of his chin. They waited.

Eira's breath stuttered in her throat. The adoration for Alfie that she once held close to her chest flared to life.

He was stubborn, and often unkind, but he cared for her, in his own way.

Silver Rings murmured something incoherent under his breath to Split Knuckles, who then passed on the message to Ale Breath. The man dhacked spit in his throat before he let Eira go. For a few awful seconds, the heiress wondered if he would rear back and expel the contents onto her.

Eira feared what rules she would forgo in answering with her own anger.

Ale Breath backed away from her, from the both of them, with a look that promised trouble the next time they weren't protected. He scowled at Alfie on his way out, dropping a handful of coins in the pool of spilled liquor in front of him. The resounding, almost comical, *plonk* rung in the air for a few moments after the group of five left, door slamming behind them.

The whole interaction was so charged, so quick, Eira was almost shocked when everything returned to normal after that. Just as fast as it all happened, conversations rose to fill the empty space in the air. Some customers got up to help Alfie clean the mess.

He waved them away, disposing of the broken half glass behind the counter.

No one paid any mind to Eira or Meilin, deciding whatever the problem was to not be of concern enough to warrant a follow up with the pair.

"I'll do my best to clean up here," Meilin said suddenly. The previous hysteria was gone—her expression was rendered with a sort of disappointment, sadness softening her features. There was relief there, too. When Eira opened her mouth to protest, Meilin nodded in the direction of the bar. "Please, go help your friend."

Friend.

Eira stood, hesitant, as Meilin took off the fine gloves she'd worn that evening, using them as a thick wrapping to collect the shards of glass in one spot. She was slow and meticulous.

The heiress left her to it, as much as she hated to do so.

She knew that it would be a losing battle to attempt to argue with her.

Alfie's eyes met Eira's as she approached the bar. He threw her a spare hand towel, which he seemed to pull from thin air, and she got to work.

He refused the help of other offering patrons.

But not from her.

She guessed it was due to the fact that he, internally, blamed her for the disturbance. She was at fault for bringing trouble to his door.

Unwanted thoughts of her shadowed companion came to mind. Eira wondered if he would've done the same thing for her. Or if he, like those men, would've questioned the time that she and Meilin spent together.

After cleaning the spillage that made it to the floor, and anything left over, Eira took it upon herself to come around the back of the bar. She dumped the swollen piece of cloth, heavy with liquid, into a bucket already filled with rags in need of a wash.

Alfie didn't object to the familiarity of it all.

He just watched Eira, a hundred unasked questions dancing behind a gaze that was anything but stoic, despite his best efforts.

Eira took the moment of peace between them to see what changed in his working station since her last time as a server. A few things were rearranged, though the shelves still retained their classic state of organized chaos only Alfie could truly navigate. But it was something new that caught Eira's eye—a small, gilded frame on the lower shelves of the bar, propped between two bottles. A drawing of a man, bushy-haired and blushing, looked back at her. It wasn't a self-portrait. Eira knew that much.

"We protect our own here," Alfie said, simply.

Eira just nodded, something tight in her chest unwinding, just slightly—letting in room for air, to breath. When she turned back to her table, to Meilin, she saw that the heiress finished collecting the pieces of glass and had soaked any liquid with the cloth napkins the drinks were served on.

Eira watched, in a sort of dazed fascination, as Meilin brought the rim of her drink—the one she'd nursed during the confrontation—to her lips. The feeling of a passing kiss danced across her cheeks like a breeze may do.

We protect our own here.

Alfie protected them from his own kind but Eira hadn't been able to do the same for Meilin when she was suffering at the hands of Durante. She didn't believe herself deserving of either of them—of Alfie, an unsuspecting mortal friend or Meilin, a fellow fae heiress she kept in the dark about everything that truly mattered.

She'd gotten herself too involved with mortals, too involved with those she should've considered as her enemies. She was too far gone, with too little time left in Erebus to really grasp the enormity of her circumstances.

The immediate danger had disappeared when those men left Amzi—but in reality, Eira's situation saw her so far from safety that it was almost laughable.

CHAPTER 9
TO BE WARY OF WARNINGS

They didn't talk about that night.

Not in the times they sat in Amzi thereafter, in the same booth, drinking the same drinks. They didn't talk about what the men implied, about what *their* understanding of one another was outside of simple companionship. They didn't talk about the unexplained ecosystem under Meilin's floorboards. Eira's thoughts weren't occupied by that of her missing shadowed companion.

She no longer dealt in secrets or traded in mortal misery.

Eira and Meilin just continued to enjoy one another's company—both in public and in private. Whilst the encounter hadn't turned Eira off Amzi entirely, it made her wary of how often they went there, more conscious of who else may be watching, and of the vexed men trying to seek them out again.

Luckily, the pair found a new familiarity in spending time together in their homes, where the forest shaded them from the eyes of mortal onlookers—and they could almost convince themselves that if they looked at the skyline through the window, with squinted gazes and too much optimism, they could be anywhere else in the world.

Though Meilin was happy in the cleaning of her home, despite the unanswered questions that lay rotting underneath the floorboards of it, the heiresses preferred to meet Eira at her place of residence.

Unsurprisingly, Eira's cottage seemed to welcome Meilin in as if she had always existed there.

Even from the first time she came over, its walls were open arms, rays of sun dancing inside and across the floor in something of a warm smile.

Meilin padded around, gaze drinking in every inch of the place like she'd never seen anything quite like it, and that made Eira don a small smile of her own.

Something about Meilin being there felt *right*. She fit in amongst the terracotta-toned furniture and the gilded window frames. The cottage was humble—leagues away from comparison to the monster that was Meilin's aged mansion—but Eira couldn't deny that it had, begrudgingly, become something like home to her.

Sharing that piece of home with Meilin was the most vulnerable she could be in a city like Erebus. In here, Eira opened the door as if it were her rib cages, and she let her fellow heiress walk atop her heart, inspecting every detail of her arteries and veins with careful curiosity.

There was a hint of scrutiny in her gaze, too, that Eira couldn't ignore.

"Is something not up to standard?" she questioned, voice light despite the sudden flurry of mothwings in her stomach at the thought that the other may be disappointed in what she was seeing.

Meilin met her eyes. "I find it hard to believe that *you* can keep a space so tidy," she retorted, one eyebrow raised, "and I'm starting to wonder if there's another guest you're hiding from me."

Eira barked out a laugh, the tension slowly beginning to ease from her body. She couldn't remember ever worrying so much about impressing someone. "I can assure you that it's just me. The place is small enough that I don't struggle all that much to keep everything in order. There's no woman I'm deceiving in bringing you here whilst she's away."

She watched Meilin's face in expectation as soon as the words left her lips.

Woman.

Eira tried to be bolder in her admitting her interest since that night in Amzi. It was a slow, tentative process. This was the most upfront she'd been since then.

Since the accusations.

Would Meilin react to the word? Would she notice the lilt in Eira's voice, the sudden hitched breath of expectation?

Meilin didn't falter. She just dismissed the other with a half-hearted roll of her eyes and turned around to continue her inspection.

Their interactions became a routine after that.

For the next few weeks, they circled like stars in each other's constellations. Days became intertwined. Mornings were Eira waiting at Meilin's door, or vice versa. Some days, Meilin would play the piano. Then, they would talk and sit with the peace that came in whatever bouts of silence thereafter. The heiress hated the quiet, but with Meilin, it was relaxing. At Eira's cottage, they would make an activity out of washing clothes or perusing the shelve of books that Eira had long left untouched before she spent time with Meilin.

Afternoons could be trips to Plentiful Pastries or walks around the forest. Eira would listen with equal measures curiosity and intent as Meilin pointed out the names of plants the heiress would've never known the origins of otherwise. The leaves around them continued to grow deeper and darker in color. Some started to fall.

On colder days, they ate inside the bakery, always keeping a respectable distance between them, despite the urges that Eira had to hold Meilin close. Silvia always regarded them with curiosity.

When the touch of the sun was plentiful and warm, they would sit in grassy spots along Celimene's river, tucked away on large rocks that kissed the bank of the rushing water.

Nights were spent star gazing and drinking.

They opted for the alcohol stored away in Eira's cabinets, leftover bottles that Alfie gifted her in her early working days. Clearing out room for more recent imports was the reasoning he gave her—but the heiress always thought it was his way of thanking her for working through busier days without complaining, especially considering that they were almost always full.

With Meilin, she would share a glass or two. They would cook dinner at Eira's cottage.

The activities that filled their days were painfully, perfectly, mortal. Mundane.

Eira wanted to make the absolute most out of the short time they had together.

Slowly, Meilin unfurled before her. She began to trust her, just a little more. The heiress watched the wounds on the other's skin become less tender with time. Meilin's mortal injuries were slow to knit themselves back together. Eira didn't ask about their origins and Meilin didn't talk about her pain. But Eira knew; she knew, and she noticed when Meilin stopped trying to hide a wince, or a sharp intake of breath, when her pain was worsened.

If she knocked a particularly tender part of a bruise against a piece of furniture, she didn't immediately dismiss an instantaneous reaction.

Meilin became comfortable with revealing her soft underbelly.

Her vulnerability was clear to Eira, even in those small actions, and it made her own guilt at their circumstances grow stronger every day.

That worry surmounted into a physical manifestation the day Eira last saw Meilin.

The evening started, as it always did, with the smell of cooking food and a freshly poured glass of juice. They often drank in the evening, but it had become more sporadic as of late, as Eira found she quite enjoyed the sweetness of fruit juice.

The stew was almost at a boil when Meilin entered the kitchen. Eira swiveled in her direction, away from the pot she'd been manning, ladle still in hand and bowl in the other. Ready to prep a serving of stew for the other.

The cottage air was heavy with the scent of carrots, potatoes and herbs. Eira's enjoyment in cooking—in sustaining herself outside of the bare minimum her body required to survive—grew thanks to Meilin.

Now, the air between them was heavy. Tasteless. If anything, it was bitter.

"What is this?"

The tone of Meilin's voice made Eira's stomach drop.

A flash of white fabric and twinkling jewels made the heiress lose her appetite all together.

Meilin said nothing as Eira pieced together her own foolish mistake—why she hadn't burned that mask the same night she arrived back home from Durante's palace was beyond her understanding. She kicked it into a pile, hiding away the shame of the night in an undiscernible pile, leaving the mess to a future version herself.

When Meilin began to take up place in Eira's home, filling in the gaps perfectly with her presence, it was expected that things in her environment would change. Clothes shuffled and furniture moved, cutlery was put in a different spot and Eira made room for Meilin because a pair had been crafted created from one.

She didn't usually like to have others in her space, but the fae was an exception to that rule.

Eira couldn't be certain how the fae heiress came across the incriminating piece of evidence, but she also wasn't particularly surprised. She knew of Meilin's curiosity and of the familiarity that grew with each visit to the cottage.

Meilin's fingers clutched the fabric, and she bore a gaze so sharp, cut from a deadly mix of betrayal and hurt, that Eira felt as if the walls of the cottage around them were going to crumble inwards.

She had no excuse.

How was she to explain that the mask connected them in the most twisted of ways? How could Eira possibly convince Meilin that she wasn't the same as the other mortals who watched her being tortured at the hand of Durante—that she wasn't mortal at all, really.

Anything she could fathom to say would sound like an excuse at best, and a lie at worst.

That was the foundation of their relationship, after all.

Deception.

Meilin recognized the accessory in the same way Eira did, but for reasons much worse, and nothing the heiress could conjure in way of excuse would make up for the pain that made Meilin's face contort.

"Are you going to explain yourself?" she asked after a few moments of terse silence, the words barely above a whisper.

Eira wanted to speak, and yet, her lips wouldn't pry open.

Her tongue was as heavy as a rock in her mouth and her pulse ricocheted in her throat, making it hard for her to swallow around the gravelly mass. She felt pathetic.

Small.

The corner of Meilin's lip curled up, betraying the anguish in her eyes. She was a storm of both emotions. Eira couldn't even find it in herself to offer up something, *anything*, in compensation for the hurt she was inflicting.

Deciding she wasn't going to get anything more from the other, Meilin dropped the mask to the ground. It clattered awkwardly, weighed down by the small jewels that had been woven amongst the lace detailing. Echoes of the sound rippled around them. Eira's eyes fell to where it landed, a few steps in front of her.

That's how close she was to Meilin. Eira could reach out, if she really wanted to. She could touch Meilin, grab her hand, beg her to stay.

She couldn't.

She didn't.

Meilin turned on her heel and left Eira's cottage without another word.

A stab of pain ricocheted in Eira's chest at how softly the heiress closed the door behind her. Meilin didn't slam it. She didn't curse Eira into the next lifetime before leaving. There were no theatrics to amplify the situation—only the air, lined with electric emotions, and their chests, heavy with unsaid words.

And that made it all a thousand times worse.

CHAPTER 10
TRUST IN ME

Eira began to scab over.

For the weeks following their fallout, she was a wound. Too raw to be touched, too sensitive to be treated properly; but healed enough to not weep with every movement and aching breath.

Her skin didn't break every time she got up from bed, every time she stomached food and faced the sun again with wincing eyes. Yet, it felt as if it did.

It felt as if bits of Eira were falling off her each day.

It was all too dramatic.

Too embarrassing.

She was too worried to fall back into the habits formed at Amzi. Too worried about running into Meilin, or what Alfie would say should upon seeing her.

Besides, with no companion to make profit off of—and very little of her own money left—Eira didn't have the luxury to spend her coin elsewhere.

Like the way she fell for Meilin, Eira let herself rot both pathetically and promptly.

She spoke to no one, not even able to muster the gall to slink out of her shroud of misery to seek out Meilin—to apologize, to explain the truth.

Neither of them owed that to each other. They lied through their teeth, all whilst bearing smiles and shy eyes, as was the nature of whatever relationship they'd formed.

In Durante's city, neither of them truly held the autonomy.

Truth was never a choice. It had never been theirs, even if Eira had once tried to trick herself into believing she could choose it.

Her time with Meilin taught her that the worst habits were the ones you didn't know you'd formed; and thoughts of the other heiress became just that—a habit that Eira herself hadn't known was one until she couldn't go a day without her mind swelling with *Meilin, Meilin, Meilin.*

The sway of the limp branches outside her window somehow began to remind Eira of the sweep of Meilin's hair. A sky full of stars that twinkled and winked down at the heiress mimicked constellations of the freckles across Meilin's cheeks.

Eira wondered if she was eating well. If she drank enough water, if she chose to stay away from Amzi. Or if, when she passed the seedy joint, perhaps thoughts of someone with fiery hair and emerald eyes lingered in her mind for a moment too long.

Long gone was the heiress to the ice court.

That part of Eira was missing for a long while before Meilin. She tried her best to come to terms with that. She reached a mutual understanding within herself, accepted that Erebus— that the city of Celimene—took away that bit of her being.

At least for now.

This should've been all too unfamiliar to have become a habit. She hoped to have more productive things to worry about. But that wasn't how the weeks following progressed.

It was always Meilin.

The only time she'd been prompted out of bed was to answer the door.

Someone knocked three days in a row, always just as the sun set in Celimene, always coming at the same time.

Eira managed to ignore it until the fourth day.

She was greeted by a body clad in a dark navy uniform, detailed with gold stitching and buttons, which made it clear to Eira who he was here on behalf of—as if anyone else knew where her cottage was. Durante's servants always looked the same. When their faces weren't shadowed in some extravagant mask, their slack-mouthed expressions and dead eyes were off-putting mirrors of one another.

This man was no different.

"I come with a message from the king," he said in the exact tone she'd expected. Flat. Distant. The lack of greeting was standard—she'd encountered many versions of the same run-in with Durante's staff earlier in her stay in Erebus.

Eira just sighed. "And that message is?"

She cringed against the light of the day, so much stronger when it wasn't filtered through the panes of her mostly shrouded windows.

His face contorted just slightly. When his eyes clouded over, Eira could've sworn she saw something unfamiliar flash behind them—something *alive*— but it was gone as soon as she'd taken notice.

"There will be a celebratory ball," he started, reciting an announcement that rolled off his tongue with ease, despite the blocky tone in which he spoke. His eyes were on Eira and still, he looked right through her.

"Tomorrow night," the guard continued, "falling on the eve

of the new week. A celebration of The New Reign, one last time, before they leave us and return home."

Eira abhorred being referred to in the third person.

He must've known who she was—what she was—and yet, he referenced The New Reign in a way that made it seem like Eira wasn't the one being celebrated. Like she didn't deserve to be titled as one of the nine fae due to leave.

Eira nodded her understanding and accepted a wax-sealed letter—which could've appeared from literal thin air by the way it materialized—from his extended hand.

The exchange took all of four days to occur and it was over in three minutes.

Why they couldn't have just slipped the damned thing under the door, Eira didn't know. Durante proved, constantly, he was as dramatic as he was impractical.

As soon as she was alone again, Eira cringed away from the invitation as if the act of opening it would cause her physical pain.

Really, it was her last obligation—her last *hurrah* in Celimene, and in Erebus, before she would return to her court, heart made heavy with the ghost of memories she'd never share with another soul.

The letter was just a repeat of the details she'd just been told. Time and location confirmed, with an additional note of instruction to '*dress for the occasion*'.

Bile rose in her throat.

Eira would be seeing Meilin for the last time.

Of *course* she would dress for the occasion.

CHAPTER 11
THE NEW REIGN

The night of the ball came, and Eira thought her mother would've choked had she seen the dress her daughter was wearing.

As a result of pride or indignance, the heiress was unsure.

It was a satisfying thought, nonetheless. *Any* thought, really, was a welcome distraction from the nerves that danced atop her skin.

A beautiful gown that took far too much effort to muster the willpower to step into it—to muster the energy.

The heiress decided quickly that the effort was worth it, at whatever cost.

Fabric clung precisely at every curve and dip in the line of her figure, and when Eira took a moment to really *look* at herself—at the body that filled out the dress—she felt a sort of gratification. She took less care of herself over the few weeks prior. But faithfully, stubbornly so, her body still clung to the softness that came because of the food her and Meilin shared in quantities larger than Eira ever previously allowed herself.

Her chest tightened. She shook away the feelings—thoughts of Meilin were not as welcome as the others.

Instead, Eira focused on who stared back at her in the mirror.

She was clad in a gown the color of a starless night and so, so different to how she'd arrived in Erebus three years prior. Lips, which she'd coated with a darkened cherry red. Eyelids swept over haphazardly with a paint-like shimmer of silver. Cheeks flushed because of the courage drink she'd poured herself in preparation to leave to face the ball head on.

Eira could break out of her brooding streak. She *would*. It wouldn't kill her.

I deserve this, Eira told herself. *One last night.*

A knock at the door signaled the arrival of her accompaniment to the palace, a particularly dramatic addition that Eira wished the king didn't account for. Guards and a horse-drawn carriage to a destination that was a sturdy twenty-minute walk (if done at a brisk pace) away seemed unnecessary.

Eira sucked in a breath as she turned away from the mirror, figuring that transport was the least of her worries—it was what awaited her on arrival that would work to concern her more.

An undercurrent of sweet liquor and the tang of mingling perspiration clung to the air inside Celimene's palace.

Tall, cream pillars held up the high ceiling, blurring into one another, a haze of smoke distorting the edges of where the corners met.

Rich copper draping hugged the artfully crafted window-panes, but they could as easily be seen as no more than a blood-hued stain on the otherwise pristine walls.

The palace felt different compared to last time she'd been there.

It could've been the sheer number of bodies that filled it, or the extra detail given to less subtle shows of extravagance. Nothing was off limits.

Walls that were previously closed off seemed to fold apart, like the inner body of the building was theirs to wander. Eira was instantly overwhelmed though she did her best to act as if she belonged, which was easy enough if she considered the appreciative stares she was regarded with upon entering. Some courtiers were unabashed in their gazes. Some guards tilted their chins higher when her attention turned to them.

Maybe her nature *was* less of a secret for the night.

After all, it was Eira's ball. Eira's celebration, thrown in honor of her and the other cursed fae, bound by misfortune.

Scents of smoke and sandalwood only got stronger the further she ventured into the mouth of the venue. Her stomach sang at the sight of exuberantly decorated mouthfuls of food being walked around atop detailed golden platters. The workers that carried them donned the silks of the palace staff—material that was nice but not *too nice*—and bore emotionless expressions, faces covered with slashes of gold paint that appeared simultaneously purposeful and messy.

Working in such proximity to Durante and the courtiers that surrounded him with no days of reprieve was a very intimate and unforgiving sort of torture. As if being born a mortal wasn't punishment enough.

Eira could decipher the emotions behind their vacant gazes. She watched them as she walked, noting each time they were brushed off by someone in attendance—waved away like bugs. Their neutral masks stretched out a little thinner. She noticed the twitch of a gold-covered eye. A vein in the neck that protruded in the light.

She would have to study this sort of façade, and perfect it, to survive stepping up into the responsibilities of her own court.

All the same, the heiress decided against stopping any of them to grab food for herself. Instead, she set her focus on finding the bar, planning to avoid absolutely anyone who looked remotely like Meilin on her way there.

Eira weaved through the foyer and down some hallways, being guided by smell and sound and sight, not in any real rush. All of it was enough to keep her mind occupied. Whenever she felt herself on the verge of being overwhelmed, she sought out a darker corner of a quieter hallway. There, she would pause and focus on her breath as it moved in and out of her lungs, like clockwork.

It didn't take long for her to find her way into the grand ballroom, the prime location for the night; and like a reward for her having sought it out without much trouble on the way, Eira spotted what she was looking for through the parting crowd of women in glittering garments and men in fine-cut cloth. The elongated necks and curved lips of both tall and short glasses glittered all the same under the twinkling light of the fifteen chandeliers she counted adorning the roof.

She set her sights on the oasis and took one of the paths available on either side of the floor reserved for dancing couples. Swaths of fabric and heavy perfumes brushed past her with every step. People whispered and laughed whilst they twirled in each other's arms, their conversations following the movement of their choreographed routines. Eira, unable to help herself, caught wind of what was being said, close enough to the edge of the dance floor that she heard the tail end of discussions from a handful of couples.

It made the surprisingly long trip to the other side of the room more interesting.

"You look beautiful tonight."

A smile tugged at the corner of her lips, but Eira kept her face angled towards her destination, not daring to disrupt the special sort of magic that was eavesdropping on unknowing mortals.

"I wonder if we'll be served desserts after the grand dinner. I've heard that the king's cook makes his legendary lemon pie for special occasions."

Her stomach groaned.

But it was the end of one discussion in particular that almost made her stumble.

"All this for the *fae*! You would think the king truly liked them—"

"Anything for the show, really—"

The fae—the heiresses—were nothing more, really.

A show. Animals made to perform. Put in cages and placed on display for everyone else to marvel at.

Had the past three years of Eira's life been a spectacle, of course her kind were the *main attraction*. The punchline of a joke they never asked to be a part of.

To make matters worse, Eira only managed to succeed in achieving one of the two goals she set for herself. She did, in fact, make it to the bar. But it was when she drew closer, only able to stop a few steps shy of it, that the heiress spotted something—someone—else that snatched her attention away from everyone else in the room.

She recognized her immediately.

No one else could make her breathless the way Meilin did.

Bodies continued to walk by Eira, moving to and from the dance floor and around the ballroom with a giddy restlessness. She was nestled in a spot that meant Meilin wouldn't yet be able to see her, even if she turned her back to the bar. When Eira noticed her, she was leant over it, elbows propped up atop the dark wood.

When Meilin turned around only a few seconds later, her gaze angled down at the colorful drink she nursed in her hands, she was so painfully close and so far away in the same instance. Eira's stomach swooped. Any false sense of bravado was pulled from underneath her skin with such a force that she struggled to center herself.

The edges of the room swayed.

She couldn't turn away, despite the fear that Meilin would soon look up from her drink and catch her in the act of doing so.

Golden embellishment started to take shape from the dip in Meilin's waist and trailed up her stomach and around her sternum, sitting against the dark fabric of her dress like a bodice carved from the light of the sun. The spindly material was as delicate as it was demanding, like an armor of sorts.

Eira tried to remember the time that she'd helped the other clean her home—if this was a gown she saw among the others stacked away in her closet.

Even just at her resting point against the bar top, Meilin was the picture of royalty.

Under the embellished outer corset was a lustrous silk, slip gown that shimmered with even the slightest of movement. The twinkling array of ballroom lights reflected off the material, capturing the reflection of everything around her within it, like an endless vortex.

Unintentionally, but deliciously so, Eira noted that they were a matching pair.

The heiress wanted to push through the remainder of the crowd to meet Meilin, to ask that they take to the dance floor. They would move past tightly embracing couples and servers that would shift out of their way without blinking an eye because both Eira and Meilin were all too accustomed to making space, to taking up as little of it as possible in return— and this would be the night they claimed *their* space.

Maybe she would have the courage to apologize, the humility to ask for Meilin's forgiveness, and the will to ask for more time.

Then, Eira would sweep the other up in her arms once on the dance floor, if Meilin saw it fit to grant her another chance. Under the exceedingly warm overhead lighting, the pair would sway around the floor, the movement of their gowns around them exploding into a flurry of stars.

The ballroom would be a detonation of dizzying colors that soared past them as their bodies became flightless birds. Light enough to soar through the sky, just without the means to do so.

If they could, they would have flown far from there.

Together.

Eira didn't know what she'd say to get Meilin to agree with accompanying her to dance—if she could muster the words to do so at all—but it didn't matter, because the potential for what could've and couldn't have been in Eira's fantasy was snatched from her before she even managed to make it to Meilin's side.

CHAPTER 12
THE CREATURES WE'VE BECOME

The mass of bodies rippled around them as they tore through it with none of the subtlety that Eira tried to use only moments earlier.

She couldn't squirm out of the grip the stranger had on her.

Even worse, she couldn't identify who they were, as everything in the room spun and shifted to match the speed of their movement.

It didn't take long for them to divert off the dance floor and down a hallway, arriving in some nondescript corner, far enough away from the noise and light of everything in the ballroom that Eira could quickly readjust the dizzying mess that the trip made of her mind.

But she hadn't expected the flash of familiarity that caught her off guard next as she faced the stranger front-on.

"*Alfie?*"

The name came out sounding like a question, but Eira *knew* this man.

She knew him in a dim tavern as well as she knew him in an exquisitely lit ballroom. She knew him even though he was dressed in the colors of a server, face painted in streaks of gold, mirroring the theatrics that she'd seen on others in the hall.

She would know him anywhere.

Alfie, the mortal stain on her fae teachings. An unlikely friend who stuck around, and who she stubbornly began to care for, whether she chose to admit it to herself or not.

He didn't look nearly as surprised to see Eira, despite her shock at seeing him.

Alfie wasn't invited to events held by the king and he definitely didn't work at them, either. Durante *tolerated* his citizens —but unless they were his staff, of high standing, or played a coveted part of his personal court, they weren't getting casual invites to his celebrations (though it wasn't like Eira particularly fancied being there either).

The barkeep himself wasn't shy in his open distaste, and distrust, in the king. He was smart about who he told but Eira *knew*. She assumed it was why he let her operate in her secret dealings inside of his establishment.

No, Alfie shouldn't be attending an event like this. Eira shouldn't be facing him in this hallway.

Unless someone else brought him along—or taught him how to make his own way in. How to blend in. Someone who had the resources to do so.

Ah.

Ah.

"Listen to what I have to say before you open your big mouth," Alfie said, tone somewhat softer than his usual default. He saw her work it out. Watched as she pieced everything together, bit by bit.

Noticed the change in her expression; the firm set of her mouth, the crease in her eyebrows.

"You knew him," Eira stated plainly.

His eye twitched. "Know him, yes. I *know* him."

"It's more than that, though, isn't it?"

A moment of quiet.

"Yes," Alfie admitted. Sadness clouded his gaze. "But he's not gone in the way you're presuming he is. He *is* in Exilis."

"Has he told you that?"

"He told me that was where he was going—"

"No," Eira interrupted, anger making her muscles tense, "has he called for you since leaving Erebus? Have you received a message on his behalf? Any sign, at all, that he actually *made* it there?"

With every question, Eira saw Alfie shrink further and further into himself, appearing as if he regretted approaching her altogether.

This was not the man she knew. Being softened by love—and fear—made him unrecognizable.

Alfie's silence was answer enough.

It only took a few seconds, though, for him to shake off the semblance of care and revert back to speaking to Eira in a way that was entirely *him*.

"I didn't come here to talk to you about my love life." Alfie's resolve hardened as he spoke. "I came to pass on a message."

She wanted to be angry. Angry that this was hidden from her, angry that neither of them ever told her, angry that she didn't realize it earlier.

Angry that Alfie had to harbor this burden of worry alone.

Eira wanted to be bitter, to be hurt about this betrayal. It seemed hardly fair, considering all that she hid from him—from her own . . . *non-platonic* companion.

Yet, she couldn't muster any of that. Instead, an odd mixture of despair and adoration consumed her.

Alfie was so good at hiding it. His concern, his fear—all of it. Grumpiness was the default characteristic she assigned to him.

But Alfie hid his pain in the face of work. Eira never would've known of his suffering otherwise.

Amzi continued to run.

The tavern didn't crumble, even if its owner fell apart inside, whilst Eira had spent the last few weeks rotting of her own accord.

The framed drawing she spotted behind the bar came to her mind.

It was obscured, sure, but the details were similar enough. A younger version of her shadowed companion was captured on that piece of paper.

Eira *should've* known.

"I'm going to assume that you don't have any more questions," Alfie bit out, growing impatient with their back-and-forth. "Look, the message is that you should be careful who you trust."

She scoffed. "Clearly."

He grit his teeth. "Meilin, you fool. I'm talking about Meilin!"

"What, he told you to warn me about *Meilin*?" Eira heard the disbelief in her voice. She was entirely unconvinced. "Great job you've been doing at keeping us apart. I'm sure he'd be proud that his message got to me so late, but noted. Loud and clear. Can I go now?"

"Eira . . ."

The sound of her voice falling from his lips, and the exasperation that weighed heavy behind it, made her pause. "I know that you and I have had our"—he thinks on the right word to properly acknowledge the whirlwind that had been their acquaintance—"quarrels."

"Quarrels are what lovers have—"

"But this is information that I'm asking you not to disregard," Alfie pushed on, choosing to ignore her. "It is just best that you remember who is safe to share your secrets with—and that she is *not* one to trust."

Eira didn't think the advice was much to heed, both considering that the one who shared it was now gone and that Meilin owned her own little slice of Eira's good conscience.

"Well," was all she could muster in response, "I will . . . keep that in mind."

Alfie wasn't convinced. She could see it in his face. Yet, in all fairness, there wasn't much of a message to take from. The heiress knew well enough that she shouldn't trust Meilin. She shouldn't be anywhere near Meilin. It's just that this was all too little and entirely too late.

Before her companion could push for further reassurance, Eira wanted to ask questions of her own. "You didn't go with him?"

Neither of them needed to address the 'him' being discussed to know who was being referenced.

"He is more than grown enough to be capable of taking care of himself," Alfie spat back.

"Don't you love him?"

The curiosities poured out of Eira. She wanted her musings answered. Wanted, so badly, to know what was going through their minds—the both of them. These mortal men, tied together in a way that was special to them, tied to her in ways she'd never expected. Eira wanted to *understand*.

He was taken back by the question. Confused by it.

"Don't speak to me of love, as if you understand it at all."

His bitterness was astounding but not unwarranted.

This interaction was *exactly* what she wanted to avoid—it was time that she could've been spending with Meilin, maybe, but it was time wasted.

Whilst he stewed on his response, Alfie's face was tightened by a seriousness that irked her. Mortals were always *so damn serious.* Everything was serious and unfun with them. Eira herself had started to feel like one as of late—all her problems started and ended with mortals.

Their moment of quiet continued to pass. Eira waited for him to bite out another response, to maybe curse her for her insolence. Instead, his eyes, previously shadowed with a mix of rage and disdain, took on a silent plea.

It was entirely uncharacteristic of their circumstance, courtesy of her impatience to get back to Meilin and his lack of explanation.

She was almost dizzy with the emotional shift.

"He warned me too, you know," Alfie admitted. His eyes moved from her to plant themselves on a faraway spot on a wall behind her. Eira could almost see the cogs turning in his head, the memories of his precious time with the other a sacred thing to hold onto. "But I have people here. I can't just leave up and leave so easily. Even I don't know the full extent of what he's seen or heard, yet I've always, *always*, trusted him. His word is good, and his warnings ring true."

Eira didn't particularly know what to do with that. She asked the questions and then couldn't handle the sudden overbearing weight of their intimacy—of a relationship that she could never have with Meilin.

"Your opinion is biased," she said, simply, as if it were the clearest answer of all. The heiress hoped that the bluntness of it would cut clean their complicated conversation.

It was best not to entertain these sorts of things.

He was gone. Her shadowed companion was gone and all that was left was the missing man's messenger. She wouldn't find herself caught up in the affairs of mortals again—she couldn't.

Eira had a life to go back to so very soon and became resolute in spending whatever retched time remaining in Erebus, at the very least, in the company of Meilin.

She leant in closer. "When you meet him again in Exilis," exaggerating the *when*, because Eira couldn't deny the feeling that resounded in her bones, promising her that they would, in fact, be reunited, "you can let him know that his worry was wasted on me—but that I thank him nonetheless."

Alfie's next breath came in like more of a hiccup, his eyes wet with emotions she could only wish to decipher. Taking a moment to commit his face to memory, Eira stood. Waited. For a response, for a plea to stay. For anything.

Silently, she thanked him for Amzi. For his company. For what he gave her and took from her.

The last thing Eira saw of him was the firm set line of his mouth and the singular tear that streamed down his cheek. She turned away from him, her stomach tight.

If what he's prophesied as happening in Erebus is as bad as he imagines it to be, I truly hope I never see you in this kingdom again. I wish for you to make it out.

The pleas were silent. Her own, private things.

Then Eira walked away. She left Alfie, abandoned, in the shadows behind her, once and for all.

On her way back in, she did her best to feel steady again. She breathed.

In and out.

It would have to be enough until the heiress got her hands on some alcohol.

Drawn back into the path of commotion, Eira found that the ballroom teemed with life, as it did when she left it.

Music of a more feverish pace and volume erupted around her. The air of initial awe and flurry shifted to give way to the heart of the night. A feverish joy that was a rare commodity in the Kingdom of Erebus seemed to make them all drunk.

Durante definitely knew a thing or two about throwing grandeur parties—and the display was so distracting and marvelous that Eira almost forgot about the interaction she shared with Alfie moments beforehand.

To be expected, it was only those of apparent status—whether courtiers or the king's royal ass-kissers—who got to enjoy the frivolities of parrying in such a free environment. Those who were there, despite the resounding bitterness Eira knew was ever-present in the hearts of all of them, *were* genuinely enjoying themselves.

It was a special occasion, after all.

She thought of her own onyx dress as she waded through the crowd, how she chose it for the night as a symbol of both celebration and mourning. Eira never expected to be leaving someone behind in the kingdom—to be leaving behind more than one person alone was overwhelming.

When her eyes flickered over the crowd, she was swallowed by the blur of dizzying colors and sounds, smells and *textures*. The heiress brushed arms with more dancing couples who had no concept of the space around them, and she felt the pace of her heart quicken along time with the upbeat melody of the music. Its power had infected all the attendees with a need to move, to wind along with the grand space like glorious, uncaged birds. She supposed that's what they were, considering it'd been one of the few occasions the king wasn't seated at his dais, watching over them.

Eira knew she'd be seeing him soon regardless.

She continued to push through the crowd, resisting the urge to yelp every time she'd had a toe danced over or a particularly slick part of skin brush against hers. There was something alarming about the frenzied nature the ballroom took on in her absence.

It was beautiful from afar, but swept up in the center of it all, Eira found herself in even more dire need of a drink and a familiar face.

After arriving in a break in the unrelenting ocean, Eira scanned the faces of those nearest to the bar. "Please tell me she hasn't left," she muttered to herself. A muffled prayer to The Deities that had yet to listen to her.

There's always room for a first, she told herself.

Luckily, Meilin was easy to see from across the room, still in the same spot, as if looking for someone.

Waiting.

And it was utterly devastating the way that her face fell upon spotting Eira.

Expected, sure, but that didn't make it hurt any less.

Eira wanted to cross the room. She wanted to push through the swell of mortals again, faster this time, with no worry for the sweat slicked skin she'd brush along the way. It would take nine, maybe ten, strides if she moved with purpose. Eira wished that, when she did so, she'd act on her fantasy. They would dance and laugh and rekindle something that could never be.

None of those things were hers to have, though. That much was clear in the fire that roared across Meilin's expression. They only had a moment to process the surroundings, to truly acknowledge the sight of seeing one another again, before a scream broke out in the crowd.

A startling, sudden thing that was stark against the jovial flute and chorus that played moments prior. Almost comical.

Meilin's eyes were the last thing Eira saw before the ballroom fell into chaos.

CHAPTER 13
A TRAIL OF CRIMSON

Eira knew nothing more than the adrenaline that poured through her veins.

It thrust her into action. As it wrapped around her limbs, she thought, foolishly so:

Wow. My body does *remember the training.*

As if her bones could ever forget. As if her muscles could ever unlearn such an integral part of her life. As if the strained nerves could untangle themselves from the sharp points of pain they'd caused her so many times.

Her body would never forget, just as it would never forgive her for putting it through all that it withstood.

The parts of her that remembered—the ones she thought she'd sacrificed in her transition into mortal life in Erebus—pulled Eira in the direction of the bar. The heiress pushed aside mortals that cowered in small circles.

Eira shook away any worry reserved for them as she pulled herself up and over the bar top. A mixture of spilled liquor and blood stuck to the once-polished wood, and her hands, when she lifted them off.

She didn't know whose family member, who's loved one,

she now had a bit of slotted underneath her fingernails, drying against her skin.

This was not a brawl in a training field.

Not spilt blood from an open wound that was made because of careful, characterized technique and skillful sparring.

This was messy.

This was unfair.

It was not a battle she prepared herself for. Eira wasn't ready to face this kind of ugliness.

Especially not sober.

The extent of her own cowardice was not yet so over-whelming that Eira couldn't bring her focus back to the situation at hand. Behind the bar, there were members of the king's staff curled into balls, using the small space to hide away. She wanted to tell them they would be better off trying to find an exit, like the other mortals she'd shoved away in her efforts to get there; wanted to pull them to their feet, to prompt them to move towards safety.

She didn't.

There's no time, an insistent voice in her mind prompted, *hurry.*

Choosing to heed the call of that voice, Eira focused on finding a suitable weapon. She doubted—no, she *knew*—that nothing easily accessible in the space around her would rid the ballroom of whatever had come to life before them. These things made something sinister from the broken bones and warped skin of mortal guests and left the torn fabric of fine dresses and artfully crafted suits strewn across the dance floor.

It all happened so fast, the shift spreading like a fire across the space of the ballroom.

Eira didn't have time to grab weaponry from Durante's guards, who were nowhere to be seen either way, their king much the same.

So, she sought solace in the one weapon she knew more intimately than most.

Eira's weapon of choice crunched under the weight of her boots—which she suddenly felt incredibly smart for wearing, despite the way they clashed horrendously with her dress—and it proved to be a mission to grab a hold of a shard large, and sturdy, enough to brandish.

Even the largest Eira could find may not vanquish the creatures, but it would at least aid her in the meantime to push through the chaos, to distract them.

To find Meilin.

Fearful mortals watched her with wide eyes and slack mouths, confused by her actions. They pushed themselves further against the shadows provided by the bar-top, willing their bodies to blend into the darkness.

For their sake, Eira could only hope that the creatures on the other side of the ballroom had poor senses of sight. And smell. She heard them draw in sharp breaths as she bent and grabbed hold of the best piece of glass she could find, not flinching as her fingers curled around it.

The skin of Eira's mortal palm was malleable and soft. Instead of the expected golden ichor that always spilt forth from her veins in Seelie, the broken shard she chose left blooming pools of crimson. She was still so unused to the grotesque color, even after three years of it cycling through her body like a toxin.

Eira's mortal blood marked her path out from behind the bar and towards the center of the ballroom. She left the cowering mortals and a trail of red in her wake, and there was no pain—only determination.

And fear.

The combined cries of Erebus's citizens and the gurgled calls of the creatures was an alarm that kept time in Eira's mind. As she ducked, maneuvering through the ongoing destruction with careful precision uncharacteristic of her surroundings, Eira was plagued by the reminder that she hadn't seen Meilin since the ballroom fell into chaos.

They were separated on the dance floor for what felt like years prior. No matter how hard she tried to recall how much time passed since that moment, nothing made sense in Eira's mind.

Everything roared around her.

In her peripheral, mortals were being ravaged. The ones that hadn't yet split and cracked at the seams to transform were bearing the brutal brunt of the creature's wraths.

Heads were pulled from necks as if they were connected with little more than crinkled streams of colored paper.

Screams were cut short when clawed hands, grown two sizes too big for the indigo skin that stretched around them, came in contact with tongues and yanked. They seemed—much to Eira's horror—to be enjoying themselves. The deaths that they dealt were not swift, for the most part.

The creatures preoccupied themselves, in groups and alone, with drawing out the torture of the mortals they procured.

The air, previously tinged with scents of vanilla, heady smoke and expensive liquor, was suffocated by copper. Eira's lungs heaved in metallic air.

She choked on every breath as she moved.

Eira slashed at creatures that came too close. Those that broke away to get a look at her were bold, or bored, with blood smeared across their dislocated jaws and a feverish look in their eyes. It should've been impossible, considering they were all but ink-hued pearls lodged in hollow sockets.

Her aim wasn't as erratic as she feared.

Instinct told her to aim for the amalgamation of flesh and skin that bore the closest resemblance to the throat, which was not so easy to decipher when what was in front of her was anything but a normal mortal body.

Whether as a result of the adrenaline, or by benefit of her training having kicked in, Eira was able to keep the creatures at a distance. Their curdled cries were short and sharp as she slashed. The blood that spilt from their open wounds—their *own* blood—was the color of silver.

Confusion pushed her further and faster.

When the world around her slowed, and everything was covered by a sickening sort of crimson, Eira could only think of Meilin.

Could only think of what was lost in not taking the chance to tell her the truth. Could only think of the look Meilin gave her before everything fell apart.

As if by the act of her intention alone, a split in the seam of the bodies that blocked Eira's vision made Meilin come into view. Her dress was torn, a large strip of the luxurious fabric haphazardly tied around a portion of her upper arm that leaked red—mortal blood, binding them both—and her eyes were set on Eira. A broken heel was brandished in her hands like the most fearsome weapon, her face set with anger and resolve.

It only made Eira move quicker.

"Why do I always find you in the face of danger?" Meilin shouted at her, the words tumbling out over the chaos of the room. "Why is it that trouble follows you?"

Eira huffed out a breath, hit by a sudden wave of exhaustion and relief. Besides the injury being held together by the fabric of her dress, Meilin seemed otherwise unharmed.

"I could say the same thing to you," she said through clenched teeth, circling the space around them, trying to focus on both Meilin and anything else that could be coming their way. Neither of them talked about the mask. They didn't make up for lost time with an embrace. Now wasn't the time.

The mortals in attendance—ones that hadn't turned and were, instead, being attacked—dwindled in numbers so fast that Eira couldn't be sure how much time passed since everything fell apart.

Was it an hour or ten minutes? Was it a few weighted seconds that dragged out to forever?

Whatever it was, they didn't have much time.

There were easily over two hundred bodies that occupied the space beforehand. Attendees, servers, musicians and guards; and whilst Eira didn't have the capacity to count the bodies that lay strewn across the ballroom floor, she was numbly aware of the profound loss in the room—as well as the fact that she and Meilin would be next if they didn't move quickly.

But where was there to go?

What other choice did they have?

Where in Deity's name was the king?

The creatures that weren't still cornering their victims or making the most of the meals they did secure began to turn their attentions to those who still stood. There weren't many.

Eira found that when she turned over her shoulder, Meilin's back was against hers. They were skin to skin—interlocked by sweat and blood—and neither knew what to do next.

"This might be the first time you haven't got anything annoying to say," Meilin murmured. Eira didn't have to see her face to know that she winced through the words. Maybe she was in more pain than the heiress could see. "I'm impressed."

"You're bleeding," Eira hissed back, like that was enough of an explanation as to why she didn't have enough handy remarks available to spare in the life-or-death situation they suddenly found themselves in.

"So are you." She felt Meilin's face turn against shoulder.

"Are you admitting that you're worried about me?" Her breath was hot against Eira's neck.

The warm kitchen flashed to her mind. The look of burning despair and betrayal on Meilin's face.

The heiress swallowed. "I'm more worried about us both getting out of here no more harmed than we already are."

A bitter chuckle from Meilin. "At least we're both in agreement on that."

For what felt like hours after that, they slashed at creatures that inched towards them. They screamed in their faces, like the noise would make them scuttle away. The only thing that kept them back was being able to make a slash in the creature's skin. They howled in pain when touched with anything wielded by the mortal hand. The people they'd already killed hadn't been a problem because they were weaponless—but those remaining were different.

Whoever was left standing in the ballroom did the same as Eira and Meilin, grabbing whatever they could get their hands on to use as a means of defense.

But Eira didn't know how much longer they could all go on like that, fending off these inconceivable beasts with broken shoes and shards of glass.

Nonetheless, she held strong in her resolve.

Until she was caught off guard.

The sound of Meilin's scream—one of pain rather than intimidation—made Eira stutter in the careful sequence of moves she'd curated. Her eyes sought to find her, to see what happened, if she was badly hurt—or worse.

It was then that a creature came close enough to grab her. Somehow intelligent enough to know when to seize a moment of distraction, the thing leered at Eira. Claws sprung out of its disfigured fingers, wrapped around her neck and *squeezed*.

She sputtered for air.

It lifted her higher and higher in the air as she struggled. Eira could hear Meilin, somewhere close by, scream her name. Again and again. The shard of glass in her hand was still there —she hadn't yet lost full control of her limbs—and whilst her arms hung limply at her sides, her right hand clenched tighter around the broken weapon.

The creature brought her closer to its face, which was made up of the distorted features of someone that was once mortal. Human bones broke and re-shaped to make way for what emerged from inside of it, and Eira could swear that she heard a moan of pain rattle from deep inside its elongated throat.

When her vision blurred, she steadied her grip on the glass. With a surge of energy, her survival instinct flaring up in her chest, Eira slashed in a wide arc. Her aim was accurate, and the last bit of strength impactful enough, to lodge the shard into the side of the creature's neck.

Her own blood glittered on the edge of the glass, which looked comically small when planted into something so unnaturally large.

But it was enough.

The creature wailed in agony.

Its face reared away from Eira, and after a moment of very brief consideration, flung her across the length of the ballroom. Meilin's voice was a constant throughout the whole ordeal.

The heiress only stopped hearing it when her head collided with a wall, and everything was swallowed by darkness.

PART II
THE DEMIR TRIALS

CHAPTER 14
A FOOL, A DISAPPOINTMENT, A TRAITOR

As if it had never truly existed in the first place, the room around her fell away.

And for the first time in years, Eira knew she was dreaming.

Everything from the walls, with their spectacular glass paneling that was dressed in curtains of a deep russet—all of it melted down, and when the heiress blinked, it was nothing. It was just her, stood against a blank canvas of a landscape that stretched as far as the eye could see.

In this vast emptiness, Eira dared to dream of Meilin.

For as soon as she wished it—wished for her—she was there. Dressed in the gown she wore to the ball, taking Eira's hand to be led out onto a dance floor that didn't exist, to spin to music that didn't play.

Then they embraced, arms looped around each other's necks, swaying side to side.

"Do you ever wish you were normal?" Meilin whispered, face nestled in the crook of Eira's shoulder.

"What's normal to you, Meilin?"

"I don't know. Anything but what I am."

"And what do you perceive yourself to be?"

"A fool." The word came out cruelly, like Meilin had heard herself be called by the name too many times before.

A fool. A disappointment. A traitor.

Eira knew the feeling all too well.

Was this what falling for the fae heiress would make her?

"A fool, a dagger-wielding pianist, a firecracker donning the face of a cherub—nothing is normal about you, and I'm glad for it," Eira cooed, "because who else would sway around with me in a shabby little cottage to music that no one else can hear?"

That's where they were.

Eira's forest home. The night Meilin left.

Except she didn't leave, because she never found the mask. She never felt the betrayal that saw her distance herself from Eira.

"It's not that shabby," she laughed softly.

"It started looking a lot livelier from the first day you burst in."

Meilin pulled back from Eira's shoulder to ensure the other could see her as she rolled her eyes.

Silence trickled in as they continued to sway.

But Meilin broke it only a few heartbeats later. She had a lot of questions.

"Is there really a need for romance in a place like this?" she asked. Feeling brave, Eira smiled.

"Of course," she answered, pulling back so that she could dip her head to meet Meilin's. "If anything, I think it's needed here the most. Don't you agree?"

It was cold.

So, so cold.

Even for Eira, an heiress born to a land dominated by ice, this sort of cold felt like sleet, occupying the space inside of her left by her stolen magic. It created icicles in place of her warm, soft insides.

She bit back a cry of pain as her eyes opened for the first time, seeing anything but the magnificent ballroom and the carnage that was left behind. Everything around her was dull and frigid, blanketed in the sort of darkness that made it near impossible to know where she really was.

But it clearly wasn't the same location as before.

Memories flooded in, all unwanted, and Eira wanted so badly to scream. The pain of them was unrelenting and constant. Her head thrummed with a special sort of anguish, only amplified by the injury she sustained after being thrown like a ragdoll.

The dream—or delusion-fueled fever dream, more like—of Meilin hadn't helped.

Meilin.

Eira moved to stand, driven by the sudden need to find her, to know that she was okay, only to find that the mobility of her body wasn't as it should be. Her ankle, which she thought healed, seared with a visceral pain. Worse than that, her movement was restricted by the manacles that had her hands bound at the wrist. When she moved even a little, a burning sensation flung her back into stillness. The smell of her own seared flesh made her want to gag. Looking down to her legs, stretched out before her, only confirmed that the heiress was bound at the ankles by the same burning manacle.

Iron.

But who would do that? *How?*

Even remaining still didn't ease the pain. Her insides were cold but, on the outside, her skin seared. It was a uniquely cruel —and targeted—torture.

The iron-inflicted agony also told her that, whilst she was still very clearly without her powers, Eira was no longer in her mortal form.

There was no palpable relief.

Power didn't reside in her. Again, she was empty.

She'd waited for this moment for three years, but now, Eira wished for nothing more than to be in the cottage in the forest, unknowing, thinking of the next time she would hear the sound of Meilin's knock at her door.

Anything but this.

Her body felt like a shell of what it had been when Durante forced her into the skin of a mortal. Her magic was not returned to where it rightfully belonged, and the hole it left in Eira's very being made her want to scream.

And she wasn't alone.

The white noise that rumbled high and overwhelming in her head dissipated as she fully came into her consciousness. Only then did she hear the low moans and whimpers of those around her.

They, too, were stripped of one mortal form to be thrown into another variation of the same thing. A mockery of their heritage, of the glory they were destined to touch.

This was not the freedom they were promised, nor the circumstances any of them had envisioned.

"Ah, you're all awake," a familiar voice crooned from somewhere close by. "Finally."

In an instant, the room was flooded with just enough light to paint a clear picture of the trap they were all ensnared in. Eight other bodies, bonded both in the identical shackles which kept them in place and the bone-chilling coldness that suffocated the entire space, seeping through the ruins of their ballroom dresses.

They were set up in a semi-circle formation on the floor of the underground caverns Eira discovered with Meilin.

Except, when Eira looked up, there were no floorboards overhead. No hole to show that she'd fallen through. No streams of daylight fighting to get through the broken wood. The same rocks that made up the walls ran all the way over their heads, an impenetrable fortress.

But she knew it was the same spot. She knew.

Just as Meilin did.

Recognition of the space, and the person who was shackled directly across from her, flashed across her features. Eira saw her cycle through a colorful array of emotions, all the while trying to steady her stomach.

This isn't how I wanted you to find out.

I wish I told you earlier.

I'm sorry.

The unspoken words weighed heavy in her dry mouth.

None of it would be enough. Eira knew as much. The distrust—and hurt—that Meilin's contorted expression conveyed was proof of that. She curled her lip back from her teeth and bared them at Eira. They were bloodied, her lips cracked. The thought of her sustaining another attack from the creatures once Eira was blacked out made her chest constrict.

The heiress couldn't look at anyone else. Couldn't bring herself to focus on the fact that the secrets hidden from her all her life were sat so close to her, all the truths on an ugly, cruel display. She couldn't drag her gaze away from Meilin's.

Slow footsteps came from the darkness, the voice from before moving closer and closer. With the movement came slinking, inky tendrils that emerged from the shadows. Like snakes, they coiled and twitched, winding along the ground.

Eira heard other fae hiss and murmur curses under their

breath. Anytime they tried to scurry closer to the wall—anything to put more space between them and the quickly approaching tendrils—the sound of pops and snaps filled the air. Their mana-cles catch on larger bits of skin, pushing further into the burn marks already formed around their ankles and wrists.

"The more you move, the more it will hurt." Durante's face emerged next, a grin splayed across it. Eira knew. She *knew* from the first moment he spoke, and she still hoped by some power that it was *anyone* else. "I would suggest staying still."

The king looked sickly in Erebus—eggshell white skin pulled taut over his skeletal frame—yet, now, the hue of his skin was *iridescent*. It was stretched just as thin, though, like he was in some sort of recovery phase. Eira saw silver ichor move through his veins. His blood shimmered, just slightly, when he paced under the dim light of the cavern.

His existence, in this form, was in opposition to the very nature of the gold-blooded fae.

Eira didn't know what he was. She couldn't say for sure.

But he wasn't mortal. He was anything but.

Eira's gaze only moved from him to the other heiresses around her when the king stopped to examine them all. She scoured the room, the same as he did, trying to see The New Reign from his eyes—what made them so susceptible to his hate.

The only feature they shared, a giveaway to their heritage, was the elongated tips of their ears.

With the little knowledge she *did* have, Eira was aware that each court had a defining feature that was passed along through bloodlines. It was never the same for each royal, always being altered as royal generations shifted through time. Her own marking was the first of its kind in her family. The silver streak of hair told the story of an heiress who was born into the wrong court, one whose magic betrayed her lineage. Her image betrayed her.

A symphony of ice and fire. She wielded flames but was born of the snow.

"Eira Isolde, Court of Isolde."

As for the others . . .

Durante listed them off, one by one, voice grating.

Seven petal-shaped birthmarks, dusty pink in color and no bigger than the size of her thumb, started from Meilin's left ear, trailed up and over her left brow bone and disappeared into her hairline.

"Meilin Azelie, Court of Azelie."

The heiress with shoulder-length hair the color of autumn leaves had two antlers that sprouted from the crown of her head, draped in spindly vines of a deep moss.

"Silvia Herminia, Court of Herminia."

Silvia.

Recognition winded her once again.

How many of her own had Eira talked to without ever knowing any better?

Silvia's face fell when their eyes met. She spared a cursory glance at Meilin, on her other side, and then shook her head, as if acknowledging the curse that was their doomed companionship.

Eira swallowed.

Next to Silvia was a fae with intricate markings on the skin of her knuckles that travelled up the back of her hand. Whatever ink they were created with pulsated with an aqua hue, as if the very essence of the ocean was flowing through her veins— and with a head of hair that resembled the currents of an unsettled river more than follicles, her affinity was unmissable.

"Etsumi Eimi, Court of Eimi."

Next, the heiress with the head of hair so full and thick that the plaits she wore looked to be genuinely heavy. An indiscernible marking, made of a few circles, shone on her right cheek.

"Sila Atuat, Court of Atuat."

A stark opposite to her was the next fae, whose skin resembled the surface of a dormant fire, ready to spittle at any given moment.

"Akela Kalama, Court of Kalama."

After that, the heiress with sparkling strands of silver lightning running through her head of tightly wound coils and dark brown skin adorned with complex markings that reflected off the light.

"Tufani Faven, Court of Faven."

Two minuscule horns, which looked to be made out of solid gold, sprouted out of either sides of the head of the sixth heiress.

"Enyo Telema, Court of Telema."

The last one, shackled closest to Eira, had different colored eyes. One pure black, one pure white. Constellation-like patterns covered both her cheeks, covering raised scars that may have once marred the soft skin there.

"Haneul Eodum, Court of Eodum."

Some deep part of Eira *knew* who was seated around her—knew which courts they came from—and knew that each and every one of them was her enemy.

Meilin included.

"How lovely it must be for you all to finally—formally—meet one another." Eira dragged her eyes back to Durante. His grin never faltered. "I've satiated your near eighteen-year-long curiosity. You're welcome."

When no one responded to his prompt, unsure how to even properly fathom the situation they were in, Durante frowned. He appeared the disappointed Deity, unimpressed with the lack of enthusiasm at his words. The murderous rage deep inside of Eira's chest struck at her frozen-over insides, burning her from the inside out.

"The lack of gratitude I'm feeling is quite disappointing, I will admit. You're all quite vile to deal with, even when sedated *and* immobilized—it wasn't easy work getting you here." Durante sighed, as if exhausted by the whole ordeal. As if he did any of the work.

The creatures, clearly, worked in favor of him.

Eira couldn't say she was surprised. She just wanted to understand how they came to be—and how he, who was supposed to be mortal, wielded them. How he got them here, to the abandoned shrine underneath Meilin's residence. How he walked with tendrils of darkness in tow, silver moving quick in his veins.

Silvia was the first to speak up, her eyes alight with a loathing they all had in common. "What *are* you?"

His eyebrows raised.

"You can't recognize one of your own?"

CHAPTER 15
WILTED WORDS, WARNING SIGNS

The Unseelie Court would be, in the mortal world of Exilis, a campfire story—a warning hidden behind layers of plot points and a building climax.

For Eira, Unseelie was a word never explicitly uttered. Not directly to her, at least. But she heard it in passing. A word, wielded as a weapon, and a place that didn't truly exist—had *never* existed, for all that she knew. A word used by vexed parents to fae children prone to misbehavior.

"If you don't stop, your father will send you to the gates of Unseelie to answer for your actions."

It was a drunken joke, made in passing.

"Deities, sometimes I could swear she's born of Unseelie."

A rumor, at best.

"I heard that there are hidden texts, depicting the rising of the Unseelie, in the archive."

Whispered amongst young fae who needed something to fear, something to drum up a sense of adrenaline in unsuspecting peers. Whispered by drunken husbands. Whispered from the mouths of bored, lax guards, who began to tire of their jobs.

Nothing more.

Unseelie was nothing more than murmured words.

And yet, if Durante was one of them—fae rather than mortal—he did *not* hail from Seelie.

Whilst the pendant he wore in Erebus was no longer anywhere to be found, there had to be some sort of explanation for how he obtained his power—if it truly was his own. But what sort of reasoning could there be make sense of a mortal, claiming fae heritage, to manipulate the darkness that clouded him.

How did this version of Durante look like he'd aged backwards one hundred years but still appeared fragile enough to be threatened by a small breeze?

"Why would we have any reason to believe you?"

The voice belonged to the fae closest to Eira. Haneul. Her eyes were ablaze with anger, her cobalt dress tattered and torn against her skin. Dried blood and darkened bruises were a common sight amongst the group, and she was no different.

Durante stepped towards her. "Your kind has always been stubborn when it comes to acknowledging truths that do not benefit you." *Your kind*—as if the type of fae he claimed to be was fundamentally different. "No, I'm not akin to the night like the Court of Eodum, but *my* kind is kindred with the shadows." He gestured to the space around them like it in and of itself was explanation enough. "We are still fae, even without the same pecking order that Seelie has established.

All in Unseelie are equal."

For a few moments everyone was quiet. His words settled in the air with all their heavy, confusing implications and no one seemed to know how to even begin to unpack—or understand —the extent of what he'd admitted.

It may have even been amusing, had they been anywhere else, in any other context.

Silvia broke the silence, her hiccup of laughter a reflection of the grim humor that Eira herself pondered just seconds prior. "How foolish do you think we are, Durante?" Ire lined her words, seeping from her tongue. "Concussed, perhaps—and in pain, most definitely—but I can say with certainty, for myself at the very least, that every word that comes from your mouth is a lie. You've given me no reason to believe otherwise."

"That's what mortals are best at, right?" Tufani chimed in. "Lying."

Silvia nodded. "Do not act as if you don't know that this is a gross violation of the Treaty. Mortals are punished just the same for forsaking it. You will not be spared that punishment."

The original shock from having woken up chained, shackled and injured, wore off. The heiresses, Eira included, were so focused on their anger that the words poured out with an intensity so visceral that even the king seemed perturbed.

Maybe he wasn't as strong as he claimed to be.

Not yet.

Though, as soon as the weakness showed itself, it was gone just as quickly. The king's face crumpled into something uglier, his rage contorting his features to relay the frustration he must've felt at The New Reign's immediate refusal to fall at his feet, even as the odds appeared to be stacked against them.

Durante looked at them, forged pity in his eyes and venom lining his words. "How can there be such rules for a place that doesn't exist?"

His gaze bounced between Silvia and Tufani, a sudden still-ness permeating through their prison. The sound of constantly sizzling skin amplified and Eira watched the two fae cringe. Their pain was worsening. They didn't crumble but it was abundantly clear that he was forcing them to endure an addi-tional level of torment, simply for speaking up.

Haneul shrunk in on herself.

Eira wondered if she was grateful to be left alone.

Durante continued to pace forwards. Small rocks crunched underneath his heavy footfall. He stopped once he was positioned in the middle of the semicircle of fae. Now that he was even closer, Eira could see with more clarity the dark coils that danced in his eyes, which were otherwise void-like pits.

Definitely not what they'd looked like before.

He clasped his hands at his waist. Maybe to avoid the urge to reach and throttle the heiresses who questioned him before. Another added punishment. He seemed like the type.

Durante cleared his throat before speaking again. His smile was rot. It was the type of expression that Eira wanted to cringe away from. She didn't plan on giving him the satisfaction.

"If you'll just suspend your disbelief for a moment, and cease your interruptions, I would be able to relay the messages I came here to share with you all. Unlike what you may think, my duty to you here is not just to gloat."

Even if she wanted to speak, Eira quickly realized that her mouth would be unable to form the words. Her lips felt like they were sealed shut. That oppressive weight lingered atop her skin again, and the idea of Durante being anything but mortal began to feel much more feasible.

Was *that* his power?

The heiress suspected it was the same for the others. Alarmed eyes and hurried glances were shared amongst the group of nine, enemies in all senses but the same in their aversion to the king.

Whatever other power resided in Durante clearly extended to that of language manipulation. In Erebus, they shared the common tongue of the mortal kingdom. A gift of communication bestowed upon them during their arrival, sometime in between the period of being stripped of their powers and being sent off to their residence promptly thereafter.

But here, they spoke in the tongues of their own courts, still able to understand one another *and* him. He bonded them with this too, so there would be nothing left to mistranslate.

No room for misunderstanding.

"As annoying as you all are, I will let you know that you're right in one assumption," Durante droned, tired of having to address them—like he didn't love the sound of his own voice. There were dramatics to his cadence that never seemed to disappear, even when he tried to appear disinterested. "I'm made of blood that is both fae and mortal and am, therefore, unlike any king that has ever existed before me. I will bring about the resurrection of this court, and you will all play an instrumental part in that."

It was impossible.

It went against all Eira knew—and yet, so did the existence of Unseelie.

When she truly thought about it, there was so much about herself that Eira didn't know.

But fae and mortals . . . it was written in the Treaty. They were to never harm one another, maybe, though that didn't mean they were allowed to procreate. In fact, she knew that was one of the very specific requirements noted in the sacred agreement.

Frightened gazes turned frantic. The heiresses were, again, on the same page of disbelief.

Durante was amused by their reaction. "There is more to come, so please sit still so that I can get through the rest of what must be said. I would hate for another interruption to see one of you without the full functioning use of your ankles."

Haneul, who was spared from his punishment minutes prior, began to jerk.

Her mouth tore apart in a silent scream, and the very much *non-silent* sound of her skin being blistered filled the cavern.

When she realized the rest of the heiresses knew of her pain, of Durante's targeted attack, she bit down on her tongue. Despite the binding of her wrists not allowing room for much movement, Haneul dug her blood-crusted fingernails into the skin of her exposed thighs.

Eira doubted any of them would think her weak, enemy or not.

Whatever point Durante was trying to prove in his capacity for cruelty was clear enough—it always had been, considering the way he'd initiated them into their stay in Erebus.

Eira saw tears run down Haneul's cheeks. Inside, she burned with the vitriol of all the unsaid words she wished to spew at him.

The king seemed satisfied. "Now, as I was saying, there *is* a reason why you're all here now. To understand how to best utilize you, I had to have you close before the Rite. The limits of your powers are not yet fully understood, neither by yourselves or your families—who, just so you're all aware, will be unable to find you here. Thus, I would suggest that you do not ponder over your inevitable rescue. It's not happening."

That much, at least, Eira understood with terrifying clarity.

How would they know to look somewhere that didn't exist?

What happened to Erebus was another question entirely.

She couldn't grasp the extent of his power and didn't want to, at that moment. It would only see the heiress diving deeper into an endless well of despair.

"To get your chance to obtain immortality, to take part in the Rite, you must survive." Durante clapped his hands together, the rings on either hand making contact with an echoing *clink*, like that of two wine glasses. "I've been waiting for this moment for years, you see. Planning this *dissection* since the moment the nine of you were born."

Maybe they wouldn't be at mercy of this unstable man had

their families been brave—brave enough to overcome their own prejudice and fear—to rely on one another. Brave enough to truly protect their daughters, despite not understanding them.

Eira never even knew their names until then. Even so, the heiresses were pinned against one another since birth; she was fed vague tales of the other's vile nature, told it was her duty to protect and represent her court with the pride they all lacked. Meeting Meilin was enough to disprove all she'd learnt, and it became clearer and clearer to her that her knowledge of everything outside of her court's high walls was next to non-existent.

Humiliating.

"Everyone wants to rule in some way or another—but I don't want *mortal realms*. I want what's rightfully mine." Durante continued to ramble, the darkness that coiled at his feet getting thicker and thicker. "Unseelie is only the first part in all of this. Why would I stop at just one court when I could have all nine?"

Unseelie wasn't enough, it seemed. If that wasn't rightfully his, then what was?

"Really, I care not for the Treaty or for your cross-court feuds. If you wish to see your families again, I implore you to heed these words. Time matters not in Unseelie. Your concern should be on whether you will make it out of here to complete the Rite, or if you will die unremembered, a fae whose name will be forgotten when the next wind blows—or if you will be one known for greatness."

His eyes were alight with maddened joy. The more Durante talked, the more frenzied he was. Even more enjoyable to him was how the others weren't permitted to object—all the heiresses could do was sit and soak in the completely otherworldly nature of his words, and this made the king even more ecstatic.

The oil slicks at his feet thrashed and twisted with renewed energy. Eira hated how they almost seemed to have a life of their own. She wished to put more distance between herself and them, though their reach continued to spread.

"I will judge you in the ways that mortals judge one another," Durante explained, "using their morals and ethics—the things you despise, what you believe yourself above. And after I do so, I will punish you with the methods of the fae. You will suffer the humiliation of being treated like both, and neither, all at once. You will think me cruel, but what you must understand is that I seek the strongest out of nine—and I won't stop until she is revealed to me."

Durante's smile was violence incarnate.

"Welcome to the Demir Trials."

CHAPTER 16
THE GHOST OF A MEMORY

Eira couldn't be sure of the exact moment she was free of the manacles.

The relief never came to her because the pain remained.

She didn't know her ankles were made to walk—how her knees didn't buckle and crumble—but one moment she was fighting an unfamiliar weight, relentless in pushing her further and further down into unconsciousness, and the next, she sat in front of a vanity.

This wasn't the altar the heiress was stolen away to. In fact, it felt like another world entirely.

Partially thanks to her delirium but mostly credited to the horrifying fact that she came to understand very soon after—Unseelie was more than just an abandoned ceremonial site.

The court was comprised of an entire underground network, so much beyond the looming darkness she initially saw upon waking in captivity.

Whilst being transported in her lucid state, Eira saw hallways that stretched on forever and rooms with closed doors, one after the other. But the further Eira went, led by the oppressing and indiscernible figures on either side of her, the more structure her surroundings took on.

Gilded archways, lit up by wall-mounted torches, came into view. The smattered sounds of hissing and clicking followed.

Mumbled words were exchanged out of earshot, as if she had the capacity to comprehend meaning from a fragmented conversation when she could barely focus her eyes without feeling like her head may implode.

At one point, Eira remembered that cold hands gripped her chin with no amount of gentleness. When her lids fluttered closed again, she wasn't saved from the rotting smell of decay on the breath of whoever she came nose-to-nose with.

All of what led her there was a confusing, melting pot of memories and moments that were poorly stitched together by her fragile mind, with nothing being *quite right* enough for her to understand.

She couldn't be sure if Durante's speech was yesterday or years prior. All she recalled thereafter was that his welcome to whatever trials he set up was followed by an all-consuming darkness. The seal over her mouth retracted but it didn't matter if Eira screamed. She could shriek and thrash.

She didn't, though.

It would be energy wasted.

Her shackles remained the same, the pain constant even after Durante disappeared, leaving the nine fae in what felt like a never-ending, fitful sleep.

No one spoke to one another.

"There used to be so much *more*," someone whispered into her ear. Eira was frozen. She was silenced by Durante, stilled by another. Her limbs were no longer her own—she'd expected it had been this way since she was first moved from the cavern—so there was no way to identify who the voice belonged to. Even her reflection in the vanity was hazy.

It was hard enough to recognize her own face, let alone anyone else.

Wheezing laughter crawled over her skin. "This is only the beginning of the restoration that will bring Unseelie back into the light."

Perhaps her thoughts were no longer just hers to have, either.

She could barely fathom that a whole hidden city existed without someone in Seelie knowing. To think that there was *more* yet to emerge was another thing entirely.

Just how big was this place in its former glory?

Two figures burst into the room then. Whatever—whoever —murmured words to her a few seconds prior seemed to dissipate into thin air. Their presence was a weight lifted from Eira's shoulders, despite her unease at now finding herself in the company of more strangers.

They hailed from Unseelie and served the king.

Whether they were mortal or fae was another thing entirely.

The pair got to work on Eira without hesitation. She couldn't angle her head away from the vanity to get a good look at them, only able to catch hazy glimpses of their uncovered faces in the reflection, and that made her even more restless.

Why Durante obscured the identities of his staff in Erebus but not in Unseelie was another question left unanswered.

Muttering in a tongue she couldn't understand, the two figures flitted around Eira with purpose. Steady hands pulled strands of sweat-slicked hair off her forehead, braiding the front pieces with nimble ease and bringing them to meet at the back of her head. She felt fingers loop the ends together with something—maybe ribbon—and then the familiar tug of a brush as it made its way through the rest of her hair.

Eira couldn't remember the last time someone brushed her hair.

Sickeningly, the next thought that sank in was the one that led her to look down at her body, which was no longer clad in the ruins of her ballroom gown. She ignored the raw rings of red that encircled her wrists, placed with purpose in her lap, and the matching ones adorning her ankles. Her skin, though still bruised and scraped, was void of the dried blood and caked dirt from beforehand—and the plain cotton slip dress she wore was not her own.

Someone *washed* her.

When she was insentient, no less.

Eira swallowed back bile, doubting her immobilized state would even allow for the expulsion of her empty stomach.

Unaware of her heightened distress, or perhaps just unbothered by it, the figure who wasn't in charge of her hair moved to make something acceptable of her face. Instinctively, the heiress shut her eyes. Pigment was pressed against her eyelids. Her cheeks, eyebrows and lips were covered with other cosmetics that she couldn't identify.

The heiress was afraid to open her eyes.

Afraid to think too much about the hands on her, the unfamiliar skin against her own, the thought of bath water and wandering fingers.

It was a violation so severe that Eira could barely process the magnitude of it all.

Satisfied with their transformative efforts, the figures looped their arms around Eira in a joint effort to hoist her up and out of the chair positioned in front of the vanity. It was by some sort of sick miracle that her body stood upright once they managed to do so, like her figure was nothing more than clay to be molded as they pleased.

Eira didn't protest as the plain slip she'd found herself in was pulled from her body. It wouldn't be the first time, apparently, that the people of Unseelie saw her like that. Exposed.

Vulnerable.

She didn't protest when they shimmied her into another gown, not much unlike the ones that gathered dust in her closet in Erebus. She didn't protest as they left the room promptly thereafter.

She didn't protest because *she didn't have a choice.*

The fear of what—or who—she was being preened for rushed into her veins like a hit of adrenaline. Eira tried to will her body to listen, to respond to its rightful owner and to *run*, but nothing heeded her call. Being able to move her eyes around the room proved to be enough of a struggle; the heiress couldn't even lift a finger or stretch her face into a smile, so it was hopeless to try and use the moment of solitude as the time to escape.

Besides, the feeling of never truly being alone was one she suspected she'd have to quickly become familiarized with. Especially here.

Nowhere was safe.

No *one* was safe.

Thoughts of Meilin began to make her heart pound, only worsening the panic bubbling beneath the surface of her skin.

She groaned. The sound was low and garbled, not quite right.

Not the time.

I can only afford to care for myself.

She resents you.

The thoughts did nothing to quell the visions of silken hair and freckles that burned behind her eyelids. Every time Eira closed her eyes it was just Meilin.

Meilin, Meilin, Meilin.

She was at war with her own thoughts.

So much for my survival instinct.

Meilin should be the least of her concerns. Still, that didn't make it so.

A murmured conversation occurring on the other side of the still-ajar door made Eira pause. From the sounds of it, a heated exchange was taking place. But just as she began to take note of it, the noise quieted all at once.

Gooseflesh covered her arms.

Another figure nudged the door fully open and stepped over the threshold. Eira was positioned in such a way that she could see their face, despite being unable to move any other part of her body.

All at once, the air in the room disappeared.

Alfie?

The surprise on his face was only momentary. "Is this the first time you've been stunned into silence? I'm honored."

How was he here? How was he *so casual* about it?

Alfie, all but the same since she last saw him in Erebus, closed the space between them in a few broad strides. As soon as his hand brushed her skin, Eira felt feeling rush back to her limbs.

The world around them came to life.

Before she knew what she was doing, the heiress enveloped the mortal in a hug. He stilled against her touch before quickly softening, reciprocating the embrace.

Wetness pooled in her eyes. She couldn't understand how he'd done it, but the gratitude was both all-consuming and overwhelming.

Alfie smelled painfully familiar. Sandalwood and something else. Something stronger. Spilled liquor, likely. It was what he always smelled of. Amzi.

The tears came hot and fast, then.

Alfie cleared his throat against her. Eira sniffled, swallowing the salt of her sobs. "As much as I would love to catch up, you and I are going to have to move." His hands were gentle as they pulled her back, the cool touch of them on her bare shoulders a grounding technique that he most likely didn't even realize he was utilizing.

"Quickly, now. There's not much time."

So, the heiress abided, swiping at her cheeks with the back of her palm and interlacing her fingers with his. The callouses on his palm pushed into her own.

Eira didn't know why she trusted him entirely.

She shouldn't.

But she did.

"How did you find me?" she asked, the sound of her own voice unfamiliar. The words came out scratchy and slow. Her tongue tripped around them.

Alfie was already moving ahead of her, taking the lead. "I know a lot of people in dark places," he remarked, which felt like a non-answer, "and it seems that you're exceedingly hard to get rid of."

Eira took that as a compliment.

Choosing to be satisfied with that amount of information for the time being, Eira let herself be led; even as the hallways began to blend together, even as the sounds of chatter and hisses filled her ears; even as Alfie's grip tightened exponentially on her hand and a feeling of dread began to rise inside of her throat like sickness.

She swallowed the saliva pooling in her mouth. "Are we almost there, Alfie?"

He looked back over his shoulder at her, eyes crinkled. "Soon."

Then, the mortal moved so fast that Eira worried she'd trip in trying to keep up with his pace. Gathering bundles of fabric from the annoyingly long dress she was forced into, she pushed forward.

Alfie's hold on her fingers didn't give her much of a choice, otherwise.

Together, they wound through open entryways and, eventually, the walls around Eira seemed to expand, growing to fit more than just the two of them. Lights in the near distance bloomed in her vision—and after what could've been an eternity, they were in a hall as great and wide as the one in Erebus.

But unlike the spot she'd become familiar with, this place boasted rows of wide seating on each side, starting at the floor and going up almost as tall as the ceiling. Bodies filled each tier, all eyes on Alfie and Eira. When her eyes adjusted to the jarring change of setting, the heiress saw that, whilst the space was lit up with more light than she'd seen thus far in Unseelie, it was shadowed with a darkness that felt like a veil of smoke. Smothering her gaze, it was intangible, but undeniable, nonetheless; and when she found Durante, seated along the far back wall, the murkiness made sense.

Wherever he went, an eclipse followed.

His lanky body was draped tastelessly, almost childishly, over the silvery arms of his thrown. When their eyes met, the king offered her his signature toothy, terrible smile.

There was no string quartet nor bar. No wandering servers and gossiping mortals.

And when Alfie's fingers untangled themselves from Eira's, the heiress *knew.*

She knew, whatever this situation was, Durante played his hand in crafting it; and Alfie wasn't going to be assisting in her escape.

How could he do so if he, too, was trapped?

A few dreadful moments went by.

When her only friend turned on his heel, not looking back

at her before he walked towards Durante's dais, the world around Eira grew cold. There were others following his path. She craned her neck, turning to see who they left behind.

The other eight heiresses stood in various spots beyond the threshold of the hall, all in extravagant gowns and bearing expressions that were scrunched in several shades of agony and rage. A sort of dazed bewilderment passed amongst them by the time they properly acknowledged one another, faces painted as if they were preparing to spend a beautiful evening under the moonlight.

Her heartbeat began to thunder with a strong ferocity when her gaze brushed over Meilin.

Why Durante felt the need to make them don these costumes, Eira didn't know. She couldn't pretend to understand the true intentions of his mania.

The bodies filling the stands roared in excitement, a sudden wave of noise cascading through the hall. As the puppeteer companions of the heiresses reached Durante's side, all falling to kneeling positions at his feet, the crowd clapped and hooted.

It was a show.

Eira thought she wouldn't recognize anyone else in the line —yet, amongst the other unfamiliar faces, there was someone who looked alarmingly like her; and upon closer inspection, the heiress realized it *was* her.

A copy.

Accurate enough to be disorientating, and convincing, though not all the way correct.

Eira's eyes sought out Meilin's once more.

Was she made to trust this fabricated version of the heiress?

Did Meilin put everything aside for the prospect of escape, or because—deep down—there was some part of her that still cared for Eira?

Meilin's cheeks flushed a deep crimson. Her fingers pressed

hard into her clenched palms, undoubtedly leaving half-moon imprints on the skin there. She refused to meet Eira's—*the real Eira's*—gaze.

So the heiress decided that would be a situation to confront another time.

If they ever had the chance to do so.

The others all looked so *real*.

Their faces were positioned towards the crowd, towards the heiresses, and their mouths continued to move. They murmured, quietly enough that Eira couldn't decipher what was being said—but it must've been some sort of repetition of what Alfie mentioned before leading her there. The shape of his lips formed those same words, the ones she'd believed in for a few foolish seconds. Now that she was of somewhat sounder mind, the inconsistencies in Alfie's appearance were stark.

Durante was powerful—this whole performance was as much a show of that—but there were gaps in his mirage, which he hid with dark veils and intimidating words. Eira knew he wasn't as powerful as he claimed to be. Not yet.

Kneeling alongside Alfie and Eira's copy were seven other women and men—friends, or lovers, maybe, of the other heiresses.

She couldn't know what relationships the others in The New Reign forged inside Erebus. Their raw displays of distress were clue enough that they, too—like Eira herself—failed to keep themselves untethered by mortal ties of companionship.

"I'm so glad you all found your way here," Durante said. As soon as he spoke, the room quieted. Eira turned back to face him. "A gift, from me to you, was a familiar face escorting you to be presented to the rest of my court. I hope that their guidance will aid you in your journey to become more accustomed to my power—and to my home."

She couldn't make sense of his words. A *gift*?

The king's mockery was salt rubbed in the wounds of every other fae around Eira. They were dressed up and, even so, their skin bore the effects of his actions: cuts and bruises, puckered and still healing patches of their bodies that may never truly recover.

Had he not hurt them enough?

"Is *this* the trial you threatened us with?"

Etsumi's voice rang clear. All eyes fell on her, Eira's included, and she didn't shrink back from the attention. Etsumi's anger was a solid thing, her scowl unwavering.

"You strip us of our powers, keep us chained with silver and taunt us with memories that can walk and talk," she continued, her words pointed, "and you call this a fair trial?"

Durante cocked his head to the side. "When did I ever give you the impression that this trial would be fair?"

Barks of laughter and jeers aimed at the heiresses came from the onlookers.

Etsumi's lip curled but she didn't respond, deeming him unworthy of the fight.

When her eyes fell back to the dais, at the bodies knelt before it, Eira met the gaze of her off-putting replica. Sickness rushed through her as Durante let out a bellow of his own. The sound of his laughter was grating.

Durante was still himself—the bleak pallor of his newly translucent skin was as unpleasant to look at as it was the first time, his hair hadn't become any fuller and his gaze was like that of death. There was something different about the king, however.

A vigor that wasn't present at any other points Eira had been subjected to laying her eyes on him.

Being in his court was giving him back bits of lost life. Bit by bit. Slowly but surely.

But at what cost to those around him?

"Do *not* offend me with your feigned disinterest," Durante spat, sitting straighter in his throne. His hands flew out, pointing at each heiress. "You are as curious of one another as I am of you—what makes the fae around you so revered; what qualities you share; what powers you have that they don't. This is all information you've been denied your entire life." His audience guffawed and taunted in response. Their noses twisted in the face of the heiresses, their scorn unavoidable. "And, for what, exactly? Out of *fear*? Pathetic.

So, I must ask that you don't underestimate, or misunderstand, my intentions. I didn't bring you to my home to intimidate you. My prior words were not a threat. No, they were a *promise*—because I will find the strongest of you all—and in order to do so, there will be stages to these trials."

Durante stood. "And this, this is just the beginning."

Deafening applause came next, the room rising from near silence to ear-splitting noise in a matter of seconds.

Something else happened, then.

The companions of The New Reign stopped moving altogether. Their lips pressed together in a thin line, and simultaneously, they got to their feet. The king smiled knowingly before the figures in front of him *changed*.

The same way the mortals in Erebus had done, the bodies of these beings quite literally tore apart; and out of them crawled something that should've never resided.

Eira was too slow to squeeze her eyes shut.

The sharp intakes of breath—and gasps—from her fellow heiresses told her they'd made the same mistake.

It's not him, is what she told herself as she watched Alfie's skull split right down the middle.

It's not him, is what she told herself as his blood—crimson, mortal blood—sprayed across the hall's marble flooring.

It's not him, is what she failed to believe, when what may have once been screams came out as muted, muffled groans, bellowing deep from the belly of the creature he'd become.

And, for whatever sake, it wasn't him. What Alfie became was far from how she'd known him.

Was it better to watch? Would it add fuel to a fire that burned so viscerally?

Would this pain give her the power needed to find a way to make it out of Unseelie?

She wanted to resent the other heiresses for not falling to the ground and screaming. Eira wanted to hate them for not allowing their pain to be put on display. If they did so, she'd have a reason to mirror them without shame. If she were brave enough—certain of herself enough to not care about saving face in front of this wretched king she wanted so badly to prove she wasn't afraid of—Eira would grieve openly.

But she didn't. She couldn't.

So, she watched.

Even if she'd wanted to close her eyes, it wouldn't have saved her from anything. The horror was on display, and it was unavoidable. The collective applause became thunder, booming in her ears. Or maybe that was the sound of her heart as it beat erratically, uncontrollably, against the confines of her ribcage.

There were discarded organs and bits of muscle strewn across the floor.

After what felt like hours of listening to the painstakingly loud cries of pain, which mingled with the sounds of shifting, cracking bones, the creatures finally settled. Their agony was only second to the cheers, which never stopped.

Eira felt like her head was about to erupt.

All the while, Durante basked in the theatrics of his own making. His grin split the leather skin of his face, and he nodded approvingly at his creations. He stepped down from his dais, now stood in the middle of the line of misshapen bodies.

When he raised a finger in front of his lips, silence came once again.

"You will learn more of my home as you progress through the Demir Trials, rest assured. But you should know, as I wish to learn of your powers, what it is that makes my own so special."

Durante's expression was smitten. Maybe he expected them to be grateful for the knowledge.

"The power of Unseelie is that of manipulation," he explained, voice carrying across the hall, "of the body, the mind, memories, even time. Of the heart and of light."

She shouldn't have suspected anything less, though that didn't make the truth more digestible.

If it even was the truth.

Eira didn't know what to believe.

Durante's gaze trailed over the heiresses. "The people of Erebus were not what you expected. That city, those mortal bodies that occupied it, were nothing but a mere veil to cover the true nature of what was growing underneath it. The citizens you came to know, and love, weren't alive in ways that you can understand. They are nothing but souls. The lives that you saw them living were nothing but a carefully constructed limbo— and in it, they moved back and forth between memories of their past and a false reality. They have always been mine to control as the manipulation of death, too, is that which Unseelie specializes in."

Durante nodded to his creatures. "This," he said, fondly, "*this* is the result of agony incarnate. This is what stagnant souls morph into if they're unable to pass peacefully—my pride and joy. I do this with the ones who no longer prove to be useful contributions to my cortege."

No.

When Eira's eyes wandered to the stands, she saw what she

thought were mortals shedding their costume. Fractured images of what lay underneath. Some had pointed ears and skin that shone with an unnatural undertone. Creatures of Durante's creation—housed by the bodies of undead mortals—and fae of the Unseelie, existing all at once. In the same space.

It shouldn't have been possible.

Not in the world Eira was raised in, which seemed to prove far more withdrawn than she'd ever imagined.

"You think I didn't know what all of you did, every moment you spent in Erebus?" The sneer in Durante's voice made the slap of the words hit a thousand times harder. "The mortals of that world were my puppets—*are* my puppets, even now—tasked to entertain you until the time was right. I implore you to understand that no choices were ever truly yours to make!"

Durante's sudden laughter became the loudest sound of all. The joy he got from mocking them was unbridled. It came only second to how much he reveled in making them suffer.

All Eira could see was a boy in a man's body, drunk on too much power. *He* shouldn't have existed.

"I confide this in you—my secrets, my truths—because my goals are clear. One of you will survive. For those of you that don't . . . well, I shouldn't have to explain why there is no matter of concern for me there, and it's not as if the truth of Unseelie will remain forever hidden. Not for much longer."

Durante paced closer to them as he spat the words, creatures in tow. All eyes in the hall moved with him.

"You *will* hold onto your bitterness and your vitriol, you *will* keep your mouths shut, and you will play your part, because I *demand* it."

Eira's body had long stiffened, control over her own limbs relinquished as Durante indulged in his speech. Her lips were glued shut.

As the king came closer, Eira thought of her shadowed companion.

I'll tell him you made it to Exilis, she said, to only herself. *If I see him again, I'll tell him you made it. He will be heartbroken that you are not with him. I'll say that you had a change in heart. It will be a more bearable ache, than to know this.*

It was the best way she could think to mourn.

It was the fantasy she allowed herself; the reality where she didn't understand the concept of Durante's power, and of his realm. It was an existence where her companion and Alfie were mortals who truly lived and loved one another, a pair who escaped the grasp of an unkind king, who had their own happily ever after.

The ending they deserved when their reality was anything but.

The complexities of the suffering Durante captured in his kingdom was not for Eira to fully understand. Not now. She couldn't wrap her aching head around it all.

She was so *tired*.

And so, when darkness came, Eira didn't fight.

She let it in because she didn't have a choice.

CHAPTER 17
BONDS THAT BLEED

What were they supposed to say to one another?

Would they be punished for trying to do so?

Those were the thoughts that plagued Eira upon waking up, bound by the same iron cuffs around her ankles and wrists; but instead of the abandoned altar underneath Meilin's house, she was in a narrow cell. The stone wall and floor were cold against her skin, which wasn't at all protected by the flimsy fabric of the evening gown she still wore.

Everything ached.

Her head throbbed, eyes straining against even the smallest slither of light. A lamp must've been lit in the pathway to the right of the cell block. The spill off from its orange flames, though dim at best, made Eira's eyes water.

It was as if her body had already accepted the darkness, now struggling to adjust to any source of light. She groaned, trying to shift the mess of her limbs into a less uncomfortable sitting position.

Eira supposed it was safe to assume that Durante had ways of monitoring her, and the rest of The New Reign constantly, no matter where he was.

Not that it mattered.

There wasn't much she thought she could keep hidden from him, regardless.

Like an itch between the back of her shoulder blades or a persistent headache, Eira was painfully aware of the other heiresses' proximity to her. She didn't need to see them, or to be sat directly across from them in a ceremonial semi-circle, to know they were there.

The nearby sounds of stirring—accompanied by moans of pain and spat curses—only confirmed her assumption. A bitter tang, one Eira immediately associated with sick, filled the air.

The soft, almost unintelligible, sound of crying followed it.

Eira laid her head against the wall and cringed, torn between sympathy and annoyance.

None of them wanted to wake up in the position they were in. She wanted to convince herself that everything thus far was nothing but a convoluted, carnivorous dream; that her body was set on tearing itself apart from the inside out and that it planned on doing so by breaking her mind, first.

But that wasn't the case, and the distant show of vulnerability made her angry.

Why was *she* allowed to fall apart? And how could Eira keep up her conviction in viewing the other heiresses as her enemies if they did this?

It was much harder to pretend that the other fae around her were expendable if she was made susceptible to their agony. Especially when she could barely swallow, and keep down, her own anguish.

Maybe that made her weak.

Maybe that didn't matter, here.

Nonetheless, she wished she was brave enough to speak.

She wished she wasn't a fool. If she were of stronger mind,

Eira would hold onto the underlying bitterness; the fervent dislike that was bred into her and the other fae.

It would be wise of her to remember that the other heiresses were not her friends.

Not her comrades.

All the same, as was her struggle, Eira *was* a fool. She couldn't help but wonder why it had to be that way. Durante was wrong in many things—though his delusional oversight wasn't completely off the mark when it came to the judgement he passed on their families.

Could the tension between their courts end with The New Reign?

Was there any harm in trying?

They were her enemies. It wasn't her prerogative to fight for them and all the same it felt wrong not to.

Despite being bound together by the same tragedy, the heiresses would continue to regard one another with caution. Fear would make their limbs tighten and their skin take on a sickly pallor, whereas hatred—the emotion they'd been conditioned to feel—would make their eyes narrow and lips draw back from their teeth.

Both emotions made it impossible to trust one another, to open up, all whilst being caught in the same web of darkness that Durante spun around them.

Shouldn't such a situation bring them together—and wasn't the opposite exactly what the king wanted?

If they allowed their distaste towards one another to fester it would make room for their survival instinct to hinder reasonable thinking; and that would see them tear one another apart and take their knee to him rather than team up with their fellow fae.

At least here, away from the physical presence of Durante,

Eira felt like herself just a little bit more—which meant she could afford to strategize.

How would it be possible to foster reliance amongst The New Reign when they were only tethered by deceit and death?

"How *could* you?"

A quiet voice, laced with undeniable hurt and searing familiarity, stirred Eira from her thoughts.

Meilin's words wobbled as she whispered them. They echoed through the chambers like an accusation, painfully loud despite the volume at which she said them.

As if sensing that the question was not directed at any of them, the other seven heiresses were silent. No doubt that they were all awake and tuned in, though.

Blood rushed in Eira's ears, and her fists clenched in the fabric of her gown. It was not the time for her to feel humiliated but the public nature of the conversation that should be anything but made her cool skin burn hot.

Eira didn't know what Meilin was referring to. An array of betrayals had been committed in the short time they'd known one another, so she took a stab in the dark.

"I kept my identity hidden from you, just as you did from me," Eira said, doing her best to speak without allowing her voice to quiver, "and although it was the nature of the circumstances we met in, I *am* sorry for deceiving you. You must believe that."

The other fae didn't need to question the circumstances of their relationship aloud, despite the fact it shouldn't have ever existed in the first place.

They all, in their own ways, broke the rules that Durante set.

Meilin scoffed, the noise closer than Eira expected. But she didn't interrupt, so the other heiress continued to address her.

"I cared for you, the version of you that I was lucky enough to meet—"

"You know *nothing* of what, or who, I am!" The words were harsh, biting, and lined with the serrated edges of a wound Eira couldn't blame her for wanting to pry open. They pushed the air out of her lungs. "You *lied* . . . you misled me into believing I knew someone who was anything but what they claimed to be. What was the point of luring me into this—this false sense of security?"

Meilin's voice got louder. "Did you plan to make a head start on Durante's work? Knock one of the nine from the list to make it a little easier for him?"

Eira's chest constricted. The sound of rattling chains and sharp breaths made it harder for her to form the right words. She squeezed her eyes shut.

"I had a court to protect."

It was a pathetic response, but it was the truth—one she knew the others could relate to. She had to hide her identity.

She had to.

"And I didn't?" Meilin choked out. "Maybe you're not stupid enough to side with Durante, but you should know this: no amount of glory you get from all of this will ever make you *belong.* You can play the part of mortal merchant—selling secrets in a dingy tavern—and you can seek out excitement in courting a woman who doesn't know any better, but at the end of the day, you're a drunk and you always will be. You're no better than a mortal, Eira. You don't deserve your title."

Her words rung out.

They congealed in the air.

Rotten, pungent things.

Tears slipped down Eira's cheeks. "You're hurt."

Weak words, again. Reasoning that wouldn't make Meilin's

accusations hurt any less. Worst of all, it wasn't as if she was *wrong*.

"Silvia here. Are you just about finished?"

Another familiar voice. Eira had almost forgotten that they weren't alone. "Deities, you're both just as annoying now as you were when you were mortals."

A few snickers echoed after her sentiment. Eira sucked in a hiccupping breath, feeling even more pathetic.

"We're all stuck in this unfortunate situation," Silvia continued, "so the pair of you taking the first chance we have to actually process all of this shit to air out your grievances isn't making this easier. We're *all* hurt. We've all been misled, in one way or another. Let's steady ourselves, and figure out what comes next, before tearing each other apart."

Eira couldn't say she'd ever expected Silvia to be the voice of reason in a dire situation, but she was immensely grateful for it (despite the fact that she'd never admit that aloud).

Some heiresses murmured their agreement, clearly moved by Silvia speaking up when the rest of them wouldn't. Eira figured she'd probably feel the same way if she were any of them—but she couldn't stir the sadness from her bones.

She wanted nothing more than to make it up to Meilin, despite the sting that her words left; but Eira couldn't deny that she actively, consciously, played the part in the deception that left her so hurt. Of course, Eira considered the circumstances of her lies catching up with her—but she also hoped she would never see that conclusion, or have to face what came after it.

Now, forced to be face to face with the consequences, all Eira could do was cower.

Pathetic.

"Haneul," another heiress said, as if they were sat for roll call. It made it easy to keep track of everyone. "I've had my fair share of angst today. Let's talk about the problems we all have in common instead. Maybe it'll help us bond."

"Bonding over shared trauma will not make us best friends," Meilin spat back.

Haneul scoffed. "No, but like Silvia already said, it will help us form some sort of understanding of the larger situation at hand, outside of the lens of our own personal grievances." Eira could almost hear the eyeroll in her words. "How would *you* suggest that we pass the time, Meilin?"

Meilin hissed air through her teeth but didn't push any further.

Tufani chimed in, then. "Tufani. What is his angle?"

She asked the question they all pondered on.

Durante's intentions were clear enough. He would put The New Reign in a life-or-death situation, cull them one by one in an effort to understand the full extent of their untapped power, and in doing so, would use the last one standing—the most powerful heiress—to bring about the true resurrection of Unseelie.

But there had to be more to it.

More to uncover and to understand about how such a plan, and such a place, went on existing without any of the powers that be finding out.

Would Durante give them back their magic in order to test them?

Did he know *how* to?

"Akela. There is no reasoning to be found behind the actions of that mad man." Akela's tone was spite-filled. "It may be more productive for us to try and think on ways to escape, rather than to overcome."

"Enyo here, wondering how you propose that we plan to escape a place that isn't supposed to exist?" Enyo questioned

Akela flatly, though there was an underlying bitterness that may have extended past the confines of their situation.

Etsumi made a noise of agreeance. "Etsumi. Escape is not an option. None of us know anything about the true extent of power this court may hold. Its layout, people and king are just as much of a mystery, despite what we've already been told. We would just be walking further into the darkness, and that would most likely take us out before Durante got the chance to."

"Speak for yourself," Haneul murmured.

That earned a soft chuckle from someone else, though Eira couldn't be sure who.

"Since when are we all on the same team, anyway?" Enyo retorted. "I'm not disagreeing with Silvia's comradery concept—"

"No offense taken," Silvia chimed in.

"—but I also don't trust any one of you more than I trust that slimy man. I can't afford to."

That, Eira understood. They all did.

Everyone seemed to consider Enyo's confession for a few moments in quiet, and just as Eira prepared to open her mouth to counter it, the sound of heavy footfall made her pause.

Whatever movement they'd made, as small as it may've been, came crashing to a stop.

Eira had the sinking feeling that they wouldn't have another chance to pick up whether they left off from that point onwards.

CHAPTER 18
A HUNTRESS AND HER HUNTED

Durante's presence warranted an unpleasant shift in the air.

No one wished to acknowledge he was there, and yet, he was impossible to ignore.

The king didn't need an armed guardsman in his wake. There was just the sound of him, alone, as he walked with no amount of grace down whatever steps led the way to the chambers where he'd locked The New Reign away.

He hummed as he approached, the sound growing louder by the second, until he was in view. Durante stopped on the other side of Eira's cell and peered in at her, no more than a predator being observant of its prey.

She swallowed down an inclination to spit at his feet.

The king was dressed simpler than when he confronted them all in the great hall.

Gone were the trousers trimmed with purple threading at the ankles and the high-collared blouse that appeared as if it was choking him. The set of caramel-colored clothes he currently wore made him look like a wealthy aristocrat, more prone to spending his days in an art gallery and drinking expensive bottles of liquor.

Eira was still yet to see the pendant from Erebus around his neck, unless it had been artfully hidden beneath the frills beforehand.

It definitely wasn't there now.

Those were the key points in time that Eira chose to focus on, taking bits and pieces from the haunting interaction because she couldn't truly be sure of the capability of her own mind—not in the presence of a fae whose power was that of manipulation.

How much of it was real?

Not that it mattered.

She'd fallen asleep after that encounter with thoughts of Alfie on her mind.

Alfie wasn't in Unseelie. In truth, Alfie had never really been in Erebus, either. He was nothing but the fragmented parts of a mortal soul, stuck between the thickening veil of death, unable to fully cross over.

Truthfully, Eira didn't know much about how mortals experienced death.

When someone died in Seelie, there were ceremonies and celebrations, all at once mourning and cherishing a life that was expected to have been lived long and lived well. But what happened to them after death was not so ambiguous. The Court of Isolde passed on their deceased not by burying them under dirt.

Instead, their bodies were frozen.

Whatever was left of them, if it was death brought on by fighting or sickness, or simply a case of sleeping and never waking up, it was always the same.

Ice would consume their body, crystallizing their form. A manual task, extremely taxing on the fae who did it. Nonetheless, there were only a few who possessed the power to do so, and it was considered an honor to be bestowed with such an important job.

Then, at the ceremony held to acknowledge their passing, the frozen bodies were placed on a dais. A staff crafted from the magic of Isolde's first queen was driven through the remains, which would shatter, its fragments returning back to the foundations of their court.

Eira remembered the experience like it was something beautiful.

Bits of crystal and snowflakes, as big as her face, rising and rising into the sky. She was so young when her grandmother died—and despite it being a part of her duty-born right, her father insisted on keeping her out of ceremonies for any of the fae who passed since her.

"She will see enough death in her lifetime," he'd pleaded to her mother, "and she has plenty of time to learn. Let her say her goodbyes to family and live without the burden of the others until the time is right."

Eira didn't understand what was so fearsome about it. After all, her grandmother was sacrificed to the sky. All she could think of was the glint of the crystals.

Perhaps she'd blocked out the memory of the tears that glistened on her mother's face as she was tasked with driving down the staff into the crystallized body of the queen before her.

From the bodies of the deceased, flowers would bloom to life.

Their sapphire leaves would push through the snowy terrain of the Eira's home, only sprouting in a field nearby the palace. She made a habit of keeping track of how many bloomed there, as all queens should.

Bodies gave back to the court, even in death. Souls—which

was what mortals described them as—became crystallized flowers in Isolde.

No fae lingered or wandered. No one found themselves lost between life and death.

It wasn't an option.

And how Eira, the fae born of ice with the blood of fire, would wield the staff when it came time for her to see her citizens off to their frozen afterlife was another problem entirely.

But that wasn't where her mind should be; and even so, her heart ached for Alfie.

After deciding he was done with staring at her, Durante moved further down the line of cells. The pause in his footsteps told Eira that he repeated this action, of stopping and watching, with each one of them.

Whether this was to intimidate or simply do a headcount, she couldn't be sure.

Copper tainted the atmosphere in his wake. It was as if the scent clung to him—his skin, his clothes.

Eira longed to inhale the morning sky air; smells she'd taken for granted in Erebus. The earthiness of the soil in the forest surrounding her cottage; the waft of freshly baked bread that travelled on the wind upstream, all the way from Celimene's city center; the smell of rain, of liquor, of smoke.

Anything but this, Eira thought.

Once satisfied with his findings, Durante moved back to the middle of the cell block. From where she was positioned, Eira could see him lean against the wall, only half of his body visible.

Half of his shit eating expression on display when she'd hoped there was none.

"Now that I suspect you've settled more *amicably* into your surroundings," *whatever that meant*, "and you've all learnt more about this precarious situation you've found ourselves in, I wanted to offer you the chance to dine before taking part in the Demir Trials."

Eira's stomach groaned at the mention of a meal.

She couldn't pretend to understand the way that time passed in Unseelie, and though it felt like her body aged years in the time she was in Durante's captivity, a whole lot of her exhaustion could be chalked up to the fact that her last proper serving of food was before she attended the ball.

The heiress was so focused on survival—and so consumed by her affliction—that the dull ache of hunger was easy enough to ignore, especially whilst everything else ate away at every bit of her focus, at every part of her resolve.

"I would rather starve than accept food from you," Silvia snarled, her voice low and dangerous. Eira could picture her expression. The tight furrow of her eyebrows, the fire in her eyes.

Durante tsked disapprovingly at her response. He didn't resort to instantaneous violence as a way to punish Silvia for speaking out of turn, like he'd done during past interactions. Eira felt herself brace for the impact of the heiresses' screams of pain.

When nothing came, she took in a deep breath of coppery air.

"That's a shame," Durante said, despite sounding completely unapologetic. "I hoped you would understand the dynamic that exists here, by now. If I wanted to hurt you, I would. In fact, I *will*." The relief quickly dissipated. "But I'm not offering you food as a ploy to poison or harm you. Would you not prefer to start the trials on a full stomach?"

Her insides began to protest the idea almost immediately.

No one else acknowledged the king's offer, which he took just about as well as Eira assumed he would.

"Being stubborn will not serve you well, heiresses." Durante paced down the line of cells, closer to the confines this time. "I hand you information, and it's not enough. I provide you with context, and still, you're unsatisfied. Now, you reject an offering of food because you're too prideful—no, *fearful*—to accept what you know that your body needs?"

"We will not eat out of the hands of the man who keeps us caged," Akela said, suddenly. "We are not *birds*." She spoke on behalf of The New Reign, but none of the heiresses objected. It was strange, Eira thought, to hear them being referred to as a collective by one of their own.

Strange but not entirely unenjoyable.

Durante seemed to think on this for a moment before he turned to face away from the cells. "That may be so," he countered, "but you *are* fools, and you are fools who will go hungry because of this choice."

Eira bit down on her tongue. The only reason he wanted them fed was so that he could get the most out of whatever show he had planned for them to participate in—Durante didn't care for the wellbeing of the fae. They were cattle for him to prep for slaughter, and what good would they be if they died from hunger before he got to them.

Even so, the others were right.

The king kept walking, only addressing The New Reign once more when his footsteps receded far out of view.

Eira strained to hear his voice.

"I look forward to welcoming you into the trials tomorrow."

CHAPTER 19
GASTRIMARGÍA

Eira slept fitfully and was only aware that morning had come because she was uncuffed, moved from one cage to the next.

Her vision remained hazy as the heiress was sat in front of a vanity, not much unlike the one from the time prior, and was tended to by the people of Durante's court. Eira felt acutely aware of the way her muscles seized in the presence of others and realized that this, most likely, was a way to protect those that serviced them in preparation of the trials to come.

A foolish inclination to talk to them, to try and gauge their capacity for empathy—and their willingness to betray their king—struck Eira. As she emerged further and further out of sleep, she planned on the best way to approach such a topic.

Unfamiliar hope surged under her skin, giving her new life. She didn't know if it was due to the hunger making her spiral, or whether it could be because the understanding that Durante's power had limitations—however small—but all the same, the drive was not an unwelcome change.

As long as thoughts of Meilin stayed out of her mind, Eira could muster her courage.

She hadn't known the limitations of control that Durante

wielded over her body the first time she'd been sat in front of that vanity, only knowing the freedom she felt once Alfie's skin touched hers.

She couldn't move but. surely, she could speak.

So, when a pair of unfamiliar faces entered the room Eira was in, moving with a quiet efficiency, the heiress thought on what to say. Would begging really work in her favor? Would there be a point in trying to plea? Were these workers the mortals whose souls were trapped in limbo, or were they fae of The Unseelie court? The king didn't make it any easier for The New Reign to differentiate between the two, and Eira figured that couldn't have been a mere coincidence.

He loved to balance them on the precipice of knowledge; any more than necessary would see the heiresses tumble over an edge they'd never be able to recover from.

As their hands worked through her hair and fingers brushed against the skin of her face, Eira noted that these two didn't speak like the others had done. In fact, they didn't talk to each other at all. Whether that was because they didn't need to or didn't *want* to, she was unsure.

Just the same, Eira figured she'd try her luck with one of them, rather than with both.

If there was some pre-existing dislike that simmered between the two, she would work it to her advantage.

When one half of the pair left the room momentarily—the woman who smelt strangely of jasmine and brandished a nasty scar across her cheek, the skin puckered and angry, as if the injury was only recently inflicted—the heiress swallowed the dryness in her mouth and forced the words out, even though they felt like daggers being drawn up the length of her throat.

"Do you know what these trials are going to entail?"

The fingers on her face stuttered in the surety of their moves but no response came.

Eira tried again. "Do you fear your king?"

They weren't the most important questions she could be asking—but the heiress assumed that jumping straight to prying out knowledge of escape routes wouldn't work in her favor.

Nonetheless, it was a start.

Her words didn't prove enough to warrant a conversation. Eira threw out a few more queries, not contemplating on the fact that the language she spoke was not the same as the other. Durante made sure that The New Reign understood one another, despite their different tongues—the same couldn't be said between the language of his people and the fae from Seelie.

Another measurement to ensure they were kept at as far a distance as possible from salvation.

Eira shouldn't have expected any less. The bitter sting of failure ached just the same.

The heiress kept her mouth shut when the missing half of the pair came back into the room, and the two made their final touches with readying Eira for the day. She avoided meeting her reflection in the mirror, choosing only to focus on the still inflamed rings of redness that marred her skin, wondering if they'd ever fade.

It wasn't Alfie who came to collect her from the room she was prepped in like the last time; the creature—a maimed soul of an undead mortal—arrived instead.

The pair that prepped her made room for the creature, who sauntered into the room with a sort of purpose Eira was both unfamiliar with and perturbed by. Its body was stretched to full height, head near brushing the ceiling. A line of them had followed Durante in the great hall, slinking behind him with a patience that was unlike how they'd appeared in Erebus. Here, they were even more steadfast. The idea of the soul that was stuck inside of it, manufacturing its movements, made sickness surge in her stomach.

No wonder they hadn't killed the fae heiresses that night.

These creatures were Durante's *lapdogs*.

It reached out with clawed hands and an open mouth. Eira, who still lacked autonomy over her own body, could do nothing as the creature picked her up like she weighed no more than a stubborn, still infant.

Talons clasped her midsection and *dragged*. Inside of her own skin, Eira squirmed and pleaded. The smell of rot emanated from the creature, only growing stronger as she was brought closer. Her eyes watered, and though it *was* disgusting, the part of her consciousness that knew what made the creature as it was ached with sadness.

But that empathy evaporated once the creature placed her inside of its mouth.

Teeth closed over her—not harsh enough to pierce flesh, not gentle enough that she'd be able to roll out of its grasp—and Eira cringed against the warmth that encapsulated her.

She'd have preferred to be dragged by the hair, or something more dramatic.

This was just humiliating; and considering Durante's history, it made perfect sense. Who would he be to deny himself as many opportunities to belittle them, even in the times he wasn't directly present to witness it?

The creature carried her in its maw for what felt like a solid twenty minutes before they reached their location. When the muffled sounds of chatter and the high pitch of jovial string music became clearer—louder—Eira knew she was about to play her part in the first of the king's trials.

"I can admit that I'm greedy," Durante announced.

His voice boomed across the amphitheater they were dropped off in. All eight of the other heiresses, delivered by the jaws of their own creatures, dressed in equally formal gowns, with their hair and face adorned in such a way that, again, felt so stupidly out of place.

Once The New Reign were left in the center of the amphitheater stage, it took a few moments for feeling to come back to Eira's limbs. She pulled herself up from the immobile, discarded pile that being dropped from the creature's mouth left her in. Each creature had retracted, one by one, into a darkened entryway that opened from the mouth of center stage and wrought iron bars fell in their place after all nine heiresses were accounted for.

Their only exit had been cut off.

This area was smaller than the great hall Durante called them into prior but it still had spiraling rows of seating that went from up and around the center stage, capturing every angle in a compact circle. This time around, though, the seats were empty. No bodies filled the space, despite the sound of chatter and music Eira heard beforehand.

Durante's seat, perched in the center of the middle row, made the scene all the more haunting. His words were as crisp as they were loud.

"I am greedy because I want to *know*—I want to understand what power looks like in your hands, the revered New Reign. You're all different. But different can no longer mean unknown," he pushed on, voice tinged with a delirium Eira now believed was a characteristic of the king, "and I'll make sure of that."

The monster that had long ago made a home in Eira's stomach—the one that favored Meilin—stirred uneasily at the sound of the king's voice. It seemed more restless as of late, and understandably so. Beyond everything else that hindered her mind, Eira was constantly aware of its weight. Always displeased, always clawing away at her insides, like it blamed her for the situation they were in—as if she wanted to be in Unseelie any more than it did.

An unfamiliar burning sensation at the base of her throat made Eira's hands fly to her neck.

As if they materialized from thin air, her finger felt the leather cord tied there. She looked down at the silver medallion attached to it, which seared the skin against Eira's sternum, rising and falling with her rapid breaths.

The other heiresses wore them, too.

They were all standing now, defensiveness stiffening their posture.

"The silver is a protective measure," Durante explained, "as I can't guarantee the extent of your will just yet."

The will to *what*?

Will to live? Will to escape? Will to hurt one another—or him?

Of course, there was no follow up to give context as to how the cursed necklaces appeared on their skin to begin with.

The questions swarmed and expanded in Eira's mind. They took up too much space, and a throb of dull pain burst behind her eyes.

"It will mean that you can only access the very limited power I've given back to you to borrow for these trials. The more you try to reach, to extract, the more pain you will feel. The silver feels your resistance—and it will drain you even more, should you try to aim harm in the direction of anyone other than your fellow heiresses."

Air hissed out from between Eira's teeth.

"To *borrow*?" Sila sobbed. Her words were filled with anguish.

"We can't borrow something that is already ours," Etsumi added, tone steely.

Perhaps they, too, were emboldened by the rage of a new day; or maybe they were angered by the meagre power that sizzled through their veins.

Eira felt it there. Her fire. She should've been relieved at the familiarity of it—yet, it wasn't as it should be.

It was as weak as it was timid. It didn't recognize its wielder.

"You will have to do your very best to unlearn that thinking. Nothing is yours anymore, dear heiresses." Durante spread his hands out, palms facing upwards. "After all, what's yours is mine. That's the whole point of this."

He spoke as if they should already know—should already understand—his plans. His vision. His twisted, fruitless experiment.

The king wanted to break them for the fun of it.

No amount of clarification would make her believe otherwise.

Eira's fingers brushed the pendant burning her skin once more. But this time, she pressed her thumb down on its flat surface, ignoring the pain. How could Durante manipulate their power like this?

How could a power that even she couldn't understand be extracted and molded into something so small, so delicate?

In taking her magic for himself, did Durante understand why Eira was born with fire instead of ice in her blood? Would his own desperate, delusional search for knowledge give Eira the answers she'd sought her whole life?

"You have to get out of your head," Silvia whispered harshly. The sudden sound of her words cut through Eira's focus, and her eyes found the other's. "This is what he wants.

He's trying to manipulate us. Turn us against one another. Whatever you're thinking, stop. Focus."

When Eira looked to the others scattered around on the circular stage, some looked to be fighting their own interrogative thoughts, unsure which voice to heed. Unsure which ideas were their own.

"Show me why you're revered," Durante cooed, addressing all of them at once. "Gorge yourself on the powers you've been granted and prove to me your worth."

His directions were unclear, to Eira at least.

Nevertheless, others launched into action. Something in his words—whether it was the instruction or the taunting—flung them towards a decision.

It was Haneul who moved forward first. She broke away from the formation their bodies created.

The heiress turned her back to the king and eyed the rest of The New Reign, gaze trailing across them. Her mouth formed the shape of something like an apology before she settled on Etsumi. In the next moment the other heiress was on the ground, the palms of her hands pressed against her eyelids whilst she wailed in pain. Panic flared inside of Eira's body as she looked between the two. Haneul's pendant was alight at the base of her throat.

The other fae started to curse and scatter, trying to distance themselves from the chaos. Some seemed to consider going to Etsumi's side but then thought better of it.

Eira was rooted to the spot. She met Meilin's alarmed gaze.

"*What are you doing to them?*" Silvia screamed at Durante, hands fisted at her side.

The king's laughter was booming. Etsumi continued to scream as he said, "It is not me wielding this power, though I am impressed at your initiative."

Haneul cringed, her focus waning.

Eira *knew* it wasn't Durante inflicting the pain. She was sure that the others knew that, too. Maybe denial made the situation easier to comprehend.

Despite being rivals, there could still be parts of the other fae that chose to believe that they wouldn't direct violence to one another at the king's command. The small hope inside of her that wished for comradery seemed to die, getting further and further with the resounding echo of Etsumi's screams.

"Seeing stars," Haneul spoke the words through the gritted teeth, "is the lowest form of attack I can manage, with the power I've been given. She's experiencing extreme pressure in her eyes, but it will not blind her."

Eira saw Durante nod behind Haneul's head. He appeared impressed, despite the non-committed expression painted across his face. Eira could only assume that stealing their powers didn't mean the king recognized how they were utilized in confrontation.

Fury colored Haneul's face, but she didn't speak—and the worst part of it all was that Eira couldn't tell whether that anger was directed at Durante for enabling her to do that or for restricting her from being able to finish the job.

Haneul turned from the heiresses to the king.

Once she faced him, Etsumi's cries turned to whimpers, her hands still pressed against her eyelids. She knelt her forehead to the wooden floor beneath their feet, mumbling unintelligibly.

Durante tilted his head to one side at this, displeased at the fact that Haneul's focus was on him and not her fellow heiress. "I don't recall telling you that you could stop."

Eira saw the fae's fingers twitch at her side. "You expect us to do this to one another until we're all incapacitated? How does one *win* this trial?" Haneul hissed.

"I am the only winner in these trials, child of the night. You should know that by now." The king grinned. "Moreover, I haven't allowed you the capabilities to truly impair yourselves. I just want to see a little bit of everything—of your power, your tricks—and you will only stop when I say so. When I've had my fill."

The grim, slack-faced faces of The New Reign radiated hopelessness.

Deities, Eira thought, *he truly is delirious.*

And there was no other option than to heed his wishes.

Moments passed before anyone moved. Haneul shifted first, turning from Durante to face the heiresses one more, her cheeks flushed with rage. But the resolution in her eyes showed a sort of understanding that made gooseflesh rise on Eira's skin.

She appeared ready to accept an attack from another fae. An expected punishment.

Silvia raised her arm next. Her open palm faced towards the sky, the fae focused in on Haneul, eyes narrowed. From the center of her hand rose an owl—at least, it looked like it was supposed to be an owl. Its body was smaller than that of the regular bird and the talons that sprouted from its toes were twice the size that they should've been. Feathers of a deep gold ruffled and shook as it came into creation, shimmering in and out of focus like an illusion.

But when the bird leapt from Silvia's hand, a shriek escaping its gilded beak, Eira knew it was anything but.

Three beats of its wings brought it to where Haneul stood, her gaze widened. The owl dove at the heiress, talons outstretched. Eira felt her jaw slacken as the bird clawed at Haneul's eyes with precise strikes.

Any order in the amphitheater dissipated, the chaos brought on by the owl's attack.

When Sila turned to face Meilin, Eira knew that she was next.

Something in her recoiled at the thought—and before Sila

could do anything, and before Eira could think any better of it, her magic sung to the large chandelier above them, which blanketed the whole stage in a warm light. The wick of one candle, nestled between the delicately crafted limbs of the chandelier, burst into a flame too strong for the waxy body to handle.

Eira concentrated hard to harness the magic—to command it—and she worried her ribs would crack from the pressure that weighed on her chest. So rarely did she access this magic. So rarely was she able to wield it.

Shame only fueled the fire, and her own will to make it listen.

Faster.

The candlestick, still alight, molded into that of a thin dagger. Eira willed the flame from the wick to cover the body of the makeshift blade, and as it did, the newly made weapon slipped from its fixture.

It plummeted from the chandelier, and with a bit more motioning from Eira, plunged directly through the Sila's foot.

The fae wailed, focus shifting from Meilin to the burning wax that managed to pierce through the skin—and bone—of her foot. She tumbled to the ground. The wax spread and set itself around the hole in her foot. The fire continued to burn.

Guilt seized Eira, its grip tight. Their bodies would heal, as was the nature of the fae. Unless the injury was fatal, their bodies *would* recover. It would just take time, and it would hurt like nothing else.

The Rite was the ceremony that immortalized them—that gave them the power to withstand even the worst injuries. The only thing that would threaten their life thereafter would be a strike from a weapon forged of iron, and those weren't so easily procured in Seelie.

But The New Reign hadn't been through the Rite, and they didn't have full access to their magic. Their bodies were weak and malnourished, their minds traumatized and unsure of everything around them.

There was only so much that they could heal from.

All the same, Eira couldn't afford to feel that treacherous remorse, even as Sila's screeches of pain and anger filled her ears.

Meilin's gaze was both accusatory and grateful when their eyes met. Eira knew it was pointless to try and protect her.

It was foolish.

None of them were leaving the amphitheater unscathed, and now, Eira may've unknowingly subjected her to powers of a worse nature. But that was the problem of her magic, her downfall as its wielder—it was sporadic. Made more potent by her emotions, it wasn't easily wielded, even on a good day. The fire never truly felt like her own, and this scenario only made it feel further from it.

The fire controlled Eira. It wasn't the other way around.

She could only wish that The Deities would protect that secret for her.

Durante hooted from his prime viewing location, finding everything happening before him entirely too amusing.

Next to strike was Tufani, who wielded a bolt of blindingly bright light, the same way she may do a dagger. The light slithered out from under the surface of her skin, and it materialized into something tangent once grasped between her fingers.

She struck at Enyo, who seemed to take the hit with an uncharacteristic amount of grace.

No, it was expectancy. She's readied herself for it.

The cycle would continue if someone didn't do *something* to stop it.

Hurt heiresses would hurt other heiresses; they'd heal after a few lapses in time and would strike again.

Beyond the restless beat of her own heart, Eira heard the

cries of The New Reign, anguished and enraged. She heard the sound of her own rapid breathing and the king's unceasing laughter.

Then, air was being stolen from Meilin's lungs. A recently recovered Sila, still on the ground, had her gaze set on the heiress. All at once, Meilin's own knees buckled. A scream trapped itself in Eira's throat. She, too, felt as if her breathing had become restricted.

Meilin began to claw at her own sternum, the skin there having turned a disturbingly vibrant shade of indigo. Her hands caught on the leather string of her cursed necklace time and time again, but it never snapped.

The medallion pulsed with light.

Whatever Durante was doing to them, it appeared as if they didn't have full control of their body or their actions; the same way they were immobilized during the times he'd sent people to prepare them for the trials. He had granted them their power and enough consciousness to act out his will, but not enough stability of the mind to truly grasp the consequences of what they were doing.

Surely that was why it had come to this.

Eira couldn't fathom the possibility that the other heiresses *enjoyed* the brutality.

If they did, did that make them strong?

Did the thoughts she was having make her weak?

Meilin was released from Sila's targeted act moments later. She sucked air into her lungs, heaving and sputtering—it was at that same moment that Eira felt her own begin to fill with water, like some sort of humorous higher power took amusement in taking her for a fool.

She felt her insides become home to the liquid, and though she couldn't *see* Etsumi, the small taste of her power was unmistakable.

Salty.

Suffocating.

It didn't take long for it to overwhelm her; once it retracted, Eira's vision was already going dim. Every breath was agony—they rattled around in her chest, wet and weak. She'd fallen to the ground at some point.

Oddly enough, it was thoughts of her mother that flashed to mind.

Eira wasn't going to die—*not yet, at least*—but the near-drowning-on-dry-land experience activated something in her mind. The roar of the noise around her hushed to nothing, and behind her fluttering eyelids, visions of the silver-haired queen burned bright.

She met Eira's eyes in the reflection of the mirror, fingers halfway done with the braid she was crafting. It was so rare for her mother to style her hair—she often seemed as if the act of touching it alone would char her.

"It's easier to dismiss the potential goodness of someone you had yet to invest hope in, rather than give space for rage to fester," Queen Isolde said cooly, "and it would be wise of you to practice forgiveness. Anger will not serve you well."

It was a strange thing to tell someone who just turned fourteen. It didn't take a lot to upset Eira; but the recent loss of her closest friend, her only *friend, due to a misunderstanding didn't make those emotions any easier to deal with.*

Eira had already invested hope into her friend. Why shouldn't she?

And why should she forgive someone who hadn't even apologized? Where would forgiveness come from if both of them refused to confront the issue?

Her friend would rather pretend as if Eira didn't exist.

That was what most people did, anyway.

Maybe it was the easiest way to deal with her.

A concoction of smells—metal mingled with booze—made Eira's nostrils burn.

Her face, previously pushed up against the slickened surface of a table, stung as Eira pulled herself away for it. It felt like her body was working a hundred times harder to process her surroundings, despite the familiarity of the shadows coming into focus.

The curve of the bar top and the shelves behind it made the ache in her bones expand until it was all-consuming. She couldn't quite understand why the emotions sprang forward, but they did so with a vengeance, and Eira struggled to keep herself in an upright position as the figure stood behind the bar became bathed in light.

It was as if a controlled flame had been exposed to air.

With only the gnawed remains of normalcy left, Eira saw that the bartender was but a skeleton.

Alfie.

His name flooded into her mouth like bile. She pressed her hand hard against her stomach as she surveyed the damage.

Alfie's skin was pulled taut over the structure of his skull. The sockets where his eyes once sat, ever wary and watchful, were empty—nothing but sunken-in grooves that made dents in the surface of his face. His jaw was slack, giving the impression that time stopped for him in a moment of fear.

Distress.

If she were to stand and get a closer look, Eira would be sure that the flash of brown that rushed out and over the cracked skin of his lips belonged to an insect, making a home out of his corpse. There would be more where that came from.

But Eira wouldn't look to find out. She *knew*.

The scent of decay clung to him like a sickly perfume. All the same, he remained upright, caught somewhere between life and death, belonging to neither and to both.

At the sound of a chair leg being dragged across the ground, Eira's attention diverted back to the direction of whatever—or whoever—was in front of her.

She willed her eyes to focus, to adjust to the midnight that swallowed the rest of her surroundings beyond the bar, and as though compelled by her want, the light that previously illuminated Alfie shifted over.

They weren't the only bodies in Amzi.

Eight heiresses sat positioned in a crescent moon around her, draped in lavish gowns of varying material and color. Their faces were painted in glitter, lines drawn artfully around their eyes and deep shades of orange and red lined their tight-lipped expressions.

Each one of them donned the same look—gazes set on Eira with mouths firm and unsmiling, as if she had done something to displease them.

Eira's voice took a few moments to find her.

Why did no one tell me about the dress code?"

The words came out wobbly and unconfident, which she couldn't really blame herself for. Either they ignored her, or didn't hear her at all, because the heiresses remained silent.

When sickness began to surge inside of her, Eira squeezed her eyes shut. She clenched them so tightly that she was sure the vision before her would vanish when they were opened once more.

It was the sudden, thunderous chorus of echoing thuds that made her eyes fly open.

Full glasses of sloshing ale sat in front of everyone, Eira included. The heiresses looked quite pleased at the sudden arrival of the beverage at their grotesque evening gathering;

their previously tight-lipped expressions were now ear-to-ear grins.

It was alarming, if not for the fact that they were completely still otherwise, but for the overflowing level of liquid in each glass.

No one touched their drinks, despite their euphoric expressions.

Eira knew they couldn't have come from Alfie.

All the same, reason avoided her.

She was *thirsty*.

It was an abrupt kind of feeling. A ferocious one, as if she hadn't had a sip of anything in years, living purely off sheer will —and stubbornness—alone. As unnerved as she was, no other choice felt acceptable.

Eira wanted to drink.

Her hands shook as she wrapped them around the glass, lifting it to her mouth. There was an imperceptible barrier that barred any movement too far above the tabletop. This was as far as she could go, as much as she could do.

In any other circumstance, Eira would've relished in the taste of the ale. She would've sighed in satisfaction as it rushed down her throat, leaving a familiar burn in its wake.

But Eira wanted for something she couldn't place. Something else. *Anything else.*

The ale was so strong, and its aftertaste unbearably tinny, that the heiress ached to get it down in a few swift gulps. She spluttered and coughed, trying and failing to drag in deep breaths of air between swallowing.

All the while, the other fae remained unmoving. Their smiles didn't shift. Echoes of bright, easygoing conversation flutter in the back of her mind, as delicate as butterfly wings. Eira didn't know where it came from—memories with Meilin, maybe—but the brush of the impossible made her head spin. Her heart strained, ale and anguish an open wound.

She wished, so badly, that someone would speak.

This must be a test.

If she finished their drinks, too, maybe then they would acknowledge her. Surely there was some sort of action to take to make the scene before her unfurl. The arrival of the full glasses made them smile, so a sequence centered around those same beverages would be sure to stir them from their stillness.

Because that's all it was: a scene. A set-up. A sickly dream.

Eira's thoughts must've been broadcasted.

One by one, the outstretched arms of the heiresses pushed their glasses forward across the table towards her. The full glasses mirrored the same semicircle position of the seated fae. Spilled liquid marked their path. When Eira tilted her head, the dampness looked like blood.

The second one wasn't any easier than the first. Or the third.

The liquid burned as it went down, and she kept drinking despite it, swallowing bile in between.

Each finished glass would leave her folding in on herself in a fit of coughing, like it was her lungs that were full of liquid and not her stomach.

By the fifth or sixth glass—she lost count—the edges of her visions blurred, and her sense of reality scrambled further and further away.

The sight of the empty glasses didn't give Eira the satisfaction she'd hoped. Her gut, empty besides the monstrous amount of ale she'd forced into it, rumbled angrily. Something compelled her to look towards the bar.

Alfie was no longer there.

Paranoia slipped under her skin. It settled in beside the

grumbling wave of sickness, which festered, growing stronger with every passing moment.

Her fingers tightened around the handle of the last full drink. Eira squeezed her eyes shut against the unshifting image of the heiresses smiling at her, threw her head back and let the liquid rush down her throat.

It was *warm*.

She swallowed.

The impaired reaction time of the drunken fae meant the sudden change in temperature—and texture—didn't deter her from finishing her first mouthful. But when Eira pulled the glass away from her lips and her eyes opened once more, she saw with no small amount of horror that the contents inside it were crimson.

The overwhelming taste of metal coated her mouth.

Eira wanted to scream. She choked on a gag, instead.

The barrier holding her in place shifted away and the heiress was grateful for the range of movement that allowed her to toss the now half-full glass across the room. Eira could only assume that it shattered somewhere in the dark shadows beyond the reach of her vision, because the sound of impact—shattering glass or an obnoxious crash—never came.

Her legs shook as she pushed herself back from the table. The eyes of The New Reign followed her, the rest of their expressions unchanging. Eira didn't look back at them as she stumbled across the distance of the darkened venue, fumbling for an exit.

Relief came quickly when her fingers found the smooth brass of what she hoped was a door handle. Head spinning, feet fighting to keep her upright, Eira pushed down and propelled herself forward.

Crisp air enveloped her moments later.

Despite the stickiness of her skin, the soil beneath her was cool and she only realized she'd fallen to the ground because of the way her body melted against the earth.

A stifling quiet consumed her surroundings. It was broken by the click of the door and the sound of her retching onto the ground. Nothing would come up, even as bitterness gurgled in her throat and saliva flooded into her mouth. She tried to heave, to rid of the foul taste that the liquid—metal and ale alike—had left in her mouth.

Nothing offered her reprieve from the disgust.

Eira sat there, defeated, for what felt like an eternity, suffocating thanks to her own stubborn body.

The night sky above her was nothing more than fractured shards of colored glass, messily pieced together to form a dizzying picture. Stars—at least, that's what she thought they were—twinkled and teased her from their spot, high above. Untouchable.

Looking back down didn't prove to be any better.

A crowd of bodies, created from the nothingness that was there only a few instances prior, stood a few steps away from Eira's crumbled body. Using the back of her hand, the heiress wiped spit from the corners of her mouth. She was unimpressed, and unsurprised, to see that the faces amongst the horde, whilst mostly unrecognizable, all wore identical grins.

The same expression as The New Reign.

Another flash of familiarity came in the face at the very front of the mass.

Eira's mother, the picture of royalty.

Her tall, lean figure was draped in azure silk. Indigo ribbons made delicate bows in all the right places, adorning the small of her waist and encircling her wrists. Atop her head was a delicate crown that looked like it was woven from starlight itself. Eira remembered how she fawned over the piece as a child—it was the same one she always wore, the one that Queen Isolde always complained about the weight of. Figuratively, and literally, Eira assumed.

Even in her state, the heiress couldn't ignore the sneer that twisted her mother's expression.

It was a vile thing.

She always had a way of warping her facial features into the most terrifying of monsters. They were weapons she wielded, always with Eira on the receiving end.

Eira shuddered.

A second surge of sickness rushed upwards. Leaning over the small collection of spittle she'd left on the ground, the heiress opened her mouth and begged for the liquid to leave her body.

"Eira," her mother said, speaking her name like it was a curse.

Eira turned to face her. Unwiped wetness was splayed across her chin. She could feel it. Queen Isolde was now only a step away, a sizable change in distance to where she was only moments prior. The queen towered over Eira, her face still screwed up in the perfect mix of disappointment and revulsion.

"All you know is drinking your weight in ale. You're worth nothing, child." The words came from her mother's mouth, using her mother's voice, but they weren't hers. Queen Isolde's insults were thinly veiled, maybe, but they *were* veiled. They were passing comments that left you winded and remarks that made you want to shift back inside of your own skin.

This was targeted. Brazen.

Eira's mother leant in, her figure blocking the view of the stars behind her head. "Do you hear me, Eira? You're *worthless*."

Eira wanted to say something—anything—though a reply refused to find her. It didn't matter, because in the next breath, there was a foot pinned against her throat.

Queen Isolde had the point of her icicle-thin heel lodged

against her daughter's jugular. She pushed and pushed, the force making the heiress fall flat. The soil was even cooler against her back.

Eira couldn't breathe.

The queen's expression didn't shift—that impenetrable sneer seeing her all the way into darkness. With the taste of bile in her throat and the image of her mother's hateful face locked into her mind, Eira's vision blurred before blacking out entirely.

I'm going to die, she thought.

But that wasn't the death that Durante prepared for her.

It was only just the beginning.

CHAPTER 20
PORNEÍA

The house had reverted to the state it was on the first day that Eira stepped inside it.

A mismatched puzzle rather than a property, with pieces that she recognized along with bits that didn't quite belong. The heiress felt like she was peering through a distorted looking glass, the accuracy of her vision questionable as she maneuvered through the entryway.

Meilin lives here, Eira thought.

But Meilin was nowhere to be found. Just layers of dust that coated the floorboards and furniture alike. The swing of the broken front door behind her made Eira's skin crawl.

Cold air came in, following every step she took.

She couldn't think of where she was supposed to be, what she was supposed to be doing. Time was fragmented for her; she who wandered down a hallway in search of something. Someone.

Meilin, an instinct whispered.

Yes.

Meilin lived there.

If Eira found Meilin, everything would make sense.

The fae pushed on, rubbing her wrists absentmindedly as she did so.

Pieces of furniture that looked too new to belong were dotted in unconventional spots in front of and around Eira. She used their soft corners and structured edges as leverage, winding and contorting her body through gaps. The space seemed to shrink around her as she moved, compelled to continue in one direction, despite the sinking feeling that plagued her stomach.

Soft cries and illegible whispers helped lead the way and as she came closer to a source of light spilling out from an open archway, Eira knew she'd found the right place.

When she turned to look over her shoulder, the pathway that led her there was swallowed by twilight.

There was nowhere else to go.

No other option.

Something unfamiliar rippled under her skin as Eira stepped over the threshold and into the hall.

The air inside didn't carry the same heavy decay that clung to the hallways she'd roamed to get there.

Warm light cast a hauntingly beautiful glow on the scene before her.

Limbs and fabric melded into one. Eira couldn't differentiate where bodies stopped, and the crinkle of cloth started. No gowns or high-necked blouses played a part in the writhing mass of motion that the heiress stumbled in on; rather, there was a throw-over of sorts, draped over bare skin of varying shades. Thin in material and sheer in color, the fabric seemed to be getting in the way more than it was offering warmth, as if the mass wasn't already flushed in the face, skin slickened with perspiration and something else.

Something scarlet.

Blood was everywhere—and it wasn't that of the fae.

Metallic bile coated her throat. Eira couldn't quite understand why, though there was a lingering feeling of dread that came from the sight of it, something which extended beyond the initial horror of blood as it was.

The crimson stains marked skin and fabric alike. There were pools of it on the ground, dribbling into the slats of the floorboard, setting into the foundation of the house itself.

What was even more disturbing was the realization that Eira, without knowing it, had stepped closer to the group. From this distance, she could see that it wasn't just mortals making love and spilling their blood in the twisted ceremony.

There was a mixture of characteristics that forced her to acknowledge the presence of the fae in the mix. Eyes of golden hues and ears with pointed tips. Lips peeled back around too-sharp teeth, and aerate markings lit up through layers of blood, both dried and fresh.

They weren't bleeding, but they were definitely contributing to whatever Eira was witnessing.

Amongst the mortals, who were all unrecognizable to her, there were some whose faces lacked any determining features at all. Smoothed over skin, with nothing but mouths, to give and to receive love.

Yet, it wasn't just intimacy and its associated sacrifices being exchanged.

Every sickness that could come about as a result of it festered amongst the group. Some mouths were slickened with sick, though others didn't seem to notice or care. Strips of exposed skin were raised with welts and red-raw with rashes.

The heiress gripped her stomach.

No one paid her any mind.

Eira tried to think of books she'd read on this sort of thing. Sex wasn't an unfamiliar concept to her, and the illnesses that could come of it when done carelessly were pieces of knowledge she suffered through in her younger years (the risk of a tainted ruling bloodline was too high for her *not* to know), but the scene before her was unlike anything in her realm of understanding.

Eira knew that fae didn't lie with mortals—they *couldn't.*

Nonetheless, maybe this was the result of that. It could've been a warning—a premonition of what happened when the Treaty was ignored.

Eira could've convinced herself of that explanation if it wasn't for the body she finally saw situated in the middle of it all.

Droplets of her shimmering gold blood surrounded the spot she sat in, limbs splayed messily around her; and whilst it took the heiress all too long to take notice of her, Meilin's eyes had long found their spot on Eira's face.

Expectance glittered behind her gaze.

Her lips weren't on anyone else's. Meilin was untouched by the sickness of those around her. She seemed unbothered by the fingers that crawled along her legs and up her arms. That was the most they reached, though.

Meilin's exposed skin was splattered with crimson, mingling with her own aureate blood, but otherwise, she appeared to be unharmed.

Eira's breath hissed through clenched teeth.

The heightened sound of cries, indistinguishable between pleasure and pain, became deafening.

Eira hated, most of all, that nothing about Meilin's expression looked dreamlike. Every detail was too real. The crinkle of her nose and upwards tilt of her lips was achingly familiar. It provided her with a comfort that should've been unwelcome in the hall, which smelt of perspiration and blood and *wrongness.*

Her feet stepped through small puddles of Meilin's blood.

The other fae didn't speak as Eira came closer, dropping down to her knees so that they were face to face.

All at one, the soft whisper of Meilin's breath exhaling onto her cheeks made the turmoil inside of Eira's stomach recede.

Eira wasn't sure who leant in first.

All she knew was that it didn't take long for their lips to connect.

Fingers curled around her neck and into her hair, nails pressing hard into her scalp. Air hitched in her throat at the sight of Meilin when she pulled back for a second, mouth still slightly open and face painted a deep pink.

The horror of the scene around them faded out of view. Everything quieted for a few moments, and it was just unbearably soft lips, the taste of jasmine in the air and stolen breaths between embraces.

Although Eira would've been content to imagine that it was just the two of them, it became harder to keep her focus on reality when another limb slipped around her waist.

Rough, unfamiliar skin pushed against the fabric that was suddenly draped over the fae's knees. Eira felt the scratch of the gauze and an accompanying drip of something viscous.

Her fingers were intertwined with Meilin's when she turned to the side, meeting the gaze of a fae she didn't recognize.

They smiled at her, vision clouded and crimson dried into the cracks of their skin. Their lips parted and they leaned in, murmuring words that Eira couldn't decipher.

She was stuck to the spot, desperately searching for the familiarity of Meilin once more.

When their eyes met, just like that, a sweeping delirium stole all reason away.

Eira saw the pleasure dissolve from Meilin's face, a dazed expression of fury taking over.

The heiress imagined Meilin harnessing it like a tangible

thing that yawned awake in the pit of her stomach. Rage would gurgle and grumble in her gut the same way Eira's creature did when it wanted her attention. She wondered if Meilin would feel its acidic burn as it rushed up from her throat, coating her mouth.

Eira could only manage numbness. The fae's unfamiliar hands roamed, and she stilled, unsure of what to do next.

Stray pieces of ruddy jewelry were strewn across the floor, as if the bodies came into the hall with nothing but accessories on. Bejeweled pins and ornate earrings pierced into the soft skin of Eira's legs. She'd only just noticed them.

Meilin's fingers untangled from Eira's. Moving slowly, her hands danced over the gauze laid across her lap, pushing it aside to reveal the dagger casually nestled in the empty spot between her folded legs. Gold dripped off the blade, like she'd drawn blood before hiding it away.

The weapon was the same one that she'd held to the fae's throat on the day that they officially met.

The edges of the memory were frayed pieces of fabric that Eira grabbed at with sweat-slicked hands. It was there—the forest, the weight of Meilin on top of her, the blade against her skin—but only in loose threads. If Eira pulled any harder, she worried the whole tapestry would unravel itself; and if she didn't stay focused on the scene playing out before her, the heiresses' mind would retreat into an endless darkness.

That much she was sure of.

So, she watched, frozen, as Meilin's gold-stained fingers brushed against the handle of the dagger.

The other fae wasn't perturbed. Their eyes burned holes in Eira's skin. She moved her gaze from the weapon to the stare of the one who wielded it.

Resolution hardened Meilin's face.

She couldn't have a way of knowing what it was that solidified her decision, but in the next few moments, Eira's focus followed the swift line of Meilin's arm as it rose up into the air, her fingers curled around the hilt of the dagger.

The blade pushed past the resistance of the fae's eye with an unanticipated amount of ease. Extra weight distributed through Meilin's wrist saw the weapon fully lodged into its target with a gratifying *pop*.

The sequence happened so quickly that it was almost as if she imagined it but the spill of gold down the fae's face was tangible enough.

Eira couldn't deny the slack-jawed stillness that came thereafter. They didn't scream or struggle. Frozen, like her, except in a much less favorable situation.

Meilin's hand was still wrapped around the dagger. She only let go when the blood of the other fae began to trickle down her wrists. Eira saw specks of it on the other's face, in her eyebrows, and on her cheeks.

Meilin wouldn't meet her eyes.

But it's not because of Eira, is it?

A voice, terrifyingly close by, whispered the words into her ear. Yet, the intention didn't feel directed towards her. The message wasn't *meant* for Eira—and for whatever reason, she was hearing it all the same.

Recognition made Meilin's nose scrunch. The tone of the speaker honed in on this distaste.

You enjoy this—this lightlessness. It's your nature, after all.

Eira remained frozen. She felt warmth dribble onto her hands. Around them, bodies continued to move in established rhythms, unbothered by the sickness they'd manifested and the horror of the scene that the trio was involved in.

This is who you are.

Meilin smiled and Eira was overwhelmed by cowardice. She

wanted to stand and move away; wanted to turn a cheek to the strange emotion that the other heiress emanated.

Eira swore that, somewhere, at some point, Alfie's face materialized—almost comically so—in a far-off corner. But his existence didn't belong in this sequence, whatever it was. His features blinked in and out of focus, his mouth forming distorted words that the heiress couldn't decipher.

He was too out of place for a setting like the one they were in, and Eira couldn't wonder, momentarily, if it was him that was speaking to Meilin.

No.

Then, for the first time since she stepped into the hall, Meilin's face fell at the sight of Eira.

The heiress only realized that she hadn't been looking at her —rather, during the whole ordeal, Meilin was looking *through* her. But when she looked at her then, really looked at her, Meilin seemed distraught as she said,

"You shouldn't be here."

CHAPTER 21
PHILARGURÍA

The sun was brutal on Eira's skin.

Usually akin to its warmth, she didn't understand the need to shrink away from it. All the same, the rays were overwhelming in their grip on her body.

Eira lifted her palm to the sky, vast and never-ending overhead, and positioned her closed fingers in a poor attempt to block out the intensity of its light. She yearned to shield herself away, as others around her did.

They shuffled along, shadows cast over their forms from the arms they held over their heads. Some pulled pieces of fabric taut between their fingers and angled them upwards, though Eira doubted that did much to keep the beams off their skin.

Laughter escaped her lips.

She didn't even know where they managed to get the fabric, especially since they were told to pack light. The trip would take even longer if they added extra weight. Eira assumed that sheets of frayed cloth weren't heavy enough to warrant concern.

From where she stood at the top of the foreboding set of stairs, Eira saw that the others still meandered around the middle. At this rate, it would take them at least another hour to meet her where she was.

Giving in to the will of her aching feet, the heiress sat. A momentary break would serve her well, and it was what the other three that made it to the top with her were doing.

The pain didn't stop at the bottom half of Eira's body—the elbow high layers of golden bangles that chimed to mark every movement she made were unbelievably heavy. Why wouldn't they be sacrificed if the idea was to travel light?

But closer inspection of the pieces showed that they were more armor than accessory. Gilded spikes caught the rays of the sun with an intensity so strong it was blinding.

"Keep up or stay behind," someone called out from the top of the staircase. They sat close to Eira with a voice that was as commanding as it was familiar. Enyo—her name like honey in Eira's mouth—impossible to swallow and a little sweet.

The others below seemed encouraged by her words.

They pushed forward, faster. Soon enough, all nine bodies lined the open entrance to the temple. From their height, overlooking a never-ending landscape of rich greens and blues, the sun was close enough to touch. It wasn't as hot, though.

Eira was grateful for that reprieve at least.

They trailed inside the high-arched building, one after the other. The dresses they wore, structured from light linen and pinned in at various spots by golden brooches, dragged across the marble floor beneath their feet.

Wide columns of a blinding white held the weight of the vast structure's roof. They towered over Eira and her fellow heiresses. The ceiling was made of the same unblemished stone, and it seemed to stretch on forever. Somehow, rays of sunlight managed to pierce through the temple's seemingly impenetrable composition, and it dappled the floor in front of them.

The scent of vanilla carried on the air.

She didn't know where they were going but Enyo led the group with a confidence that convinced her they were in good hands.

Eira wasn't worried.

Here, no one lagged. No one strayed. The sound of in-sync steps, quiet chatter and even softer laughter was almost like a roll call. The heiress could mentally tick off the presence of each heiress. For reasons unknown, the duty seemed to be her own. She felt responsible for them, despite being unable to remember their names.

There was Enyo, and then the rest were airborne, stuck in a spot of her mind that was as vast as the temple itself.

It would come to her later, Eira thought.

When the time is right.

Eventually, quiet fell over the group like a weighted curtain over an empty stage. They walked for what felt a little longer than forever, and they were yet to see any other bodies occupying the temple. Eira expected them to sit in the corridors, tucked into corners and splayed across the wide walkways, eating fine fruits and drinking even finer liquor. Vibrant fabric and crowns that twinkled with heavy embellishments.

That vision made the most sense—a decadent space called for indulgence.

The thought of a life like that—soaked in color and warmth —made Eira's body tingle with a sort of excitement she was unfamiliar with.

As the group's pace slowed Eira assumed they were closer to their destination. A shoulder brushed up against hers, and the fae with eyes of a different color and constellations across her skin housed a panic in her gaze that was out of place. Her lips pursed as Eira scanned the details of her face.

The star-skinned heiress spoke first, her voice barely above a whisper. "Do you know why we're here?"

Eira wasn't sure what to make of the question, so she said nothing at all. The mutual confusion left them in a momentary silence that lasted that of a few footsteps. Star-skin spoke again, a little more urgently. A light chatter resumed amongst the rest of the group. Their interaction didn't appear out of place and yet, guilt made Eira hesitate.

"Do you *know*?" she asked, the second time more desperate than the first.

Eira's eyebrows furrowed. She tried not to jerk away when the other fae laced their fingers together. Their steps still in time with the others, star-skin leant in so close to Eira that they were essentially nose to nose. She was pleading.

"None of this is real, Eira."

The shock of hearing her name fall from the other's lips with such ease almost made Eira stumble. The pitch of star-skin's voice rose as the words tumbled out. "Please tell me you remember . . . *you have to remember . . .*"

But Eira couldn't remember—what was she supposed to remember?

Why did this fall on her, and why couldn't she shake away the sudden pressure pushing down on her chest?

Despite not being able to answer her questions or offer anything but a tightened expression and the slight shake of her head, the star-skinned heiress didn't let go of Eira's hand. She took a few shaky breaths of air—*in and out, in and out*—until the group came to a stop.

Eira wasn't sure what to make out of the interaction.

Only that, when star-skin slipped her fingers out of Eira's and stepped to the side, an awfully bitter taste was left on her tongue.

Enyo, still at the head of the cluster, turned around to face everyone. A smile bloomed across her face. She looked pleased. Whatever test was conducted in the climbing of those steps, the fae before her had passed.

Nonetheless, there was a sudden uneasiness in Eira's bones that wouldn't settle.

Enyo nodded once before turning on her heel. When she placed her hand on the doors, which lacked any discernible handle or way to get in, they came alive underneath her touch. All it took was a light push from her and the only sealed doorway in the temple opened before them.

The smell of coal hit Eira first.

So different from the hot wind of outside, and the sweet air that travelled inside the temple, the heavy wooden scents of something burning coated her throat with a vengeance. Instead of swallowing bitterness, Eira was now forced to stomach ash.

The heiresses were in the beating heart of a forge.

A fire roared on the right of the group, making its home in a space that had been carved out of the wall for it. Lined with cobblestone and shielded by an overarching lip the color of soot, the fire's home was foreboding—and *hot*. Completely unlike the heat of the sun.

Eira fought between admiration and fear. How it stayed burning was a whole other concern entirely.

Who could manage such a feat?

Taking up space in the rest of the forge were things that Eira recognized as anvils and chisels. Marble slabs were covered in layers of ash and adorned with a variety of tools, both big and small. Those, she couldn't name. Half-finished projects, weapons that weren't quite ready, were left discarded all around them.

On the walls—which were nowhere near as well-kept as the rest of the temple— mounted rows of golden swords, spears and bows winked down at them. There was another section of arrows of the same shade, all with heads formed in different, intricate shapes.

In the furthest corner of the room sat a pile of flat, golden coins, taller in height than her. Eira started to suspect that there was a color theme, and she'd never seen anything like it. She imagined it was being smelted to create that which was show-cased on the walls and in every part of the forge, which felt alive with an energy she couldn't deny.

Everything came together to form a very particular picture.

Eira could almost hear the echoes of clashing tools. She could see calloused hands and perspiration being swiped across ruddy foreheads. Picturing the reprieve found in a finished product made joy swell in her chest, out of place against the previous uneasiness.

Some fae broke loose from the cluster, drawn to the fire or to the tables. They explored with their fingers. Eyes ate their fair share whilst hands danced over everything else. Their curiosity seemed insatiable—and the only heiress who still stood next to Eira, unmoving, was the star-skinned one.

Eira's gaze fell to Enyo, who stood in the middle of the forge. She watched her the other's face rearrange itself—from untroubled to confused, all in a matter of a few seconds. "Why are you here?" she asked no one in particular.

The words were loud enough to make everyone pause.

She did a full circle, scanning the space and the heiresses inside of it. Eira saw something inside of Enyo crack. She shook her head, as if waking from a horrible dream, growing more disorientated and aggrieved.

"You're not supposed to be in here . . ."

Some of the heiresses exchanged glances, but no one responded to Enyo. Instead, they stepped closer to one another, forming a sort of semicircle around her.

In the corner of her eye, Eira noticed the star-skinned fae

swallow. "It was you who led us here," she said, softly. "We were trusted guests, invited into the forge—we wouldn't have been able to master the steps, otherwise. You know that."

Enyo wasn't pleased.

The fire in her eyes was just as unfamiliar to Eira as that of what roared in the pit beside them.

Enyo stepped forward with purpose and her hands latched onto the shoulders of unsuspecting star-skinned heiress. The other fae almost appeared to relax in her grip, despite the completely unfriendly nature of it. She leant forward, trying to take the chance to whisper a hurried exchange of words that Eira couldn't decipher—only to be promptly silenced as Enyo bent at the neck and shoved ahead, the horns atop her head piercing through the neck of the other.

Eira knew she should've stopped it.

But once it happened, it was all too late. No one protested. They just stood there, shoulders shadowed by the weapons mounted behind them, faces unmoving.

Enyo pulled away from the star-skinned fae, her horns withdrawing from their lodging in her skin with a sickening *pop*. The mouth of the heiress, whose neck was slicked with golden blood, remained open.

As if, even in death, she needed to say the words that remained unspoken.

Using the force of the grip she still had on the other's shoulders, Enyo shoved the star-skinned fae in the direction of the gaping mouth of the forge. "You shouldn't be here," she spat, "and neither should the rest of you. But your insolence alone will mean that you get to be the example for what betrayal brings in the Court of Telema!"

Enyo didn't struggle as she pushed her fellow fae, face-first, into the mouth of the flames. Eira's breath seized in her chest, her vision growing fuzzy.

The sound of gurgling was muffled by the burn of the coals that suffocated and consumed her all at once. Enyo pushed and lifted, maneuvering the body with purpose, as if the weight of the rest of the heiress was easy work. Once her whole body became submerged in the inferno, Enyo stood back. She didn't grunt or stutter. She didn't fumble under the weight.

Ichor dripped from her horns. It trickled down her forehead and into her eyes. Onto the ground.

There was another sickening sound—a sort of *pop*—that followed quickly after the muffled sounds subsided. For a long while after, the quiet chatter of the flames as they danced around their meal was the only noise in the forge.

No one spoke.

Not even as a stomach-curdling scent overcame that of the coal.

No one spoke.

Not even when the walls of the temple shuddered and swayed, like the building wanted to be rid of whatever—whoever—came inside and tainted it.

Enyo looked from the group of heiresses and back to the pit.

Eira watched, stricken by a wave of grief for the fae she couldn't remember the name of, as Enyo searched the coals. Her gaze scanned the spot over and over and over again, as if they would give her an answer she needed.

Eira wondered if she found anything.

When she looked to the pit, she could see only gold.

CHAPTER 22
LÚPE

Eira's body spat a thousand different curses at her before she finally woke up.

It was that sensation—of her own anatomy ready to turn on her—that made the fae's eyes fly open. The following inspection she conducted to locate the source of her body's great upset wasn't all that strenuous. Detestably scratchy fabric, belonging to that of a full-body, coal colored romper, clung to the sweat pooling in every possible crevice of her body. Her fingers were knuckle deep in warm earth and her head thrummed like she'd spent the last few unconscious hours throwing it against the ground.

Nonetheless, this new bout of consciousness felt more rooted in reality than any of Eira's previous interactions.

Her stomach grumbled and her legs itched. Her vision didn't blur, despite the pounding behind her eyes, and there wasn't a dream-like haze that settled over her surroundings like a veil.

Finally, for the first time in however long, Eira was *awake*.

Recollections of moments her body remembered but her mind refused to acknowledge made the pressing weight against her eyelids almost unbearable. The heiress wanted to sleep, peacefully, for years. Still, Eira could afford the gratitude at being grounded, even if that realization came with the understanding of her situation. The severity of it all.

Durante.

The Demir Trials.

The words relinquished any hunger residing in her gut.

She pushed herself off the ground and looked around, trying to adjust to the unfamiliar setting. Walls of shrubbery towered above, at least double her height. They were well-taken care of chunks of greenery—pruned and shaped to create angles and corners that appeared to form a purposeful pattern.

No, Eira thought. *Not a pattern.*

A path.

Hedges closed in on either side of her. Over the fae's shoulder was more foliage, cutting off any means for her to travel backwards. Eira quickly realized that the only way out of the dead end she'd woken up nestled into was through the opening laid out in the path before her.

But the unknown on the other sides of the emerald cage was just as worrisome to think about.

How could something like this even exist in Unseelie, a court system crafted into existence supposedly underground?

Then, a voice was murmuring in her ears. The words were close, but the speaker was nowhere to be seen. Gooseflesh rose along her dirt-streaked skin.

"Welcome back," Durante cooed, like it had been a long while since he last spoke to her. Depending on the nature of the horror-filled realms she'd been forced into, Eira figured that might be true. "It is great to have you all in one place again . . .

Well, all eight of you, that is."

Eight?

She advanced a few steps, unsure if there would be a point in responding aloud.

The king answered her query only seconds later. Uneasiness made her stomach churn again. "I will presume that you are all curious about the missing heiress, but I will not be so audacious in thinking that you know the reason as to *why* she is misplaced." Eira didn't like the way he danced around the word —*misplaced*. "After all, where would the fun be in giving you answers to the questions you have when you could search for them yourselves, instead—which is precisely what you will be doing."

There were other sounds now, too. Scuffling of feet and the vigorous shaking of bushes, as if the heiresses were trying to push their way through the maze's walls. The noises were still too far away to presume the fae were close by, which told Eira that this puzzle was created at a much larger scale than she originally presumed.

"This maze has been crafted to draw out the most unsavory parts of your powers. Within these walls, as you seek out understanding, you will be forced to face yourselves in the process," Durante's voice was giddy, his excitement a tangible thing.

"Think of every wrong turn, every impasse, as a mirror of your failures and shortcomings; and the more you straggle, the more suffering you will incur."

Eira didn't know how much damage a whole lot of trimmed hedges could cause.

Yet, she didn't doubt the king's ability to draw out suffering.

"The New Reign is not revered simply for the strange circumstances of your birth alone. There is something *off* about each and every one of you. Now that I've seen at least a fragment of what you're capable of, I want you to all be privy to one another's undoing. Really, what better way is there to learn about your opponent than through their weaknesses?"

Laughter echoed in the air after Durante's sentiment. Were they being observed?

Eira felt an edge of madness awaken inside of her as Durante's voice was silenced. There was a ringing that resonated in her head for a few minutes thereafter, like her body was doing its best to rid itself of his influence.

For Deities sake.

The feeling of hunger came back with surprising force as she continued walking, deciding that sticking to the one spot wouldn't do much to help her.

The fae body could withstand longer periods without sustenance—but they were like mortals in the sense that, eventually, they needed to eat. The starvation would come, no matter how long they were able to suppress it; and Eira *was* hungry.

Besides that, she didn't know how she'd been allowed to relieve herself, and who had control of her when she did so. If her body was being deprived of needed nutrients, was it even able to rid of its waste? There was no retrievable memory of doing it that would come to her mind, no matter how hard she tried to summon it.

Wrath simmered until it was boiling inside of her. Eira wanted for many things, but to use her own hands, of her own volition, to wipe herself clean of what had been done to her was a top priority.

But, instead, Eira had no choice but to dance for her food and her freedom.

Maybe he expected her to fall into old habits to survive in Unseelie—to hurt and steal and lie her way through the trials—and in spite of that vision he had for her, the heiress decided to do anything but that.

She would direct her rage at him.

At no one but him.

However, the fire that burnt hot under Eira's skin was not her own.

It came from her body, but it was . . . unfamiliar. A more untamed rendition of the blaze she kept at bay in her daily life at court. As she walked and tried to reel it in, to tamper it down, Eira found that it wouldn't heed her call.

Her own limbs felt too warm. She itched and the flames surged, rippling underneath the bruised pallor of her skin, intertwining with her nerves to make something entirely new of her inner ecosystem.

The discomfort made her pick up the pace.

A dizzying sea of never-ending green met Eira at every corner. When she turned to follow a different path, convinced this would be the one to lead her to something new, she was sorely disappointed to find herself essentially running in circles.

All the while, the sounds of nearby heiresses grew closer.

The occasional shout made her jumpy, but it was the sudden howls of pain—and rage—that really made her fire stir. Heightened by her own unstable emotions, the flames were relentless.

She felt like she'd been walking for forever before coming face-to-face with a familiar heiress around the next bend.

Shock flashed across Meilin's expression before her eyes narrowed in on Eira.

She recovered quickly. It was a practiced state of being.

Meilin's matching romper had a slash across the middle. Beneath it, an angry gash spilled out golden blood across her exposed stomach. It dripped down, leaving spots beneath her feet. A trail.

Whoever inflicted the wound would be able to find her with very little effort if it kept weeping that way.

"You're hurt," Eira said aloud, stupidly, as if Meilin wasn't aware of the injury.

The fae placed her hand against the wound, fingers pressing crudely into the split, like she was trying to sew herself back together. She curled her lip. "I don't need your help."

Beyond her own better judgement, Eira raised an extended hand. Her own fingers shook, just slightly, as they hung in the air between them. In the time it took for the pair to properly acknowledge one another, Meilin had shifted backwards a few steps. The space between them was suffocating.

But it also meant safety.

For both of them.

It was hard to form sentences. Eira's mouth was molten lava, her tongue struggling around the words she wanted to ask. "Did one of the heiresses do that to you?"

"*What do you think?*"

Meilin's rage was the same that type that they all held onto —directed at Durante but expelled towards one another because it was all they were afforded the chance to do. It wasn't unexpected, and yet, Eira couldn't let go of the desperate need she felt to make the other trust her again.

Eira knew she wasn't the strongest of The New Reign. For how long she would remain, she couldn't be sure—especially if she was unable to find a way to strike down Durante before he picked them all off, one by one. She'd be damned if she didn't do her absolute best to make the most of whatever time with Meilin she could get.

Though being lost in a murderous maze was not ideal.

The creature in Eira's stomach, silent as of late, roared awake. The force of it shaking itself out of sleep almost rocked her off her feet. Momentarily, Meilin seemed to consider whether or not she should take a step forward.

As if in reaction to seeing the other heiress—or, rather, in response to the creature in her gut—fire burst from beneath Eira's fingertips. It struck a spot in the hedge over Meilin's shoulder.

Eira recoiled, withdrawing her outstretched hand. Meilin's eyes widened.

"I'm *sorry*," she moaned, wanting the ground to open at her feet and swallow her whole. Eira cradled the offending hand close to her chest. Her fingers twitched of their own accord. "I don't know what's happening, but I don't have much control over . . . this at the moment." *This* being the hand she hid away.

Meilin scoffed, biting out a response. "I gathered as much."

But despite the air of annoyance, she stepped back. There was no fear in her gaze yet, somehow, the apprehension made Eira feel so much worse.

"Meilin"—the other flinched at the sound of her name falling from Eira's lips—"you know that I would never purposefully hurt you, right?"

Eira meant it, despite it sounding like a lie. She *had* hurt Meilin. When she deceived her in Erebus, Eira was hurting her.

This was different.

Meilin didn't answer. They stood there for a moment, quiet passing between them whilst the other noises of the maze got louder.

Closer.

Eira's eyes were drawn to the wound at Meilin's stomach. Mixed in with the gold was a moss-colored, viscous liquid. It oozed faster than the blood, pooling underneath her slowly retreating footfall. As quickly as she'd noticed it, the sap-like secretion covered her hands. Seeped from her fingers.

The grass beneath Meilin promptly wilted and died in the spots where the sap landed.

Neither of them acknowledged it.

Truthfully, Eira couldn't care less. It would be something for another time, though the horror that settled onto Meilin's face told Eira that she wasn't so ready to let it go.

Eira took half a step towards her. "Meilin, *please*—"

Meilin looked to the sap oozing from her body and then to Eira. Then, she turned on her heel and ran, moving so fast back into the thick of the maze that she was out of sight before Eira could convince her otherwise.

The fae cursed, biting down on her lip hard enough to draw blood.

Her fingers twitched uncontrollably as she started to run, unsure about the possibility of finding Meilin and even more unsettled by the idea of staying stagnant inside the maze. If only Eira wielded better control over her own power, she might just resort to burning the whole thing down. She would carve out her own path.

That wasn't an option, so Eira continued to run.

She didn't stop when she passed bodies on the ground, unable to bear the idea of having to check their pulses, of having to acknowledge that other heiresses did that. She didn't stop when snippets of heated exchanges, or fearful pleas, filled her ears. Eira wound through elongated paths, turned corners and often was faced with ends that led to nowhere.

All the same, she kept running.

Eira stayed moving until the shape of the maze was imprinted behind her eyelids and her feet ached.

"Whilst you have all failed in finding the answers you sought out in this maze, there have definitely been some worthwhile discoveries made along the way, no?"

Durante's words drew her out of the stupor she'd slumped into. A short break turned into Eira crawling into a corner and collapsing in on herself.

She ran and ran and ran—and, in the end, it amounted to nothing.

"The girl carved from ice who burns beyond her own control. The flower who roots itself in rot. The storm that can't withstand the sound of its strikes. The stream that taints those who drink from its waters. The giver of life who maims the ones she should protect. The forger who can't wield their own creation. The breeze that steals air from others. The star that leaves destruction in its wake. The fire that ceases to burn in times of need."

The laughter was loud, and never-ending, in Eira's head. She pressed the palms of her hands against her ears, driven to agony by the intensity of it. Even that effort couldn't keep the sound of Durante's voice from wiggling into her mind.

"Prove yourself worthy to me, and I will shape your flaws into your most treasured qualities. Here, you will be revered for them, instead of hidden away."

He took in a deep breath.

"In Unseelie, you will *thrive*."

CHAPTER 23
ORGÉ

Her screams never stopped.

In the altar room—the first part of Unseelie that The New Reign had truly been introduced to—the remaining heiresses were each chained to pillars. They faced the stone slab positioned in the center of everything.

There were seven of them that Eira could count; two chained on each pillar and Meilin splayed across the slab.

The New Reign was being made to watch as she was operated on.

Eira couldn't tell if she was given anything to numb the pain or to drive her away from the edge of full consciousness, but by the way she writhed, eyes blown wide open, it was more likely wishful thinking than their reality.

After all, this was where they'd awoken.

The maze left marks on them all, but Meilin was the one who suffered the most—first, inside of it, and now on the outside, too. The maze also took with it another heiress. From the information Eira was able to gather in the time she took to seek distractions from the searing rage that Meilin's cries of anguish caused, she noted that both Haneul and Enyo were missing.

Eira had, unknowingly, murmured the thoughts aloud.

"Not missing," Tufani hissed, her voice a low, hate-filled whisper, "*dead*."

But they couldn't be.

Surely.

Hope was not something to be held in that room. On that podium, where The New Reign, minus some, was forced to watch three looming figures make a show of sewing Meilin back together.

Except, they weren't helping her.

They began by collecting the sap that dripped from her fingers. At first, Meilin seemed unconscious whilst it was happening. Her hands hung limp on either side of the slab she was displayed atop. She was held in place by the same iron chains that kept the heiresses against the pillars, except they were strapped at her chest and hips, just below the open gash.

The searing from the chains hadn't yet pushed through the fabric of her tattered romper—it was when they started to target the wound itself to draw out the sap that she began to scream.

With weapons too small to see, wielded too fast for Eira's eyes to follow, the trio took turns. They sliced and pushed at the skin around the large laceration.

Every movement made it weep more.

Meilin screamed and screamed. Nearby, she heard the sobs of some other heiresses.

Closest to her, Tufani struggled to keep from retching.

Inside of Eira, the creature stirred. It fed on the unstable, depleted energy of her magic. It harnessed the rage that grew larger and larger with every slice and every stab. When Eira pushed against the chains at her chest and the sting of it searing her skin made tears slip down her face, her fury only grew.

When, at some point, Meilin could no longer cry out because of the sheer energy she'd expended in doing so, that fury doubled.

It grew to be something sizable. Bigger than the creature that lived inside of her.

Eira held it close, and refused to let her eyes stray again from Meilin's face.

She would memorize the agony the fae felt. She would commit it to memory.

Because, for once in Eira's life, her misery and the rage that accompanied it would serve her well.

It had to.

Otherwise, what hope did she have?

Eira dreamt of red and gold.

Her hands, covered in cuts and stained the color of a deep wine, continued to reach for more glass despite the pain that radiated through her body. She watched it crumble between her fingers. Relished in it breaking in the palm of her hand.

Eira felt as though her body belonged to that of another, and yet, her rage was entirely her own—it was *her*.

Perhaps Eira was nothing more than the entity that housed it.

The foundations had caved in; the shelter she once used to keep that anger at bay was long dismantled, and all that was left was her ruined resolve and the bitterness that ran alongside the spilt wine on the ground, together as one in a ruinous river.

CHAPTER 24
AKEDÍA

Eira knew her body was moving.

She knew it and had no idea why—or how—it was doing so.

It lacked the nutrients, and rest, it needed. The fae dipped in and out of sleep, plagued by the horrors of what came to her when she closed her eyes and what happened in front of her when they were opened.

Luxurious fabric that fit like a sickly second skin made artful waves of motion with every step Eira took. Her feet followed the beat of a choreographed routine that she'd never learned, but her muscles took the lead and marked out her path across the ballroom, which slowly came into focus.

Low groans filled her ears, sounding out of place with the music that progressively got louder in volume.

She didn't register that they echoed from her own chest until there was a resounding chorus which responded in kind.

Through her still-adjusting vision, Eira saw her fellow heiresses move around her in a haunting performance. They were placed at all different points in the ballroom, but dressed in gowns of a similar brilliance, stark against the sea of Unseelie fae who adorned themselves in ink-black and crimson finery.

Eira concluded, with a dull sort of panic, that they were being strung and paraded around like puppets. Again, she lacked control over the limbs that betrayed her. Her lips refused to form the shape of the words she wished so badly to spit at the feet of the cursed king.

The setting was too similar to the chaos of the ballroom in Erebus—if she would even dare to picture the place as a separate world to that of Unseelie, by this point—and it made her skin crawl. The memories of trauma that weighed heavy on her in every moment of this existence felt both fresh and entirely ancient. It armed her with the reminder of why she was so angry in the first place, but it also made her recoil in her weaker moments.

Eira felt her eyes water.

There was no sensation in her face, so she had no way of knowing if the tears were shed.

Laughter echoed around her.

The citizens of Unseelie reveled in the heiresses' slack jawed expressions, their hushed mumbles of consciousness the only sign that they were aware of what was being done to them.

Eira wanted to see Meilin.

She didn't want to think about the number of heiresses she counted in between dizzying twirls.

Six.

"Be kind to the heiresses," Durante bellowed, the words followed by snickers and jeers from the Unseelie fae who circled closest to The New Reign. "They may be dancers tonight, but soon, one of them will be up on this dais. One of them will take her rightful place—ruling by my side."

CHAPTER 25
KENODOXÍA

She thrashed as much as she could.

An unknown tightness bound Eira to the spot.

Around her was the visual onslaught of unfamiliar equipment of varying shades.

Muted whites and dull silvers. Discarded syringes. Balls of cotton soaked that looked like they'd been dipped in gold. Instead of silver chains or bindings, Eira was held down to the stiff surface beneath her back with thick straps, fashioned from what appeared to be cuts of leather around her neck. Her wrists and ankles were bound, her was splayed crudely, each arm and leg making the point of a star.

Echoes of past injuries, hidden under a long-sleeved robe of the same drab white hue, thrummed with a newfound vigor under her skin.

The entire setting smelt of nefarious hands—of the malicious touch of a king and his aim to make The New Reign hurt, in every sense possible.

Eira nursed the sense that she'd been pricked, poked, and prodded relentlessly—for how long, she had no idea; nevertheless, something was stolen. Chunks of her, here and there, that felt wrong. Hollowed out.

Worse than the stripping of her magic.

The pain was a staggering, consuming thing, and though she hadn't the capacity to truly determine the damage done, her bones *knew*. Her body knew.

A constricted sob ripped from her chest.

There was no sensation in her fingers or her toes; the heiress could barely make sense of the tongue that was a swollen weight in her dry mouth.

She thought of Isolde.

Of the familiar landscape and of her father's face. Of her mother's watchful gaze. Of the reflection she despised in the mirror.

It may have been an effort on her mind's behalf—trying desperately to salvage whatever sense she may have left with images of her home; of the family she'd have to survive in order to see again, and to prove wrong—but it did little to soothe Eira.

Along with the nostalgic imagery came snippets of Meilin.

A newfound surge of despair ripped through her at the thought of the heiress, whom when she'd last seen her, was caught in an eerily similar setting.

"*She's awake!*"

The sudden exclamation filled the void of space in the room. The words, both sharp and loud, were an agonizing stab directly into her thoughts. Muddled whispers filled the air, the rest of their interactions spoken in an unfamiliar tongue. Eira grappled at past knowledge, unable to fully piece sentences together despite recognizing the first statement.

Moments later, faceless figures loomed over her. They brought a flame directly in front of her eyes, as close as they could get without searing off skin or hair. The room was dim beforehand, only allowing enough for her vision to capture the things closest to her.

The intensity of the flame left a vivid imprint on her eyelids when she squeezed her eyes shut.

Eira wailed in pain.

A new, acute pain in her neck made the noise capture in her throat.

"That should shut you up." The hissed words were clear. Clarity was a shard of glass in her brain.

"It's time to burn your world to the ground."

PART III
THE SEVENTH SIN

CHAPTER 26
HUPEREPHANÍA

Alfie wouldn't meet her eyes.

Finally, after a drawn-out silence, he whispered, "I tried."

Like that was enough of an explanation—like that made up for everything.

Eira recoiled. "Not hard enough."

He whipped around, face drawn into a tight scowl. "You know that's not fair!"

She scoffed. "Don't talk to me about fairness."

Anger made his cheeks flush. "You came to *me*. You walked into that tavern, so in need of recognition—aching for normalcy, for a routine—that you *reeked* of desperation. I couldn't have turned you away, in that version of reality or another. You never gave me the choice. Our paths were always going to be intertwined, and I was never meant to save you."

His eyes clouded, rage stifled by sadness. "Neither was he," Alfie concluded.

Eira's companion, shrouded by darkness and held close by the light she cherished so dearly. Woven together in a tapestry she'd never truly been a part of, until she was. Until she forced herself into their world.

Alfie crossed the space between them. A veil, thin and flimsy, kept them apart. But he pushed past it, hands coming out from underneath it to grab hers. His fingers were cold as they laced through hers.

"Burn, Eira. It is not a flaw, to burn. Be bright. Be brave. Stop being your own worst enemy. Once you accept yourself, *all* of you, you will understand."

Eira grit her teeth. She didn't want to let go of his grip. She didn't want him to fade into non-existence—this was how she wanted to remember him.

"I can't control it," she said, pathetically. "I'm going to keep hurting others. Hurting myself."

Alfie tutted his disapproval. "It is not the intensity of the flame, but whom you burn it for, that matters."

Eira didn't know what that meant—if her own flame refused to burn right for her, how could it burn right for anyone else? All the fire inside her knew was destruction. It was not a soft, kind thing. It did not care for anyone.

Especially not for her.

"She does not burn for me the way I burn for her," Eira concluded simply.

Alfie offered her a knowing smile as his parting wisdom.

Again, she was alone.

Meilin's gaze was heavy.

"I never asked for you to rescue me," she said, simply. A fact she expected Eira to know, understand, and accept.

Eira felt her lip quiver.

She shook her head as Meilin continued to speak, her tone disdainful. "I didn't *have* to be saved."

Eira knew as much.

Of course.

She never designated the role of helpless heiress to Meilin when the fae was anything but. Even when Eira first saw her, trapped in the claws of Durante, she was not helpless. She suffered at the hands of others, as all of them did.

But she was never helpless.

Eira didn't intend to save Meilin. Not in the traditional sense—not in the way that made it as if Meilin never had the autonomy to choose.

But was it so wrong to care for her? To *want* to protect her?

Meilin was someone Eira wanted to be brave for.

"It was *me* who made the decision to leave the night I learned of your betrayal." The mask. A flash of fabric. Meilin's words struck hard. "I chose to trust you, despite that. I chose to fight with you in that ballroom. I choose, now, to face you, even though I have no obligation to do so—because Deities knows, you've lied to me. About so much. About everything, most likely."

Eira shook her head harder. "Not everything," she whispered.

Meilin didn't care for it. "It doesn't matter. I don't know why I've been cursed to care for you, and if I could stop, I would. But you, *you* need to learn how to save yourself before you try to stick out your neck to save others. You only end up hurting them when you do so."

It felt like Meilin was both teaching her a lesson and saying goodbye; preparing Eira for the lifetime to come and assuring her that whoever else chose to stick around may not be as patient as her.

Her voice softened but the words still winded Eira. "Trust in what I'm doing because I'm the only one who can do it—and know that I have made this choice for me."

This is all wrong.

No, Eira didn't have to rescue her. But did that mean Meilin had to go?

"Are you saving yourself?" Eira asked, suddenly. "Or are you saving us?"

The New Reign. The fae that Meilin seemed to deem unable to harbor enough darkness to qualify for what she was stepping up to do, despite the fact that none of the group had truly given one another the reason to believe that. To believe in goodness.

After a moment of contemplation, Meilin smiled. "Does it really matter? I've made my choice."

Eira's world caught fire.

CHAPTER 27
A FEAR OF FALLING APART

As it turned out, there was more of Unseelie to be discovered.

However, the last of the spaces that The New Reign were brought to was the throne room. This final time, Eira counted only four of them.

In the end it was not only Haneul and Enyo that were lost—Tufani, Sila and Etsumi were the missing figures present in the gathering of those who remained.

Eira, positioned in the middle of Silvia and Akela, sat facing Meilin.

She couldn't even spare herself a moment to grieve what may have become of her fellow heiresses.

They weren't being dismissed from Durante's trials just yet.

Eira braced herself for what may come next, already unnerved by the sight of Meilin perched atop one of two thrones before them.

She was every bit the queen her title would allow her to grow into. Now wasn't her time, and yet, Meilin was adorned with a crown. The beautiful dress of moonlight silk she wore didn't change the wrongness of the timing.

Her expression was stony.

Akela and Silvia remained silent.

Durante appeared soon after they all came to, something like pride lining his face.

"Why are we here?"

Silvia was, unsurprisingly, the first to speak. She hadn't given the king the opportunity to begin whatever spiel was oncoming. She, like the rest of them, was tired; and if Durante wanted them dead, surely, he would've made it happen by now.

He didn't waste a moment. "Witnesses are key, of course! If the bonds between the Unseelie and Seelie courts are to continue growing, I need there to be testimonials passed on of what has happened here—of Meilin's assistance to crown, the merging of our kinds. I never planned to get rid of you all. One testimonial is not credible, two can be misconstrued, but surely three will be enough to convince them of the . . . severity of the situation at hand."

Akela choked out a laugh. "You think that The Seelie Court —that *any* of our families—will want anything to do with you?"

"They will not have a choice. They will have their beloved daughters back. You will be alive. You will be safe—and with the combined power of a tie to The New Reign now residing in Unseelie, a relationship between the two will be undeniable. My efforts *will* be acknowledged."

Meilin remained tightlipped. Eira saw the tense line of her jaw, though.

She wouldn't allow herself to be scared of him. Eira wouldn't grant him the power of intimidation.

She should pity him—for he, surely, would be brought to ruin by Meilin, whether he saw it coming or not.

"This is what my ancestors planned for, with their prophecies whispering of the child who was the key to resurrecting our court." Durante shrugged. "I just had to play my part in making that happen."

His part?

"No," Eira murmured. Everyone in the room understood the implication.

"Surely you know what your own daughter looks like," Silvia spat.

He waved off her disbelief. "You should understand as well as I do that the fae form is malleable, to a certain degree. Meilin's mother looked entirely different when I met her—as did I. I take the form of what serves me best at any given moment."

"Why put your child through such an ordeal *knowing* she would experience the same as the rest of us?" The words were bitter as they rolled off Eira's tongue.

"I had to ensure she was fit for the position, didn't I? Why spare her?" Durante looked dumbfounded—shocked that they couldn't grasp his reasoning. "If her performance hadn't been satisfactory enough, I would've had to compensate with another on the throne."

Eira reeled back. "Does blood mean nothing to you?"

"Oh, blood is *everything*. But familial obligation? That, dear heiresses, is dependent on usefulness." He turned to Meilin. "Don't take this to heart, daughter. You have proven yourself plenty useful."

Meilin looked mortified.

Daughter.

The mask she wore for the entirety of the interaction chipped, bits breaking off before their eyes. "Can you not fathom the pain you've caused to those mothers and fathers who truly care for their daughters?" she cried, outraged, despite the stiffness of her body. "The children you *stole* from them in exchange for finding one who doesn't even want you in her life—who resents you for claiming a role you could never truly fulfill. I stepped up because you called on me, because it would see some of them spared, but *you will never be my father.*"

Durante turned on her.

"You use such bold words for a girl who is just as much the coward as she claims me to be."

Meilin's eyes narrowed. "I'm nothing like you."

"You're right—you're something much worse—which is precisely why you sit on that throne." Still facing away from the other heiresses, the king spread his arms to the side.

"Give me back my powers and we'll see how true that is."

"I will give you your powers back if you can prove yourself able to behave." Durante was a few steps away from her now, close enough to lean towards her, to be level. Meilin didn't break the direction of her burning gaze. "Your mother didn't hide you from others to protect *you*—she did it to protect them—the same as every family of The New Reign did. You're a broken lot, but that is what Unseelie deals in, which is why *you will* thrive here."

A conversation Eira overheard her own mother having with her father, so many years ago, came to mind. At the time, she didn't understand the weight behind the meaning of their exchange—of fae and mortals laying with one another, of creating children that shouldn't exist.

"*I think it is a matter of pride rather than predisposition,*" he said. "*Maybe our kind believes that we're superior to mortals but not for the fact that they're objectively lesser.*"

Her mother's face soured. "*You're speaking of sacrilege.*"

"*But am I not right?*" Eira's father was the only man who could push her like that. Who could question her without repercussion. "*We don't trust the power amongst ourselves, let alone by mixing it with mortals; mortals who forge weapons of iron and can be cruel and calculating. Perhaps it is forbidden because a fae and a mortal may just be the worst of both kinds."*

Then, without warning, Eira was somewhere else.

The walls around them were touched by many years of love.

Eira could see it in the carpeted floor, dented in spots where furniture had nestled into it, unmoved. Slowly chipping away paint was hidden behind ornate frames that captured the red-cheeked, smiling faces of a family frozen in time. Eira had the sudden, overwhelming, inclination to reach out and run her fingers over the delicate paint strokes. They looked so *real*. Each of the frames swallowing the walls on either side of her held paintings of varied shapes and sized, all skillfully done and exquisitely detailed.

When she did relent to the part of herself that wanted to observe them at a closer distance, Eira was shocked to find that she recognized the face, who was the featured subject of more than half of them.

Meilin.

Even all those years younger, she was unmistakable.

Eira heard the whispers of footfall; children running through the hallways and screeches of laughter; hands delicately mounting a frame to the wall; curtains being drawn with an uncharacteristic harshness, never to be opened again; floorboards that creaked, though no one walked over them; a house that shuddered awake when its rooms became empty.

So much sorrow.

She ached with it. She wanted to fall to her knees to plead for them to return—the family she never knew, the bodies that roamed her halls and warmed her rooms, the ones that gave her life. The grief roared so large and relentless inside of her that it felt like it was trying to consume her.

Eira was the bodies that were missing. Eira was the home that ached.

She was all of it at once and she was screaming before she was ripped away—and she came to with her hands atop her head, nails dug into her scalp. Her throat ached, and she only realized *she* had been screaming when the white noise in her mind was silenced.

"*Stop*," Meilin choked the word out, her eyes wet, "*please*."

The heiresses around her, locked in the same fetal position as Eira, must have been screaming, too. Akela and Silvia slowly closed their agape mouths, terror and confusion and understanding meshing together to make horrible masks of emotion.

"Don't be so dramatic," Durante huffed, a small smile playing on his face. The king watched them, having turned from his daughter to the heiresses at some point during the ordeal. He did not appear spent—not drained from the power it should've taken from him to force the rest of them into such a vivid vision.

Someone new stood on the other of the empty throne beside Meilin, too.

Queen Azelie.

The similarities were stark. But where Meilin's hair was long, her mother's was cut off at her jawline. She was tall, and even so, the emerald dress she wore swept along the floor.

She stood, back stiffened by the sort of composure that betrayed the situation at hand.

Did she play a part in what Durante did to them?

Meilin hadn't realized her mother was present. A mixture of surprise and betrayal made her face fall as the queen came into view.

The tears that continued to well in her eyes slipped free.

When Queen Azelie stepped forward to put herself between the king and her daughter, Durante's arm jutted out. She stopped.

Something in the queen's jaw ticked.

A bead of sweat gathered and dripped down Eira's brow. It stung as she blinked and blurred her vision, just for a moment. She wanted to tell Meilin how she felt. She was sorry. She was hurt. She didn't want to grieve feelings that never had the chance to bloom.

How could she mourn something that had never been?

Was this all they would leave each other with?

It was unfair. It was selfish. It was brave. Stupidly courageous.

Stupid, stupid, stupid.

"I will personally ensure that you live to regret the day you stained existence." Eira had to swallow the taste of copper around the words. "I will find you. You are not untouchable. If you are what you claim to be, then you are mortal and you *are* expendable."

"Meilin herself is partly me. Don't forget that." The king cocked an eyebrow. "You kill the king, and the princess takes the throne. Would you like to see her crowned as the Queen of The Unseelie Court?"

He wasted no time in dismissing Meilin's mother from the equation.

Was she really so expendable?

Meilin's eyes met Eira's, the plea in them silent but relentless. An echo of her words passed between them.

I never asked for you to rescue me.

Screw pride. As darkness edged into the corners of her vision, Eira grit her teeth, resolute. "I will bring fire to the door of your court before I see her sit on that throne."

Durante seemed pleased with her threat. His smile was razor-sharp.

"Let's see just how good your word is, Eira Isolde. I despise those who can't keep their promises."

CHAPTER 28

THE CHANCES WE GET, THE CHOICES WE DON'T

A young heiress was once made to believe that those who shone the brightest were the fastest, and the first, to fizzle out.

The idea had been so deeply ingrained in her that she trusted the notion wholeheartedly; that people who burned would, undoubtedly, be left as more ember than full being. The more that the fire consumed meant the less of whoever hosted the flames would remain.

Maybe Eira had been sputtering closer and closer to annihilation with each day of her existence.

But she loved to burn.

Truly, she could swallow the sun and still have the might to dance as the rays burst from her pores, her insides catching alight whilst she hopped and screamed in glee and wretched agony.

"Your magic doesn't make you special," Durante would seethe, *"it makes you broken. It burns, and burns, and burns. It will destroy everything you love before it takes you, too."*

Eira could only picture Meilin to be the sun she took a bite of to swallow, to keep that little bit of brightness to herself— selfishly so.

She was paying the price, for the sun belonged to no one and nothing but the sky—and it had been foolish of Eira to try and snatch that part for her own safekeeping.

Durante was right.

She burned and burned and burned.

Light and beauty and pain became one. They intertwined, merging and morphing, until Eira was unable to differentiate what made the emotions so different from one another.

At the center of the fire she lay, crumpled.

Even then, Eira didn't feel as though she would be best described as an ember.

She was still alight in full, glorious capacity, even if her body could no longer support the weight of the burn. Even if her bones became liquid and her muscles emulsified, Eira would claim the fire as her own.

The heiress wasn't a spitting ember. She wasn't the remnants of a once-great fire.

She *was* the flame that consumed her.

They were one.

Thus, Eira didn't mind the pain. It was a reminder that she was alive.

For as long as she burned, Eira was alive. And for as long as Eira was alive, her fire would remain alight.

Every part of her would crackle and burn and spit and sing like it did now.

Her skin was ablaze. The smell of it seared her nose and stung her throat. She had never smelled anything like it. Such an aroma should have made her gag, scream, cry.

But Eira, swallowed by the flames that danced inside her flesh with delightful ferocity, was silent.

For life—in all its grotesque complexities—was at its core a beautiful, blazing fire.

And Eira had never felt more alive.

CHAPTER 29
A SACRIFICE WORTHY OF A QUEEN

Eira's eyelids felt too heavy to pry open.

Her mind, slow to awaken from the remnants of a deep but dissatisfying sleep, pounded with a vengeance as they did so. She blinked a few times, groaning unintelligibly whilst the world around her shifted from congealed colors and shapes into something more like a landscape.

But she didn't like what she saw when that happened.

Eira hauled herself up from the moss-covered ground with a newfound fluidity; the sight of stiff-bodied heiresses' laying scattered around her was enough to warrant the sudden burst of energy.

The fae took hesitant steps towards the figures, a flurry of emotions making her throat seize up—namely present was a terror so visceral that Eira worried she'd choke on its intensity. As she got closer, she saw that their limbs marked indents in the soft earth, a sign that they must've laid for a long while prior to her having woken up.

She almost lost her footing in an attempt to kneel beside the closest heiress, realizing that she should be moving much quicker to see whether there was an active pulse thumping beneath their skin.

The soft, almost imperceptible sound of shuffled fabric and the disjointed murmuring that followed made Eira pause. At first, it came from Etsumi—the heiress she knelt by—but suddenly, there was a ripple in motion that travelled outwards.

One by one, The New Reign rose around her.

Eira fell back onto her feet, fumbling into something like a sitting position as, around her, fellow heiresses pushed themselves off the ground with unsteady arms, their faces adorned with varying stages of confusion and hurt.

But they were alive.

They're alive.

The words itched to be released from Eira's chapped lips, though all she could muster was the broken lilt of a relieved laugh.

They were alive, but the remnants of what nearly killed them sat as stark reminders atop their bodies. They all bore wounds that were frozen in time. Raw, infected skin that circled their wrists and ankles. Not-quite faded bruises that seemed to cover most of the skin left on display in the slip-gowns they'd been abandoned in. Some of the heiresses wept golden blood from unhealed, and poorly tended-to, lacerations.

Eira, herself, was tender all over.

Though something else was present underneath her skin, too.

A feeling that had long grown unfamiliar.

She was so overwhelmed by the sight of her fellow heiresses that she couldn't truly process the way her own body felt outside of the pain.

The full extent of her magic swept its way through her, as natural as the flow of blood in her veins. Her life source—as strong as it had ever been.

Stronger.

Simultaneously, the other heiresses cried out. A new pressure pressed itself behind Eira's eyelids, and all at once, The New Reign's vision was eclipsed by a shared vision. Images played out from a bird's-eye perspective before her.

Lifeless bodies appeared in the forest that guarded the palace's entrance, found in the formation of a circle.

Someone's mouth ajar after having found them. A silent scream for help.

Pools of golden liquid and moving hands that shook. Fabric floating. Whispered words over closed eyes and open books. Tears. Broken sentences and words that echoed, deafeningly loud.

"Pulses—"

"Haneul's magic—"

"Decoys—"

"My child—"

"Give the ichor time to—"

"The risk—"

One calm voice that cut through it all.

"If they are The New Reign, they will rise."

Then,

"Give them time."

Eira's mind was thrown so suddenly back into reality that she bit down on her tongue, drawing blood.

But there was something else—someone else—that was the missing piece to the puzzle that came together before her eyes as others sobbed and shouted and shook silently around her.

Meilin.

Her name was a strike to the chest. With it came the memories that weren't present when she'd first come to consciousness.

The king's speech. The throne room. The way Meilin looked at her before they were torn apart.

She couldn't rejoice in the full extent of her freedom because the one who deserved to be free was not there with her. Eira could've lived a thousand lives, and she would've never been able to rid herself of the name that got caught on the tip of her tongue.

Meilin wasn't with them because she was stuck in Unseelie.

Which meant The New Reign was somewhere else entirely.

A beat of time passed before the scenery surrounding them melted, giving way to the likes of a grand hall. Eira swallowed bile at the likeness of the occurrence to what happened to them at the hands of Durante.

The forest floor was quickly replaced with marble, cool underneath their skin.

They were *undoubtedly* in The Seelie Court, but in a place that Eira didn't recognize. Gilded walls and an ornate ceiling were all crafted to match the magnificence of a large throne, positioned close enough in the distance that the body sat in it was noticeable, but not so close that they could reach out and touch them.

Despite this being Eira's first time in her domain, she knew the face of the Seelie Queen. She was every part the divine being captured in ornate portraits, hung in various spots of Eira's own home. The same face she'd stop to admire as a young, awe-filled child.

Despite the somberness that soured her fair features, the still Seelie Queen was truly picture perfect. Her figure was composed, hands resting atop the silken fabric that pooled in her lap. Her perfectly structured hair and delicately painted face was a stark contrast to her eyes, which Eira could see the hardened reflection of from even the distance she was at.

"Welcome home," the Seelie Queen said, though her tone was entirely neutral—her expression unmoving. Cold.

It wasn't the reception any of them seemed to expect. Eira

cast a brief glance at her fellow heiresses, who looked to be as astonished—and confused—as she was.

"Your bodies are adjusting to insurmountable change," she continued calmly, not fazed by the state of shock that The New Reign was frozen in, "so I would suggest that you do your best to remain calm whilst I explain what is going on."

Everyone held their breath.

Eira's body was on fire.

"When the eight of you arrived, precautions were taken to ensure that you were . . . what you appeared to be." The words were heavy in the air, the implication even weightier. *Eight.* "As we have come to understand the nature of the power that King Durante wielded, there was hesitation in the hearts of some of our court."

Manipulation.

Some of the fae in Seelie thought that replicas of The New Reign were dumped at their gates in place of the real thing. How they came to an understanding of Durante's power was a whole other mystery.

Who told them?

"As such, an agreement was made amongst the ruling families for your bodies to partake in the Rite."

Eira already knew it. The feeling in her bones was enough of a sign, though to hear the confession fall from the queen's lips made the truth all the more terrible.

Again, a choice was taken from them.

Durante did the same thing in stripping them of their will and their magic; in giving himself the power to make decisions on their behalf, to control every aspect of their beings.

The Rite was something special. An honor. A celebration of life and resilience, a way to mark the steps forward into the rest of their eternal lives. It was the truest way to tether themselves to The Higher Courts, to have The Deities acknowledge and accept them. It was a rite of passage.

But they were cheated of that.

Instead, it was a necessity, performed out of fear. Eira could only presume that they would be expected to be grateful, too. To be thankful for the quick-thinking that most likely saved their lives.

Yet, if their bodies hadn't adjusted to the ceremony in their state of unconsciousness, what would've happened?

Their silence was sign enough for the queen to continue.

"I ask that you do your best to remain in a calm state simply because we can't be sure how your bodies, and minds, will continue to change whilst they settle back into being home. The extent of your suffering is not yet known to us. This will be something we discuss after you have rested. But, in any case, the stress and hurt that has been inflicted upon you has unknown impacts on the way you will adjust—so, firstly, I would implore you to be mindful of this."

Eira fought to suppress her laughter. It sprung up inside of her so suddenly that her head began to spin.

In quite possibly the least empathetic way possible, the Seelie Queen was imploring them to *remain calm*—despite the fact that they'd been both overwhelmed with information, and change, in an unperceivable amount of time; and still, were yet to see their families.

To see Meilin.

It was a joke, at best, though not at all a humorous one.

The Queen lifted her hands in the air. "As for the parties in collaboration that I've been referring to . . ."

On either side of the small pocket of space they were clustered in, the air seemed to thicken. An imperceivable wall formed, only visible once it began to shimmer, blinking in and out of existence as Eira registered that it was there to begin with.

On the other side of it, all around them, was a sea of people. The ruling families—*their* families.

Some fae had their hands pressed up against the transparent shield, mouths open in silent sobs, eyes wide and red-rimmed. Groups appeared to be clustered together according to their courts, enough space between them that Eira could determine who was who.

She'd never seen so many different fae in the same spot—it felt like a momentous moment in history, for an array of reasons both dire and delightful, irrespective of the gaps that separated them.

She only counted eight courts present. Amongst them was her own.

Surrounded by trusted courtiers, and heavily armed guards, Eira found her parents. Nestled into the center of their party, they nursed wounded expressions and each other, almost as if their hold on one another was the only thing giving them the strength to remain upright.

In that moment, Eira truly was a child once more. A strong-willed, young fae, with not enough knowledge to fear the world around her, who thought her parents were the be all and end all of her existence. In the same breath, she both feared what they had to say and also despised them for taking away her right to choose, time and time again—for making her play the part of a pawn in a game she didn't ask to be born into.

Tears slid down the cheeks of her parents' faces. The unbreakable queen of ice and the king who did his best to shape the daughter she detested.

Eira had always felt like a cursed child, and so it was impossible for her to know if they were crying for her, or *because* of her.

She wrenched her gaze away from them, turning her focus back to the queen. None of the other heiresses scrambled to the wall to get a closer look at their families. The shock, and pain, still looked to be overpowering everything else, including their ability to properly register everything playing out before them.

"I do not doubt that every fae present in this room has an array of questions that outweigh the relief you must feel at seeing one another." The Seelie Queen's eyes softened, just the slightest, as she spoke—now more obviously addressing the room at large in favor of pretending that she was just talking to the heiresses and them alone. "I, too, have many questions of my own for The New Reign, which is why your reunion will be kept at a distance, for now, as there is one more pressing matter to address."

If their families were speaking on the other side of the shield, Eira couldn't hear them. Even the murmurs of the fae around her quieted as a panic, all-consuming and unrelenting, welled up inside of her.

"Both the Court of Azelie and Kingdom of Erebus are currently unlocatable. It would appear that they have, as one, ceased to exist. In their place, The Unseelie Court has risen."

Eira didn't know what came after that.

The Seelie Queen continued talking, voice clear and commanding, despite the chaos that erupted on the other side of the shield. Muted shouting and enraged expressions gave Eira enough context—their families hadn't known of this. They, too, were given a partially painted picture, most likely urged to show up in person to receive the full extent of the bad news.

"Until we know more—"

"—the best interest for everyone's safety—"

"They will be in my care—"

Splinters of the queen's words pierced through the haze of Eira's mind.

It wasn't as if the Seelie Queen truly cared about the heiresses being reunited with their families. She needed the means for them all to gather without going for each other's throat—and the common denominator in achieving that outcome was The New Reign; so how fortunate it must've been that their bodies arrived just in time to have a reason to share the message.

Eira met the eyes of every one of the heiresses around her, one after the other. Silently, they acknowledged their missing link.

Silently, they swore to remember this.

To remember this betrayal, to remember what was done to them. To take healing into their own hands, both of themselves and the relationships formed between them, for better or for worse.

To remember that they wouldn't rest until all of them were home.

It was a strange thing, to be bonded to the fae she was taught to hate. To the heiresses she was made to hurt and to hunt in order to survive. None of it made sense, and yet, understanding resonated amongst them like something tangible. Something they could hold in their hands, and close to their chest, to keep them going.

So, when the queen's guards crossed the shield that kept The New Reign separate from their families and lifted each heiress to their feet, Eira didn't surrender to dread or panic.

She held that hope—that understanding—close. She didn't meet the eyes of her family, who watched her be led off in a separate direction to the other fae, who were all hauled different ways. They weren't chained, but they were being held all the same.

Captured, again.

The tethers of their unlikely bond being tested once more.

It was then that Eira made a separate promise to herself.

If Meilin worked to whittle down the rotten core of The Unseelie Court from the inside, then Eira would play her part from the outside.

She would find a way in.

No matter how far away Meilin was—nor how The Fates worked to keep them apart—Eira swore that she would find Unseelie, face Durante and ensure that the court was banished back to the realm of nonexistence, as it should've always remained.

Eira *would* find Meilin.

No matter the cost.

THE END.

EPILOGUE

"That is what happened," Eira concluded, resolute. "That is my story."

Her throat burned. Her tongue, as heavy as rocks, finally stilled in her mouth, finding respite from what felt like hours and hours of talking. Her eyes clouded with a freshly unshed round of tears, despite her being unable to wipe the wetness already dampening her cheeks.

Her ribcage was cracked open. Bones broken on either side, the slow beat of her now steadying heartbeat was on display for all to see.

A most brutal display of torture.

That's what it felt like to speak of all that happened to her in Erebus, in Celimene. At the hands of Durante and in the arms of Meilin. All of it, not sparing a single detail, despite wanting so badly to be able to.

Eira didn't know how long she'd sat there, the innermost kempt details of the past few years, months, weeks and days moments spilling forth.

She didn't know if the other heiresses were being subjected to the same grueling experience.

She felt empty by the end of it. Deflated. Speaking aloud about all that occurred somehow meant that those memories—both good and bad—were no longer hers to keep.

"Thank you for speaking your truth," a clear, almost sterile, voice echoed in her mind. Eira had no choice in saying anything *but* the truth. They would've pried it from her mind either way.

It was the truth. Her truth.

All of it.

Every ugly detail and every blissful moment in time; every agonizingly, intimate second of what was once hers and hers only.

That was Eira's price to pay.

Whether or not they believed her would be another thing entirely.

It felt wrong to let beauty grow here.

To not only let it grow but encourage it to do so.

To prepare, plant and tend to the roots that had now begun to infiltrate between the cracks.

To purposefully incite the jagged edges, the unpreened spores— to not cut them away but call them forth, to request that they swallow everything whole. The roots that, against all odds, clawed their way above the surface, unwilling to wither against the boots that hovered above them, as unwanted things usually did.

As they expected unwanted things to do.

Eira was never one for gardening, but a fae sprouting quick-witted remarks and a dash of plentiful freckles across her nose changed that. Eira was never one for gardening, but she found herself eager to dig her own grave in this case. She was propagating the soil without even realizing, as if in preparation for the ever-looming, ever-present allure of death.

If only for a glimpse of her smile before she lowered Eira into the soil's embrace.

If only Eira closed her eyes tight enough, she could eventually convince herself it was Meilin's arms holding her rather than the sweet caress of the warming soil.

As swift as a slicing breeze. The soft caress of morning air takes you to somewhere kinder.

As beautiful as an unwavering flower. The growth of hindered roots that flourish against even the cruelest of circumstances.

As free as the ever-flowing current. Still loyal to the banks, sands, stones and streams she travels back to, kissing their edges with familial ease.

As forceful as the strike of a steady sword. Wielded by those wiser, those that ponder before they smite.

As unknown as a shadowed night. A comforting presence to those not ready to face the light just yet.

As unforgiving as the strongest storm. Gifting an unforgettable show of light and brilliance.

As giving as the earth beneath us. The power to tear apart worlds under our feet but choosing to give, and propagate, instead.

As unrelenting as the winter slate. Kind in its coolness, providing solstice to those who seek it.

As brutal as an irrepressible flame. Warming those who seek shelter, alighting kindling in their souls.

ACKNOWLEDGMENTS

First and foremost, I would like to acknowledge the Traditional Owners of the land on which this book was written, the Wurundjeri Woi-wurrung and Bunurong/Boon Wurrung peoples of the Kulin Nation. I pay my respects to Elders past and present. Sovereignty was never ceded. It always was, and always will be, Aboriginal land.

Around the time that I was fourteen, I was set on taking my own life.

Now, I sit here writing these acknowledgements, knowing that by the time you, dear reader, are seeing this, it will have been almost ten years since that time. This year, I will be turning twenty-four—when, all those years ago, living past eighteen seemed unfathomable to me.

To be able to tell my stories—to have Eira, Meilin and The New Reign exist on readable pages and not just in the confines of my mind—is something I'm so immensely grateful for. It has been anything but a painless journey to get to this point, but it felt right to begin my acknowledgements with this; because I exist, and that means my stories get to exist. I persevered.

There were also so many people who were a part of making this happen.

TWBTB wouldn't be the book it is today without the help of my publisher, Britt.

Britt, you believed in the version of this story that you read back in 2022, and for that, I'm forever grateful. TWBTB was my first ever manuscript, and whilst it was nowhere near as strong as it could've been, you took a chance on me—you trusted my vision, you never failed in your guidance and you have been a better champion for this book, and my career, than I have ever deserved. Thank you for always reminding me of my worth, for your unwavering patience and kindness, and for helping me make my dreams come true. Thank you will never be enough. *(Bryan, you're also the best!)*

My Lake Country Press siblings, each and every one of you are true gems. You remind me every day why it was the right choice to sign with LCP. Outside of being genuinely lovely people, you're also all incredibly talented. I wish nothing but continued success for you all.

Dear reader, if you'd like to learn more about the catalogue of talent that LCP boasts, please check out the books written by these wonderful authors: Ashley Merdalo, Allie Doherty, Ann H. Fox, Beka Westrup, Brittany Weisrock, Camri Kohler, Clare Carter, Erin Mainord, Haley Warrington, Hannah Loraine, Hazel Marie, Jayme Phelps, Jeremey Harrison, Juliet Bridges, Kait Waterhouse, Katrina Kwan, Kirsten Bohling, Kit Karlsson, Rae Valtera, S. Reed, Tristen Crone and True Sloan. For those who join the family in future, you are in *great* hands.

Tara Sexton, editor extraordinaire. I'm writing these acknowledgements just before this book gets passed on to you so that you can work your magic, so I guess this is both an apology and thank you in advance—I know you're absolutely going to ace the copy edits on this (sorry for the imminent spelling mistakes that I know are going to be there), and I'm so grateful for your hard work, as is everyone else at LCP.

To the artists who gave this story the most beautiful cover —I couldn't thank you enough. My cover illustrator, Angi, who worked through this entire process (which was new for both of us) with the utmost kindness and excitement; I'm so grateful to have seen you bring Eira and Meilin to life. Thank you to Rae for the cover typography and to Joy for internal formatting.

To my mum. You nurtured my love for reading from a very young age, and if it wasn't for the both of us being such avid book lovers, I don't know that I'd ever be brave enough to pursue this path for myself. Seeing how much joy books brought you, and how much they have to offer to those who consume them, inspired me to create stories of my own in the hopes of having the same impact on future readers. Thank you loving me through the hard times, and for teaching me strength. I'm still too embarrassed by the thought of you reading any of my work—but when you do, I hope it can become a favorite on your shelf.

To my nan. Despite having absolutely no idea what I was talking about the first time I brought up the fact that I had a book deal—which, to be fair, was very suddenly—you were so quick to congratulate me. You've always nurtured my love for creating things, and I wouldn't be here today if it wasn't for your love and belief in me. There are a million things to thank you for, but all I can hope is that I make you proud.

To my closest friends. It's hard to list you all, as cliché as that sounds. I just hope you can read this and know that it's *you* that I'm thankful for; for reading this book, for loving and supporting me, and for being a part of my life. Writing has always been a segmented part of my existence that I was terrified of bringing into aspects of my 'real-life' because it always felt so distant. But you were all so kind and supportive upon learning that I write books. You are wonderful friends, and I count myself lucky every day to know you. Thank you.

Fellow author friends, of which there is such an extensive list that I genuinely can't believe how I got so lucky. Writertwt is in ruins but I will always be grateful to have met you. Whether it's ranting in Discord chats, beta reading the bare bones of a baby manuscript or screaming in each other's DMs, I want to thank you for all for being there for me in different ways, whenever I've needed it most. The publishing landscape often feels like a lonely void, and I think I would've given up a long time ago, had I not met you. A special thank you, namely, to Amanda, Audrey, Bella, Birdie, Deandra, Dorian, Emma, Hali, Irene, Jordan, Lia, Morgan, Quinn, Riley, Theo and Yuva.

To the community who has been around since the S*ge & S*arrow debacle, or even before that, I wanted to extend my thanks to you. Your support and well wishes have always been both heartwarming and humbling. I truly hope this story was worth the wait.

Dear reader, thank you for taking a chance on TWBTB. I hope there was something in these pages that set your heart alight—and I hope you're ready for what is on the horizon for The New Reign.

Until next time.

ABOUT THE AUTHOR

Kayla Morton is a writer based in Melbourne (Naarm). It was in 2021—after a childhood filled with reading and yearning to create stories that felt true to herself—that Kayla decided to act on her dream of becoming an author. THOSE WHO BURN THE BRIGHTEST is her first published novel. Her second forth-coming YA Fantasy novel, SEVEN SILENCED, is slated for release with Lake Country Press in 2026. Kayla is seeking to traditionally publish her other completed manuscripts. Connect with Kayla via her website to stay up to date with her social media platforms and publishing journey.

www.kaylawriteswords.com